Knight Kisses

This is a work of fiction. Names, characters, places and incidents either are the product of the author's imagination or are used fictitiously, and any resemblance to any actual persons, living or dead, events, or locales is entirely coincidental.

Cover Photos "Pretty Woman in Forest" by © Canva/Viktor Solomin."Night Starry Sky and Moon" by © Canva/Deyan Georgiev.

Published By

RockHill Publishing LLC
PO Box 62241
Virginia Beach, VA
23466-2241
www.rockhillpublishing.
com

Knight Kisses

Athina Paris

Romance

To clasp you now and feel your head close-pressed,
Scented and warm against my beating breast;

To whisper soft and quivering your name,
And drink the passion burning in your frame;

To lie at full length, taut, with cheek to cheek
And tease your mouth with kisses till you speak

Love words, mad words, dream words, sweet senseless words,
Melodious like notes of mating birds;

To hear you ask if I shall love always,
And myself answer: Till the end of days;

To feel your easeful sigh of happiness
When on your trembling lips I murmur: Yes;

. . . .

by Claude McKay (1889 – 1948)

For those I love and who relentlessly support me.

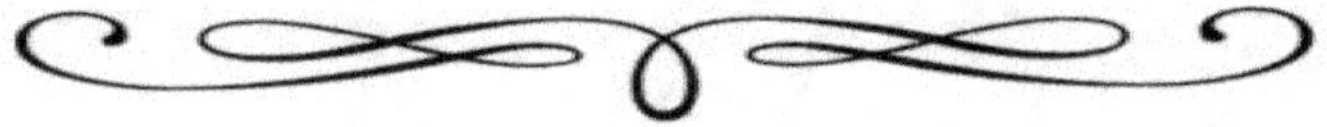

CHAPTER ONE

'Hello,' Gabrielle called, as she entered the house and dropped her bag and car keys on the hall table. Classes had been a mad rush today and she was truly bushed, but now, she had to go sit with Charles Dickens, and write a paper on why his novels still influenced modern day society.

'Hi honey,' Eleanor said from the study. 'Please come see me after lunch.'

Gabrielle knew days like this; in fact, they were becoming quite common. After making lunch, Eleanor would go lie on the sofa in the study, exhausted for the rest of the day. Gabrielle worried a great deal, but the more she tried to probe and query, the more Eleanor clammed up.

'I had a sandwich earlier,' Gabrielle said from the doorway, then walked in, leaned over, and kissed her mother's brow. 'Mom, you look so pale, you have to go see a doctor.'

Eleanor dropped her gaze, as if caught in an indiscretion. 'I have already been to see a few.'

'What? Then— what did they say?' Gabrielle sat in the armchair closest to the sofa.

'I'm very sick.' Eleanor took a laborious breath.

In contrast, Gabrielle's suspended for a second. 'What's wrong? What do you need, what can I do?'

'I have cancer.'

Fear sprung forth like a hidden monster, making Gabrielle feel weak and numb. She grabbed the chair's armrests, digging her fingers in. 'It's treatable, right? Do you need surgery, chemo, radiation...?'

Eleanor shook her head. 'I'm beyond that. It's just too late— I'm dying.'

A world-crushing hand grabbed her heart, flipped her over, and made her feel as if she were dying herself. Tears filled her eyes as she fell on her knees before her mother, dropping her head into her lap. 'No mommy, you can't.'

'I'm sorry baby, but there is nothing more to do. And you know it too.' Eleanor caressed her child's hair. 'But you will always have the happy times, the joy and laughter we brought each other. I've put everything is in order, and Charles is aware of it, so when—'

They did not have many friends in Switzerland, but there was one constant visitor, when he was in the country. Charles Knight was somehow related to Eleanor by a flimsy in-law thread, but he had taken it as his duty to see to their comfort and safety. Gabrielle liked him very much and she figured that he must like her too because he always brought her gifts, treated her like a daughter, and never told her to stop calling him daddy, which she had started doing when she was ten. Consequently, Eleanor often turned to him for advice.

She hated being scared, but right now, she was petrified. 'Stop talking like this, you are not going to die.' Tears flowed freely.

'Listen to me.' Eleanor said softly. 'It is going to happen, so you have to accept it and prepare for when it does.'

'I don't want to, I need you.' Gabrielle hiccupped, feeling so much like a little girl that she wanted to curl up into her mother's lap.

'Charles and I have already discussed everything.' Eleanor paused. 'We have decided that the best course of action is for you to go to South Africa.'

'What?' Gabrielle exclaimed. Not only was her mother dying, but she was going to be uprooted as well.

'You can't stay here alone.'

'But... Anna and Luc are here.' Anna was the cleaning, nanny, and everything else lady, and Luc, her seventeen-year-old son. Gabrielle and Luc had always been close; she had kept an eye on him throughout school, made sure he did not mix with the wrong crowd, and been his emotional support when he lost his father.

Eleanor took her daughter's chin, looking into the beautiful hazel eyes. 'You need to live, not be concerned and afraid, or alone.'

'I dreamt of going to Africa, where I should have been born, but not like this, and... What about my studies?'

'You know those can be continued and completed anywhere. Charles loves you just as if you were his child, so he will keep you safe. But if you don't want him to...' Eleanor stopped.

Even through the tears, the bad news, and the utterly helplessness she felt, she knew something much worse was about to happen. 'Mommy,' she could barely say the words. 'Please tell me you are not dying today.'

Eleanor attempted a smile and failed. 'Not so soon, but I do have to unburden my heart. Naturally, Charles is completely against it.' She moved on the sofa with some difficulty.

Gabrielle sobbed. 'Please, mommy, please don't talk like this.'

'I am sorry I lied but I wanted to protect you.' Eleanor took a deep breath. 'If you had known, if he knew— well, I don't know.'

Gabrielle looked up. 'What are you talking about, mommy? Please don't tell me daddy— Uncle Charles.' She corrected herself. 'Is my real father.'

'You should be so lucky my darling, but no, Charles is not your father. And as much as it pains me, I have to finally make a confession.'

'Yes, that you told me a terrible joke and that you are not dying.' Gabrielle wiped her face furiously.

'Gaby,' Eleanor said gently. 'I have kept something from you, something I wished you would never hear, never see, never experience, but now... I hate the way I feel because I believe the earth will refuse to eat my bones if I don't tell you.' She paused to catch her breath and find new words. 'Your father is not dead. I told you he was so you would never try to see him. And he doesn't know that you exist either because I left before you were born.'

This was the epitome of a speechless moment, because what could anyone possibly say to that? In the same day she hears her mother is dying, she finds out that her dead father is not dead. Emotions she had never experienced coursed through her. Why this horrid lie? She could not think, so all she did was fall over and break into heart-wrenching sobs.

'I am sorry baby and if I meant to rip out your heart, I have succeeded. But you have to understand—'

Gabrielle's beautiful hazel eyes swam with unstoppable tears as she got to her knees again. 'I have a real father? How could you not tell me all these years? And— you are dying and I'm going to lose you, and there is a father I don't know... why mommy?'

'If only I could undo so many things. But you, the meaning of my life, I could never, I would never want to undo, even if your father was the worst criminal.'

'My father is a terrible man?'

'Not terrible that way, but the results turn out the same. If you do meet him, be prepared, because he will eventually disappoint you. It's just how he is, and no one can change him.'

'But why don't I know him?'

'Because I did not want him disrupting your life as he did mine.'

'None of this is fair,' Gabrielle cried. 'How— I don't know what to do.'

'Know what you can do?' Eleanor told her encouragingly. 'Continue making those cute videos you like to send to Charles, but now, make them for yourself. And we will record our last times...' Eleanor's voice broke.

Catapulting to her feet, Gabrielle tore through the house, out the back door, and smacked straight into the property wall, unaware that an agonising scream had ripped through the tranquil afternoon. Then, sinking onto her knees, she buried her face in her hands.

Those who said someone's life could change in a second had probably undergone something similar, for during the course of a few minutes, everything she knew, everything she had believed in, disintegrated.

She was angry, confused, and sad, feeling so much all at once that she was incapable of concentrating on anything else for days afterwards.

While growing up, Gabrielle had often questioned their origins. Why did they live in Switzerland, why not in England, where they had blood ties? Did they not have relatives in South Africa, where Eleanor had been born? Why didn't Eleanor work? Where did their money come from? Eleanor had a myriad of answers but instinctively, Gabrielle sensed that not all were true, which was peculiar because Eleanor was no liar.

Equally, Gabrielle learnt early that her mother did not like talking about her father. Nonetheless, when queried, Eleanor told her daughter glowing stories, fuelling an innocent mind with tales of a charming lost hero. Gabrielle loved her dead father dearly.

Almost immediately everything changed in the house, Eleanor got worse quickly, becoming weak and sickly, and Gabrielle could not understand how she had hidden the pain that was so clearly plastered on the once beautiful face. She realised too that Anna had been privy to this cataclysm all along, and that she was in fact a fantastic nurse, having a kindness and compassion seldom seen. Her heart was breaking too fast, and she did not know how she was going to survive it. Crying, sobs... and pain of a different kind was all she felt.

Many days, she did not go to classes, just so she could climb into her mother's bed and lie there holding her. If she was lucky, she fell asleep and did not see, feel, or think, but other days... Tears started early in the morning and refused to stop until she drifted into a fitful slumber. Amid the unfolding tragedy, Eleanor joked as she told Gabrielle that she needed a plumber because she had some bad leaks.

She had never seen, known, or learnt that a human body could suffer so much, or that a heart could feel physical tearing as the days marched to the inevitable end. Through it all, Luc would sit outside just holding her, perhaps to remind her that there were other things to feel, but she no longer knew where to find them.

Sometimes, she remembered that he was a teenage boy. That his time should be spent being silly with friends, going to parties, dating, and kissing girls his age, instead, there sat a beautiful boy at home, loving her in silence, and making videos; that she thought she would never be able to watch.

Charles arrived. Evidently, Eleanor had called him. Gabrielle had often wondered about their relationship, but it seemed the little familial connection that existed between them was exactly that, and true friendship.

She knew he was happily married to Barbara, had one son, Jonathan, and had been her father's best friend, and perhaps still was. Now, she had an extra person to be upset with, because he too knew the truth, but he too had chosen to keep it from her.

Then, it happened. Her mother went to sleep one evening and she never saw the blue eyes again. Her rock was gone and suddenly, her feet did not know where to stand. That was also the day she lost the last piece of her heart, and there was only one word that described how she felt, numb, because she could barely feel a thing anymore.

Right there she made up her mind; she would never love again. Because loving hurt too much.

Gabrielle realised then that her mother had prepared well. Eleanor had sold everything they possessed, closed all bank accounts, and handed everything over to Charles. Now too, she discovered that the house they had lived in for over ten years of her life was Charles', not theirs, which explained why they lived in Switzerland. It was a hiding place; but a hiding place from what, and whom?

Charles was older than her father and now he spoke of how he had tried his best to influence him right but Malcolm Barker-Hayden was too much of a hot-head to take good advice from anyone. Everything she heard of that unfamiliar man was negative. After a while, she no longer knew if she wanted to meet him or stay oblivious. But he was her father and both had been robbed of the relationship they should have shared, so surely, he would behave somewhat fatherly. Besides, she thought crossly, Charles' opinion was biased, she still recalled well all the stories Eleanor had told her. Not all could be lies, or were they?

'Have you seen him and told him I exist?' She asked, as she looked out the hotel window Charles had booked her into.

He shook his head. 'No, and for all we know, he would prefer not to. Which,' he studied her for a second. 'It's not an improbable outcome as he hates responsibility of any kind. Naturally, he will ask if I knew of your whereabouts, and then just to rile me, will ask to see you and do something odd. Frankly, I wish I didn't have to tell him anything and believe me when I say that he's unworthy of you, just as he was of your mother.'

She understood nothing, and the very idea that neither he nor her mother had trusted her enough to reveal the truth or to let her decide for herself was painful and sad. She had always seen him as her father, but this— could she ever forgive them? Let him steam in his lies, she did not care one iota for his feelings right now. 'He is my father, I want to meet him.'

Malcolm reacted with the expected shock when hearing that he shared a child with his former wife. He was livid, raging in fact because who did things like that? 'And they call me irresponsible.' He spat. And how convenient, he continued, that Eleanor was absent because she needed to hear what he thought about her cloak-and-dagger adventures. Next, he went off on a tirade about her selfishness, silliness, and impossible expectations. Then realising the girl was just as shaken and clearly not to blame for the subterfuge, he did what fathers did. 'Come live with me.' He suggested then turned on Charles, the obvious co-conspirator. 'Charles,' he boomed. 'I knew someone with clout helped her, just never imagined my so-called best friend in the thick of things. All these damn years... Do not darken my portal again.'

Possibly, Malcolm told Gabrielle, as she was as much at a loss as he was, it was rather late in life for a proper father-daughter relationship but at least they should attempt it since neither was to blame for a decision based on judgemental attitudes. If she wished, he suggested further, he would adopt her, or begin a paternity suit so she could claim his name. She was touched, told him so, and said she would consider it. Although still upset with her mother, she was also too used to Gabrielle Dunstan.

CHAPTER TWO

How many times had she dreamt about this, to breathe this African air, to be under the sky where she was supposed to have been born? Now, incredibly, she wished her mother had been stronger, lied more, and never revealed Malcolm's existence. The truth, even when desperately wanted was often devastating. So was it any wonder that she was sick and tired?

For one, Malcolm had come home with a most dreadful cold the previous week, so how could she have escaped that? Second, she had not stopped running back and forth between his room and the kitchen.

Annoyingly, he wanted none of her ministrations, but she knew that she had better badger him if he was to get better at all, so he could get up from his bed, out of his room, and out the front door again. Having him around was highly disruptive. He was a bad patient, who could not lie still for any amount of time, and as for quiet... He was constantly calling her for something or other, which frequently was utterly unimportant.

Gabrielle gazed out the window. Gorgeous weather outside, but she was not in it. The white roses were in their last bloom, sending a sweet scent towards the study, where she stood, but she could not go cut any. Not that she liked doing that, because she habitually hurt herself. Selena, the housekeeper, was constantly showing her the clothes, where the bloodstains stubbornly sat.

She turned from the window and gazed around the library. The beautifully engraved wood panels had apparently come all the way from India, the Persian carpets from Turkey, the huge desk from Argentina, the chesterfield from England, and the books from all over. It was her favourite room in the house; the little haven where she hid when her father's associates turned up.

It had not taken many weeks for her to discover what her father was all about, but at least one other thing was also true, he tried fatherhood, which was a complete mystery as to what it entailed as he had never practiced it, so she forgave him for failing miserably. What she could not overlook was everything else he did.

Addictive weaknesses ruled his life. He was a compulsive gambler, bordered alcoholism, was a womaniser of note, had a short temper, and was utterly reckless with money. He had apparently been heir to a large fortune. Where was it? In casinos, racecourses, given away, lost, and a lot of it just plain stolen from under his nose.

The house was still standing because it was part of a historical trust and he was unable to touch it, otherwise, it and its contents might have already been pawned for some mindless pursuit. Gabrielle was glad that was the case because it was a beautiful and charming old house.

Here she was! Months had passed and she finally understood why her mother had been unable to deal with Malcolm's errant ways. He was never home, but when he was, eight out of ten times, peculiar characters surrounded him. As for the women— it was best she did not try to guess. She liked none of his acquaintances, and she suspected that most were involved in some type of criminal activity. It was a very disheartening situation. As with her mother and the tales she had spun and told, she had already forgiven Charles for hiding the unbendable truth.

Gabrielle glanced at the building in awe; it was a stunning example of a well-thought-out green plan. Light and beauty surrounded her as soon as she entered it, the ash wood panels reflecting the deep lustrous jade tiles. Everything had a purpose and efficiency was obviously intentional in the amazing glass masterpiece. While staring, she had a run-in with the stainless steel revolving door, so marching to front desk breathless she stated that she was there to see her dad.

The man on duty eyed her oddly. 'We have a lot of dads here. Which one is yours?'

'Sorry,' Gabrielle apologised. 'Mr Charles Knight. Tell him Gabrielle is here.'

'You mean I must inform his PA first.'

She often forgot that Charles was a businessman and that none of these people knew who she was. 'Yes, call his PA.'

Lifting the phone, he dialled. 'Mrs Stein, there is a young lady here, her name is Gabrielle— what? Yes, that's her. Sure, will do.' He returned the receiver to the desk and made a face, as if he were impressed. 'I am to make you a security card.' He took a quick photo and asked her to press both thumbs on a magnetic pad. Then he passed her a form to fill in, when she handed it back, he started on the card immediately.

She walked around while he was busy, studied some plants she had never seen, gazed at interesting art on the walls and then went to peer over a balcony, realising then that the building went down another floor. Hearing a man's laughter, she smiled. It sounded happy, as if he were enjoying a good joke. Inspecting the floor below, she tracked down owner of laughter. Unexpectedly, he looked up, straight at her, and mouthed something to his friend who seeing his gaze had strayed, did likewise, and both stared.

'Miss Dunstan, your card is ready.' The security guard announced.

She turned from the balcony and took it from him. 'Thank you. What floor is Mr Knight?'

'Top floor, turn right, it's the office at the end. His name is on the door, so you won't get lost. But announce yourself at floor desk first, and then stop by Mrs Stein, she wants to see you too.'

She studied everything with interest as she rode the glass lift in silence, Knight Industries was so much bigger than she had imagined.

Mrs Stein had two phones attached to her head when she stopped in front of her desk. Thirty-something, attractive, friendly, downright competent, Gabrielle noticed, as she stood patiently until the calls ended. 'Hello, I'm Gabrielle.'

A pair of warm brown eyes regarded her for a second, the well-formed mouth broke into a smile, and she jumped to her feet. 'Amy Stein,' she said and gave her a squeeze. 'I'm so pleased to finally meet you. Your dad—' she cleared her throat. 'Mr Knight in public, mentions you often. How are you doing, I heard you had the flu.'

She returned the smile, pleased to realise that Charles did think of her as his, and intrigued that he would discuss it with his personal assistant. 'Much better thank you. So I can just go in?'

'Yes.' One of the phones started ringing. 'Excuse me, but we will eventually get time to chat.'

Gabrielle nodded, walked to the marked door, and knocked.

'Come,' Charles beckoned, rose quickly, and kissed her cheek. 'If only I had daughters.'

'Surely, you are not sorry about your son.'

'Jonathan? No, he's a pleasure. So, how's your father?'

'Better, thank you, but the characters he brings home— I'm guessing he did this to mom as well.'

'Yes, he has always mixed with some dubious characters. And further back, he knew a very nasty Russian mobster.'

'Then he truly has not changed, because I'm a little nervous about some of his friends.'

A worried expression appeared on Charles' face. 'Do you want out? Just say the word—'

'Thank you daddy, but I'm okay; and if I do become frightened I will let you know.'

'This is how the trouble started between your parents, and it scared your mother senseless. When she discovered she was expecting, she gave him an ultimatum, to see if he would change, but he couldn't stick to it, never could, so she hid her pregnancy, filed for divorce, and left. His vocabulary is full of promises, but he can't keep any. Sorry Gabrielle, it's just how he is.'

'I know.'

'How did you get here, have you started driving?'

She laughed nervously. 'No, it's taxis for me for a while. Though, those minibuses I saw on the way here seem to be the irritation of all other motorists.'

'Yes, one must watch out for them all the time.' He went to the large window. 'So, how can I help you today?'

'I need to do something with my life because sitting in that house will turn me into someone I could not possibly stand. But I don't know if I should start working or finish my studies.'

'English Literature, is it?'

She nodded. 'As you are aware I also know French, Italian, German, and a little Romansh, so I could consider a job in hospitality or translating, but I would rather complete my degree first.'

'Yes, good thinking.' He agreed 'Have you approached the universities to see how long it would take to finish here?'

'No, and that is what I was hoping you could help me with, as I don't know the city and its ways.'

Charles paged through a diary on his desk then lifted the phone. 'Amy, what does my schedule look like today?' He listened. 'Clear the rest of the day, I'm going out.'

They were in the lift going down when she saw Mr happy laughter again. He was in the other, going up, and she imagined that he had a familiar face. However, when Charles said something, threw his arm about her shoulders, and she leaned against his chest, he was no longer Mr happy laughter. Clamping his eyes on her, she could not help but register the frigid stare.

With her credits, she could join classes the following week and graduate by yearend. Charles was pleased and told her that he would pick her up in the morning and take her back for registration. It made sense to finish what she had started, and it would have pleased her mother a great deal too. As for her father— who knew? At least now, she could be out of the house being constructive and changing her life for the better, because being around that strange man and his weird hangers-on was very demoralising.

Having joined so late in the programme, she did not have friends, but it did not bother her, as her plan was to apply herself wholeheartedly and make certain she graduated with decent marks. Charles offered to take her car shopping, but she shook her head, feeling anxious. He employed a man and told him to drive her around until she got the hang of the city or felt confident behind a steering wheel again.

Once a week, Charles took her out to either lunch or dinner to catch up on her news and to find out what Malcolm was doing.

'He's embroiled in some scheme.'

'It can only be trouble.' He said this particular evening.

She had done exceptionally well on a test, so he was treating her like a princess. 'Something about investing in a drug company, I hope he means pharmaceutical.'

'It's hard to guess with Malcolm. How much is it?'

'A hundred thousand,' she glimpsed a couple enter the booth behind Charles and thought that she had seen the man somewhere before.

'Where is he planning to get the money?'

Returning her focus to the conversation, Gabrielle dropped her gaze. She felt odd that her father had asked her for money. She had wanted to say no, but he had been so excited, even showing her a business plan and projections, and somehow also managed to make her feel guilt over her mother's abandonment. He had intimated the money was his to start off with, that Eleanor had come into marriage with a big fat zero, so if she returned some, it was no more than her daughter's duty. It had been an incredibly uncomfortable encounter.

'I made a mistake placing that money in your name, didn't I?' Charles furrowed his brow disapprovingly. 'It's yours, but you are not to give it willy-nilly, especially not to him, because he takes it to burn. A hundred thousand Rand may not be a lot in Europe, but it is still money here.'

'I'm sorry,' her eyes filled with tears.

'There, there.' He patted her hand across the table. 'He is reckless, and you know it. You are merely feeling sorry for him because he is a master at twisting conversations, but you shouldn't. Sweetheart, look at me.'

She had not heard a kind word in ages and she wanted him to tell her that everything would be okay. So all she had been bottling up for so long just started pouring out, and getting to her feet, she slid alongside him.

He wrapped his arm about her, holding her tightly as she cried on his shoulder. 'I hate his machinations, because that is the one thing he is excellent at.' He glanced at her plate. 'You are not going to eat anymore, are you?'

She shook her head.

'Then let's get out of here, and I'll take you to a movie.' Rising to his feet, he pulled her up with him.

As they walked past the next booth, she realised who the man was. It was Mr happy laughter, but right now, he looked incredibly upset. Gabrielle almost stared; with him was the most beautiful blonde woman she had ever seen. She wondered if he worked at Knight Industries, as that was where she had seen him the first time.

She graduated top of her class. Charles, bursting with pride, invited Malcolm to lunch so they could celebrate together, but as expected, and still clinging to his excuse of bruised ego, or whatever he wanted to call it, Malcolm excused himself and did not show, so it was the two of them again. Before, when he had visited in Switzerland, although caring, he had merely indulged a child's need for a father figure. Now, more and more, he felt like her real father.

'Gabrielle,' Charles began at the restaurant. 'Have you decided what you want to do?'

'Not yet, but I sort of have a plan. Although I do intend to continue with honours and masters later on, I would like to take a break now. I could teach, and I think I will eventually, but I have been buried in books for such a long time that I need something new.'

Charles smiled. 'I'm glad you said that, come work for me.'

'Really?' Excitement spread on her face. 'I would like that very much.'

'Good. As you say, you have been buried in books, and before that, there were too many other things.' He dare not mention her mother because she usually cried when he did. He watched her happy face; this was more like it, his old Gabrielle, his little darling. He felt young when in her presence.

She was a gorgeous girl, with the most expressive hazel eyes, light brown hair that shone like burnished bronze when she stood in the sun, and had a mouth that tilted slightly upwards, giving her the look of happiness. She was just above medium height, but what a fantastic figure. Everything she wore looked right, as she had a knack for throwing garments together. Regardless of her looks, she was so very smart and he loved her young and innocent sense of humour.

CHAPTER THREE

Gabrielle was having a grand time at the office. Charles had sent her down to records as she was excellent at sorting out things, making lists, labelling, and anything that had to do with filing. He had heard the head of that department complain enough times to know that they needed a new system so Gabrielle was probably the perfect solution to get that dungeon into some kind of order. When he went there to check on her, he saw the grins of satisfaction on those who had been battling to keep up.

'Gabrielle,' he called on the phone. 'Can you come up to my office?'

'Sure Mr Knight.' She was adamant about treating him professionally in public. He did not like it, but she was not going to listen to him on that.

She was already a little up in the lift when she glanced casually at the other one. There rode Mr happy laughter, also going up. Suddenly aware that someone was watching him, he turned, leaned his back against the side, and fixed his eyes on her.

His gaze was stripping, as if he were trying to dig inside her. Nevertheless, her eyes did not move for a few moments. He was good-looking, with a roguish air about him, perhaps because the brown hair and five-o'clock shadow sat so well on the well-proportioned face. He was probably as tall as Charles was and seemed to be in good shape but that smug sneer encouraged her to want to remove it off his face as she felt under scrutiny and judgement. She tried to guess what colour his eyes were. Perhaps dark, like a stormy night. Brown, and as wild as a sandstorm? Possibly green, like an algae infested lake, and just as dangerous! Or as blue as a raging maelstrom—

It was in fact annoying watching him, so she turned to glance outside as the lift rose higher. When she returned her gaze to him, he had a sardonic look across his face, as if he were questioning her. She took a deep breath, disliking him greatly. Then reaching the top floor first, she got out quickly and walked down the passage at a fast pace.

'Gabrielle,' Amy called. 'Take these with you.' She pointed to a stack of files.

Getting to the closed door, Gabrielle realised she had too much in her hands to turn the handle, so hearing a footfall behind her, she turned to ask whoever was there to open the door. It was Mr annoying happy laughter. She straightened her back, leaned the files against the door, and reached...

How it happened she did not know but abruptly, the door slid open, and all the files went flying into the office. If he had not somehow grabbed her hand midair as he had also reached for the handle, she would have gone sprawling after them.

'Gabrielle,' Charles said as she tumbled in, trying not to step on the files. Then a wide grin spread on his face. 'Jonathan. Good grief, what are the two of you doing all over those papers?'

Gabrielle stood up straight and went scarlet then she looked pointedly at Jonathan who was still holding her hand. No wonder she had thought he looked familiar; Charles had shown her the occasional photograph. Only, he had not looked this mature without that stubble.

He let go of her hand, helped pick up the files, and dropped them on the side-table.

'Have you two met?' Charles asked.

It was maelstrom eyes, and just as tumultuous, but worse, she could sense dangerous things happening behind that inscrutable gaze.

'Oh, we are old friends already.' Jonathan announced.

If he kept this up there was going to be a dictionary following Mister, because it was already Mr sarcastic annoying happy laughter. She grinned.

He saw the smirk, did not like it one bit, and then glanced at her security card. 'So, Gabrielle Dunstan, what department are you?'

'Gabrielle is sorting out records.' Charles told his son. 'Why are you here?'

Jonathan glanced at Gabrielle.

She imagined that he was wondering if he could speak freely in her presence. What he did not know was that she knew quite a few things about him, while he knew absolutely nothing about her, as Charles had decided not to share her life story with anyone. Which was also why, he often asked her to move out of her father's house. He had a point, Malcolm was irredeemable. 'Should I come back later?' She offered.

'No.' Charles turned to her. 'Sweetheart, do whatever while we discuss this. Go ahead, Jonathan.'

Obviously, Charles thought nothing of how he addressed her, but the look on Jonathan's face was one of pure dislike, as he fixed his blue eyes on her. She felt dirty at that moment, and hated it a great deal; Mr judgemental sarcastic annoying happy laughter. No, she was removing happy laughter. There was nothing happy about him, as he seemed to be making an effort to keep his troubled gaze away from her while he addressed Charles.

'Did you get to look over the Johnson contract?'

'Yes, I think...'

The two men got into a debate about all sorts of things; price, availability, producers, manufacturers, and everything else.

Instead of sitting, she sorted the files into order again. Then she went to the drinks' cabinet, opened one Perrier and an Evian, poured them out, and placed them before the men.

Charles nodded thankfully, she knew well what he drank during the day, and that he liked it in a short glass.

Jonathan stared. How did she know he liked Evian in a tall glass? No, he did not like what he was seeing here. Miss Gabrielle was a little too well versed in private affairs. Talking to his father, he took mental notes as she crossed his line of vision. She had a good figure, and as she made a movement and the slit on her skirt widened, he saw the perfect line of calf and leg. He raised his eyes to her face.

It seemed as if she was not one for too much make-up because her clear skin looked bare. She had beautiful long lashes that rested every-so-often against her smooth cheek, her hazel eyes had a hint of green in them, wide, expressive, and she had a well-formed nose. Very French, he thought. The mouth— he stopped right there, unable to focus on anything else again. Never had he seen one that screamed as much as this one did to be plundered.

'How is Amelia?' Charles queried.

'Huh?' Jonathan asked quizzically, having no idea who that was. Then he realised his father was referring to his girlfriend. 'Oh, she's fine, very busy.'

'Did she get that role she wanted so badly?'

'Yes.'

'Okay, then I will see you later. Now, Gabrielle and I have things to do.' Charles turned to her. 'I'm guessing you haven't eaten yet.' He grabbed his jacket and put it on. 'But we'll just go across the street.' Then taking her hand, he tucked it into the crook of his arm.

Jonathan stared after them. That his father did not feel an ounce of shame to flaunt his little floozy in his presence was something he had never imagined possible. He followed them out of the office, watched them disappear towards the lift, and walked over to Amy. 'What the bloody hell?' He pointed to the disappearing pair.

Amy looked up at him uncomprehendingly. What was he on about? She had no idea what they had discussed in the office. 'Excuse me?'

'Who the hell is that, and what are they doing?'

One thing Amy knew. Charles did not want everyone knowing everything about Gabrielle, and since she was not sure into which category Jonathan fell, she shrugged and reached for the phone as it started ringing.

If ever she had thought that both her mother and Charles had exaggerated, this was the moment when she forgave them every lie they had ever told. She had thought them unfair, mean, completely heartless to keep her away from a life she should have been born into, a father she should have known... Her mother had known much, and Charles was the best judge of character.

The hundred thousand was gone. Where? She had no idea, and neither did Malcolm. Now, he was asking again. She had put her foot down, and said no, as Charles had begged her to do, because if she did not, Malcolm would wipe her out. But it was not money that had her upset this time; it was the reason why he wanted more.

Malcolm had become romantically involved with a drug-addict. Gabrielle had seen her around and she knew instantly that that woman was bad news. Charlotte Richards was dirty, demanding, desperate, decomposing and a huge trouble-maker. She was plain weird and if possible, knew even creepier characters than her father did. She was unable to control her addiction in any form or manner and Gabrielle had been upset twice before when she had stumbled onto her paraphernalia carelessly tossed about, then knew she had to hold her tongue because this was not her house.

Gabrielle realised that she had not seen the woman for over four months, and evidently for the very reason she was having this horrible discussion with her father. What made the whole episode enormously worrisome was that the union had produced a baby; her father's child, her little half-sister. Who, right now, was sick in hospital with who-knew-what because the two had no decency or clue on how to look after the infant properly.

Gabrielle's eyes filled with tears. Poor innocent, how were these two untrustworthy people supposed to raise a child when both were sick addicts? One of drugs and the other of everything else.

'Will you lend it to me then?' Malcolm tried one last time as he saw the tears.

'I will pay anything and everything the hospital asks for but I will not give you money.' Gabrielle said. 'But there is something I will do to help as soon as she is discharged.'

'Anything,' Malcolm said eagerly.

Gabrielle realised that he was still pushing his luck. Her tears were a flashing neon sign as to how soft her heart was, so he would try breaking her. 'Bring the baby here, I will look after her. Bring Charlotte too. And that is my help.'

'You know she's an addict, who needs her fixes, and she can't stay in one place for any amount of time.'

'For that very reason I want my little sister here, not abandoned in some back street. And shame on you,' she told him sharply. 'How have you not suggested this yourself? But I am not putting any cash in Charlotte's palm, so get them here, before either of them dies.'

Gabrielle fell in love with her half-sister instantly. But how little Tammy showed no signs of drugs and looked healthy enough now, had to be a miracle because as she heard the story, Charlotte had been on an eight-month high and eventually gone into premature labour. Gabrielle merely shook her head disbelieving, she had not even guessed that Charlotte was pregnant.

Charles watched Gabrielle rocking the baby-stroller as he walked towards her in the park. She had begged him to come meet her. 'Are you babysitting?' He asked curiously.

'You could say that.' Her eyes filled. 'This is Tammy, my little sister. Can you believe it?'

He stared agape. 'What the blazes is that idiot up to?'

She shrugged and gulped. 'Now, I have this innocent to protect from those two because they are both a mess. Oh daddy,' she flew from the park bench and cried on his shoulder.

'Everything will be all right.' He hugged her. 'I just cannot believe that the more the years march on the more irresponsible he becomes. What does this woman look like?'

'She must have been pretty once but she looks a hundred now. She is ravaged, sick and everything else you can imagine. I told her to stop breast-feeding. She could easily get the baby addicted— I could not bear it.'

'What does your father say about all this?'

'I don't think there is a decent thought in his head. I have regretted being upset with mommy and you so many times already. I should have never gone to him, but I always wanted to know. But if I had not, who would have rescued this baby now?'

Charles shook his head, what could he say? He was sorry he had relented to Eleanor's guilt, and eventually agreed to help this wonderful girl connect with her malingerer father. They should have continued to lie and told her nothing, but with her in South Africa, fate might have engineered any number of awful scenarios and then he would have certainly lost her. 'I am guessing you bought this.' He pointed to the stroller.

'She had nothing, not even a decent bath.' Gabrielle wiped her eyes again.

'Take the week off, they will manage without you at the office, I don't think she can. But when you return to work, what is to be done about the innocent?'

'That is actually what I really wanted to talk to you about. I cannot leave her in that house; I don't trust either of them. So would it be okay for me to take her to the work nursery?'

He gazed lovingly at her. 'You did not have to ask me.'

'I just have to convince them that it is a fantastic idea.'

When Gabrielle appeared at the nursery school to get information, they told her what they needed for registration. She asked for the documents as soon as she got home that afternoon, unaware that she had just run into a huge problem. The school needed the baby's birth certificate and immunization card. They could not accept her in without those, no matter whom she was related to.

Charlotte stared at her for a moment and then announced. 'I haven't registered her yet. And I never took her to the clinic; I didn't have time.'

Gabrielle phoned Charles and told him. Both raged at the two idiots, who were going through life as if nothing but their little addictions were important. No wonder the baby had already been to hospital, she probably had next to nothing in the area of an immune system. So when Gabrielle reached the front of the queue at Home Affairs, she knew something outside her body possessed her, because suddenly, she knew exactly what to do.

'Dear lord,' Charles said when she told him the story. 'And when the two crazies discover what you have done?'

'I'm past caring. This is how I read the situation; she's putting herself in a grave, and he— not much better. His addictions are different but they are just as dangerous.'

'If they never find out, you will have complete custody, and certainly not need their signatures for anything. Did you name anyone as father?'

She shook her head. 'I could not involve anyone else in my crime. I feel as if I'm stealing her, but given facts, my actions are justified.'

'Let's hope this works, for the both of you.' He chuckled. 'I have to hand it to you, Gabrielle, you are a brave one.

CHAPTER FOUR

Jonathan turned the corner, heading to his car, when he saw Gabrielle struggling with something. He could not explain it, but when he saw her, he got into a muddle. He disliked her intensely, yet, there was something about her that just pulled him in. 'Can I help you?' He stopped in utter shock. That was a baby.

'Thank you. I have just bought the car and I'm still very unhandy around it, especially when dealing with baby things.'

What in hell's name was this? He studied the baby closely. Oh yes, definitely hers. 'What's her name?'

'Tammy.'

'I never realised you had a baby, or that you were in a relationship.' Well, he knew that bit, not this. 'Who's the father?'

Gabrielle coloured at that. What was she supposed to tell people? That she was pretending to be her little sister's mother? That their useless father was no father at all, and that the baby's mother— all best left unsaid. 'It does not matter, so we are leaving it at that. And it's not as if she's going to need him.'

What exactly was this woman all about? He could not fathom anything she did or said. 'I'm guessing he has seen her.'

'He sees her every day.'

'But you are not telling anyone who he is.'

'No one needs to know.'

That made him mad. 'Is he providing for her?'

'He'd better. I am not taking any nonsense like that.'

'How old is she?'

Why was he so interested? She told him and thought he was doing mental calculations, figuring something out. She wondered what. 'Are you still going to help me?'

'What do you need?'

Gabrielle took the baby out and held her close. She pointed. 'Unhinge that, fold it down, and put it in the boot.'

He did then looked at her. 'Something else,'

'Hold her while I sort her things.' She handed him the baby and busied herself around the back seat.

He had never held a baby so he was uncertain if there was a specific way to do it. He gazed at the cute face. She was going to look just like her mother.

'Thank you, Jonathan.' Gabrielle took Tammy, sat her in the baby-chair, and opened the front door. 'See you tomorrow.'

He could not move as she drove out of the underground parking then realised someone was addressing him. 'Paul,' He said when he recognised his best friend. 'Did you say something?'

'I asked who is driving away.'

'You would not believe me if I told you. Hell, I have never been this furious in my life.'

Paul gazed at his friend. 'Yes, something seems to be rattling you. What is it?'

'Have you ever met Gabrielle?'

'No, who is she?'

'Remember pretty face over the balcony months ago? Well, she works in records. And little angel is not so angelic,' Jonathan said sarcastically. 'She is dad's mistress.'

'You have got to be kidding me.' Paul made a face of disbelief. 'Your father has never and will never cheat on your mother.'

'That is what I thought too, but that was before I met her.' He pointed to the exit.

'No, no no no,' Paul shook his head. 'It is not possible. For goodness sake Jonathan, you know your father.'

'Yes, but you have not seen Gabrielle. She is this perfect...' he could not continue.

'Well,' Paul said. 'Guess what the first thing is I'm doing tomorrow.'

True to his word, Paul went down to records with some flimsy excuse the next morning and saw Gabrielle. He was dumbfounded. Of course she was gorgeous, there was nothing wrong with Jonathan's eyesight, but this girl was involved with Charles? Realistically, Charles could attract any woman if he wished because he was still a good-looking man, but what was the age gap here, thirty, forty years? Age aside, he was having trouble comprehending the clandestine affair. This was not Charles. Then he thought that Gabrielle watched him oddly, as if she were thinking something.

She was. She also recalled his face from the first time she had looked over the balcony and seen him standing with Jonathan, as they both stared up at her. They were both weird.

For two weeks, she found Jonathan every day in the parking area, and every day they did their little routine of getting Tammy into the car. In the third week, Paul appeared. Clearly, he was not aware of Tammy because suddenly, he looked as if he were dying of apoplexy.

Jonathan revelled in his friend's discomfort and shock, so when Gabrielle left, he ground out through his teeth. 'See what the hell is going on?'

'Are you telling me that is your father's child?'

Jonathan nodded. 'Yep, my little sister.'

'Dear God...' Paul looked sick. 'I hope your mother never finds out.'

'No, she is not going to hear it from me, and I will kill anyone who tells her.'

Gabrielle stared at her father and then at Charlotte. Somehow, they had figured out what she had done and both were mad. Wondering how that had happened, she noticed papers in Charlotte's hand. The woman must have been digging in her room, probably scrounging around for money, and found those damn documents she should have kept in her handbag. Then, both started accusing her of things she had not even thought about.

'She doesn't have her father's name.' Charlotte decided to climb onto her high horse.

'She didn't have it when she was unregistered.' Gabrielle retorted tartly.

'Why?' Malcolm asked.

'You know why. Neither of you can look after yourselves, how would you look after her? I just wanted to do what is best for her, without having to run after you all the time.'

'You are saying that we are both incompetent, accusing me of being an unfit mother.' Charlotte cut in.

Gabrielle was exasperated. She knew she had done wrong, and felt guilty enough about it, but their phoney *I'm concerned about my child* was not sticking. 'What do you want me to do now, go undo everything?'

'Can you?' Malcolm asked curiously.

'I suppose I could try. But can't we resolve this in a different way?' She was tempted to tell them that she suspected that neither would be around too many years more to look after Tammy, so her shocking deed already took care of who was to be her guardian, because she would be known as her mother, but that sounded cold and callous, even if it felt like the truth. 'I'll do something for you, something huge.'

Charlotte threw herself onto the sofa and pointed at her. 'Something huge, you say. So if I asked for all your money, you would give it to me?'

Gabrielle closed her eyes; here was their true destination. They probably were not half upset about Tammy not being registered as theirs, what they really wanted was the money. She looked at her father; he turned away. Obviously, he did not want to participate in the conversation now, even if agreeing with Charlotte. 'How much do you want?' She asked coldly.

'All of it.' Charlotte announced emphatically.

'Fine,' Gabrielle said. 'I will go to the bank and make the transfer.'

'How much is it?' Charlotte queried.

Gabrielle wanted to lie, so she could split it and give them a portion, because she and Tammy needed that money, but something happened in her head and she told them the stupid amount.

'I'm glad you didn't lie.' Charlotte said, her eyes gleaming. 'Tomorrow, all of it in here.' She gave Gabrielle a piece of paper with banking details.

Of course they came prepared; Tammy was merely the excuse they chose to get to it. She gazed at both of them with dislike; they were pathetic. 'How did you know how much I had?'

'You think you are the only clever one around here?'

'I will part with it willingly if you sign something that tells me you will never ask for her back.'

'However many signatures you want.' Charlotte made a dismissive gesture. 'And don't think that I'm a bad mother. But I'm making you sign something as well.'

'For what?' Gabrielle wondered what demands they could possibly impose, but seeing Charlotte's face, she decided not to push her luck too far. 'Fine, and after that, neither of you will say a word, ever, nor interfere in any way.'

She thought of telling Charles then kept herself in check, instinctively knowing what his reaction would be. He would not mince words, he would not feel sorry and he would find a way to prevent her from impoverishing herself, because that was exactly what she was about to do; now that she needed to create a future for Tammy.

She told him nothing, went to the bank, did the transaction, and then they sat at home writing some personal contracts. It was all insane and idiotic, but she needed to protect herself as much as she needed to protect Tammy.

What had they wanted in their papers? That she never demand anything from them. No money, no house, and who knew what else? She had what she wanted so she happily signed so they would get off her back. But four weeks later, she witnessed the horrific results of their doomed transaction.

It was Saturday and she had gone out with Tammy, as she needed new clothes. She made it a rule to never leave the baby with the crazy pair - as she thought of them - because as she had told Charles, she trusted neither with parenting skills. Besides, Charlotte usually passed out in some corner, and a screaming baby was not what she wanted to find on her return. Malcolm... perhaps there were people who were born without natural caring instincts.

Driving up to the house, Gabrielle stared. There in the middle of the gravel-yard stood Selena, their housekeeper, lifting her arms. She lived at the back in her own apartments so she always lent a hand.

'Selena,' Gabrielle jumped out of the car. 'What is the matter?'

Selena gave her a tear-smeared face, rattled off an extremely long sentence in Xhosa, and her arms waved in all directions.

Gabrielle placed her arms on her shoulders. 'Slowly Selena, tell me in English what happened.'

'You have to go, Gabrielle, you and the baby. This is very bad, and I'm going too, I have two children, I am not staying for this. You two must go.'

Selena was too agitated; she would have to go find out for herself. 'I'll go look, but please stay with Tammy.'

'Five minutes.' Selena said as she wiped the tears furiously. 'And then I go.'

Gabrielle rushed into the house and saw no one as she walked through the hall and lounge. She looked through a few rooms more and then turned into the study. All blood drained from her face.

Resignedly, she sat on the sofa and took Charlotte's wrist in her hand. There was no pulse. Her father... he still breathed but would not be able to for much longer, no matter how fast any ambulance could be. All he managed to say was. 'He wanted the money.' Then, he was gone.

She called Selena and asked if she knew anything.

'I saw him five seconds, but not well.' She turned herself sideways. 'Then I was upstairs, polishing the passage panels. They started screaming, but I could not hear. Charlotte and the man did all the screaming. Then he must have given them something— I don't know what.' Selena shivered. 'I came down but he was nowhere, only them, like that.' She pointed to the house.

What difference did it make what the strange man had given them; they were both dead. She understood Selena's urgent desire to go home to the Eastern Cape perfectly; she was not going to endanger her life for other people's stupidity.

Gabrielle couldn't cry; tears would not come. She called Charles, then managed to convince Selena to call the police, and await their arrival, while she tried to think about this calamity, which she wanted no part of.

Charles arrived before the police, not altogether surprised at the bedlam this was going to create and told Gabrielle as soon as he saw her to get into her car with the baby and go anywhere for a couple of hours, even a hotel if they became tired. He wanted no photographer catching sight of either of them.

Later, when he found them at the Crowne Plaza in Rosebank, he became raging mad when hearing what had taken place, how, and why, but what use was getting upset? The outcome screamed folly and if possible, he had to protect the girls from it. But he could not help himself and told Gabrielle. 'Did I not tell you not to give them anything? Look at what their insanity caused. And now, you have nothing.'

'I am sorry too, but not for giving them the money, for what happened. I didn't like them, but I didn't want them to go like this. But I have a good job so I think I'll manage to look after Tammy.'

'You have no idea the arduous path ahead. Just be thankful neither of you has your father's name. This way, no one will connect Gabrielle or Tammy Dunstan to him, his reputation, and this sorry mess, because, dear God, who knows who this killer is? And the police know you saw nothing, so they won't need you.'

Charles and Amy went flat hunting near Knight Industries, furnished it, and surprised Gabrielle one afternoon. This was a nuisance, but now, maybe the girls would actually have a future without their capricious father's shadow looming over them. It was all a sad and distasteful affair, but he had known that it would eventually end like this.

CHAPTER FIVE

Something had happened in Gabrielle's life because she was becoming happier as time went on. Jonathan knew this to be true, because he had seen the melancholy as well. Since the first time he had spoken to her in his father's office, he had noticed that she carried an inherent sadness around. He had tried to ask on occasion, but she never gave anything away, so he wondered if she had broken up with his father because he never saw them together as a couple anymore, except when he ran into them at the office, on their way to the odd meal.

He had appeared at his parents' house unannounced on numerous occasions, but Charles was always there. He did not quite get this relationship so perhaps the whole thing had been one of those things, a mistake. And honestly, who would not be tempted with Gabrielle? She was exquisite.

Every afternoon he waited for her so he could give her a hand, and see Tammy. The baby was growing into the cutest little girl and he enjoyed watching her go through her milestones.

Paul made the occasional appearance and Jonathan could tell that he liked Gabrielle. Unashamedly, Paul flirted openly with her, but peculiarly, Gabrielle did not fall for it. It was as if she were immune to the schemes of men, and there were quite a few in the building who had their eye on her. He boiled as he heard them speculating about her.

She might be his father's mistress, or ex-mistress for all he knew because she said nothing concerning the relationship so he dared not ask, but she was also a woman alone and his little sister's mother. He wanted them nowhere near her.

They were celebrating. Amelia had received excellent reviews for her latest stage work and when she was happy, he was happy. Everything was wonderful when it went well with her career. When it did not, it was like living in a madhouse. She cried for no apparent reason, screamed at everyone, became rude, and made an annoying pest of herself. She was in fact a very difficult person to get along with.

Her laughter filled the restaurant and people looked their way. Jonathan did not like it when people paid them too much attention but she swam in it because she was a glutton for compliments. She needed them constantly, as if she never believed them the first time. She also loved things, and measured relationships and friendships by what she received.

Her character was extremely flawed but that she was beautiful, there was no doubt. What most people did not know was that just about all of her beauty was shop-bought. Her long blonde mane consisted of extensions and an expensive salon that kept it shiny and perfect. Her legs were the product of liposuction and very painful exercises. Her enticing chest was fake, her flat stomach had been tucked a few times, and she had already messed with her face unnecessarily.

He would not have cared if she had climbed out of a plastic factory, if she were a nice person. She sort of was nice to the people she wanted to be nice to, but if one fell in her bad books— she was the meanest, ugliest voice anyone hoped not to hear.

He glanced at her; she was behaving rather well tonight. Everything was running so smoothly, he was sure he was about to slide down some trap she had set up. Some of those had turned out to be quite the experiences, but this one felt a little suspect.

Suddenly, a light bulb exploded in his face. He hated that. She in contrast, was moving in her chair as if she were posing. Of course she was posing; this was what she lived for. Sometimes, he wondered if succeeding on the stage was as important as just being known.

When the photographer moved away, she reached for his hand. 'Darling,' she purred. 'I am doing so well that I'm feeling extremely happy. I wish you would make me even happier.'

He grinned and leaning forward, kissed her. That stupid flash went off again. He made a dismissive gesture, hoping the photographer understood and went away for good. 'How happy do you want me to make you?' He asked close to her face.

'A long time happy.'

That meant that she wanted to get out of here. 'I will make you happy, all right,' He was about to deepen the kiss as a prelude of things to come but noticing hovering nuisance again, restrained himself. Hardly the picture he wanted to see in the papers.

She sighed and pulled a little away from him. 'Do you love me?'

It was not as if he had never thought about the question, but now that she asked, he did not know what to say, or if he should answer at all.

'You have to tell me if you do.' She moved in her seat strangely.

He gazed at her for a few seconds, wondering what her expedition was, because she did not do things without reason. She wanted something she had either seen or someone had and she was feeling envious about. He studied her for a couple of seconds longer then realised that her attention was focused on moving target photographer and not on the conversation.

Unable to think what she could possibly want, he excused himself and went to the men's room. He stood there a minute then washed his hands. On his way out, he stopped by the partition trellis and watched her at the table. Her looks demanded attention and she was revelling in being gawked. Then he realised she was communicating by sign language with the photographer, one finger featuring rather prominently as it tapped the left hand.

Just as dawn slowly but surely appeared, so did her mission become clear. For some unfathomable reason, she was trying to get him to propose. Clearly, she did not care about a ring right now because she knew full well that he did not have one, but she wanted the words. For a split second, he felt like indulging her then sense flooded in. Could she not do anything without it becoming a performance?

He wondered what he wanted in the woman he would eventually marry. He wanted someone like... Beauty, yes. He wanted to enjoy looking at her, and although Amelia was beautiful, there was some underlying thing that did not completely satisfy him. Respect, definitely. Chauvinistic, he did not want to be, but he wanted a woman who would look up to him, who needed his help, who asked for his opinion. She was not that woman. And he definitely wanted someone who could excite him in ways Amelia had never been able to do. She was sex, fantastic sex, and she knew things that made men crazy, so in that respect, he could not find better. Yet, how many times, after long passionate nights, did he leave her place still wanting?

Returning to the table, he asked as soon as he sat down. 'What is going on?'

She pouted. 'I want to feel special, to tell people that you want me. I want to have your ring on my finger. I want them to film and do spreads— I already have two magazines willing to follow every detail of my life.' She told him excitedly. 'What I do, wear, who I see. It's so grand to see people wanting to be like me. They are so jealous of everything I have, how I look, what I can do.'

He was not one for commitments and serious relationships, but most of what had come out of her mouth was wrong where a marriage was concerned. "Whoa!" He told himself. "She wants to be engaged, not married. At least that's what I think she wants." Evidently, this was something she saw as an accessory, and was going to push until she got it. But why was it he felt as if he were the ornament? 'We should go, and talk about this later.'

'I want to talk about it now.'

'No, I am not discussing this here.' He folded his napkin. 'You like public displays, I don't. So, coming?' He saw she wanted to protest, but realising his unmoving stance, gave in.

'How did it end?' Paul asked after he heard the story.

'In a fight that led to tears, and I didn't believe a word she said, or the tears she shed. She was trying to bamboozle me, but you know how much I enjoy being hoodwinked.'

'Maybe she really loves you and wants to be married.'

'Perhaps, but does it look like I want to be married?' Jonathan asked caustically.

'No that is not the *I want to be married* mug.' Paul laughed then. 'Women are crazy. So, where does everything stand now?'

'When she saw I was not going to be pushed, she apologised. But even the sex felt strange afterwards.'

Gabrielle looked around the parking area. Jonathan was late. Every afternoon he was there before her, so where was he today?

'Hello,'

She turned quickly, a smile on her face, which diminished somewhat when she saw who it was. It was odd, he was so much like Jonathan, even the eye and hair colour, yet they were miles apart. 'Hi.'

Paul registered the reaction. 'Can I help you today?'

'Where is Jonathan?' She looked past him again.

'I can help if you need to leave now.'

'Jonathan seems to enjoy this thing every afternoon so I'll wait a few more minutes.' She took Tammy out and cradled her lovingly.

Paul peered at the baby. 'She looks like you, very pretty.'

Gabrielle coloured slightly. 'Thank you.'

'What does her father think? Does he love her?'

She always wondered what these two men were about because they confused her with their questions. It was as if they never thought about asking proper things, both curiously fascinated with who the father was. 'Do you know anything about babies?' "Let's see how he feels."

'Not really. Is there something specific you need to know?'

'I was wondering about a teething remedy. She's not sleeping well so I'm a little exhausted.'

'What about the father, doesn't he help?' He would really like to hear the answer to that one because he could not imagine Charles staying out of the family home.

There it was again. 'Huh, don't worry, I'll figure it out.'

'Jonathan,' Paul called. 'We have been waiting for you.'

A smile spread on Jonathan's face, the idea that she had waited making him feel good. 'Hello cutie.' He spoke to Tammy.

She gurgled back and lifted her arms to him.

Gabrielle merely passed him the baby. 'Paul, if you don't mind, you can help me now.'

Paul nodded, collapsed the contraption, placed it in the boot, and glanced at Jonathan. Then, he turned to look at Gabrielle. Goodness, she was so bloody gorgeous and Jonathan was thinking the exact same thing. 'Right,' he said, but noticed that neither was paying attention. 'I'm off to the moon; I hear someone turned a piece of it into cheese.'

'Okay,' Jonathan waved. 'Have a good evening.'

'Thank you, Paul.'

Shaking his head, Paul went to his car.

'She's growing.'

'Honestly, do you expect babies to stay the same forever?' Gabrielle smiled. 'Anyway, thank you, we need to go home.'

'Do you ever get a babysitter?'

'For what?'

'Don't you go out on the weekends?'

'Not really, and if I do I take her with.'

'Does her father come to stay?' His piercing blue eyes fixed themselves on hers, and there was that weird feeling he got right in the middle of his brain.

Gabrielle sighed deeply, back to the father story. Maybe she should tell these two crazies the truth, but that made her nervous. Stories tended to liberate themselves and become something the original teller never intended. Besides, she did not want anyone to ever doubt that she had a right to be her sister's parent, or to suspect that she was not. She reached out, took Tammy, and sat her in the car. 'Goodbye, Jonathan.'

She wondered why someone was pounding on a door so harshly. Turning in bed, she half-opened an eye and listened to the din again. Did people have to be unnecessarily noisy and never think of others? It was Saturday, Tammy was actually peaceful, and she needed those extra winks. 'It's my door.' She realised.

Jumping out of bed, she scrambled for her bathrobe, and stormed down the passage, into the sitting room and looked through the peephole on the door. 'Who is this?' She asked as she saw two strange men standing outside.

'Open up, we need to talk to you.'

'Who are you?'

'I'm Calvin, and this is Dimitri.' One of the men said. 'Open this door, damn it; or must I keep hitting on it?'

Gabrielle stretched the safety chain as much as it would go. 'Why are you making this racket?'

Dimitri's first reaction was a strange one, as if he was surprised, expecting something else.

Calvin leered at her openly. 'Listen girlie, your father owes my boss a lot of money and he wants it back.'

Gabrielle tightened the robe and crossed her arms. 'My father is dead.'

'And my boss doesn't care, he wants his money.'

'Sorry, I don't have any spare to give away.' She pushed the door.

He stuck his boot in the gap. 'I'm going to tell you this only one more time. Your dear father Malcolm owes my boss half a million Rand.'

Her mouth fell open in shock. 'But he's dead.'

'So we have heard, but we also know that you have money. So missy, you will pay daddy's debt, otherwise my boss will announce his business to the world. And let me tell you, it is not pretty, or above board.' Calvin pulled a paper from his pocket. 'And this says right here that if daddy cannot pay, you will.' He pointed.

'What?' She went pale and her gaze turned to silent Dimitri. 'Can I see it?' She stuck her hand outside.

'It's a copy so you can keep it.' Calvin passed her the paper. 'As you can see, you signed it.'

'I did no such thing.' She became almost breathless. 'But, it can't be.' Her eyes ran over said document, where it stated that in case of Malcolm being unable to pay, she would be responsible for his debt. 'I never signed this...'

Dimitri finally decided to open his mouth. 'But it is your signature, right?'

She nodded and leaned against the wall. 'It looks like my handwriting, but I don't remember... I don't have this kind of money anymore; he took it from me. Or rather, Charlotte took it.'

'She did, did she? So where is it?' Calvin asked.

'How should I know? I transferred it to her bank account at,' she told them the bank's name. From the looks of them, they were serious so she was going to waste their time until she could speak with Charles.

'I tell you what I'm going to do.' Calvin gave her a squint look, grabbed his phone, and started talking. 'Hi boss,' he explained quickly. 'Boss, don't get upset, I think she's telling the truth.' He said as he studied Gabrielle. 'Can we look for it first? Can't be that difficult to find if Charlotte had it in her account. How long to sort it out? Maybe two weeks, tops.' He disconnected.

Her heart dropped and she felt gooseflesh spreading over her arms, this felt as dangerous as sinking sand. 'What?' She tried to sound brave.

'This is what we are going to do. I'm going to search for two weeks, and you do the same. You call me if you find it.' He scribbled his name and number on the other side of the paper.

She glanced at it, Calvin Ford. 'If you find it, I don't need to know, but I must tell you?'

'Okay,' Dimitri said. 'It's obvious there is a misunderstanding.' He took the paper, scribbled on it and returned it to her hand. 'Have mine as well.'

Calvin frowned. 'What are you doing?'

Dimitri made a gesture towards her. 'She's just a girl, I doubt she needs scare tactics to realise that there is a huge problem here.'

'Look,' Calvin said more calmly. 'It's not our money, it's my boss' and he does not listen to excuses. He lent your father money on good faith that you stood surety for him.'

This was worse than a mess, and how a man had lent money without knowing her, she did not understand. 'I have never met your boss, why would he trust Malcolm?'

'Because my boss can do whatever he wants and he knows about you. You brought a nice little packet from Europe, which Malcolm dangled in front of everyone's nose every time he wanted something.'

This was bad, very bad. 'I need that money too.'

'Perhaps, but this says it belongs to my boss.'

'Not all of it.' Should she have said that?

'Well, now, however much it is, it basically belongs to our boss.' He pointed to himself and Dimitri. 'Besides, you are pretty enough to find a rich husband. In fact, maybe I should work out a plan with the boss.' He leered at her.

Dimitri made a sound, something between laughter and disgust, as if he thought it was a joke. She studied Calvin closely. Perhaps he was having a bad day because he did not appeal to anything within her. Greasy hair, gold cap on one of his upper teeth, floral shirt almost open to the navel, and shag on chest. She shivered and returned her gaze to Dimitri. Oddly, he reminded her of Jonathan, just perhaps older but more or less the same height, body build, and stubble, except that it was darker and the eyes were brown. She turned her gaze back to Calvin.

'I see you are noticing that I'm quite the catch.' Calvin crossed one leg over the other and leaned a hand on the doorframe.

The only thing she would catch him with was the net they used at the SPCA for rabid dogs. 'You go look for that money, and leave me alone.'

'Trust me,' Dimitri told her. 'You want to deal with us, not the boss, and definitely not with the other guys,' he pointed to the paper in her hand. 'Don't lose it and call me.'

'Whatever, just go.'

'Nobody forgets half a million Rand, especially not our boss. And please take this seriously, because he knows how you got your hands on that baby.' Calvin announced.

She went pale, then her brain went right back to functioning. 'If he knows that why didn't he know about the money too?'

'Obviously, Charlotte was talking about the baby before she decided to pull that one on you. So you see he already has the upper hand.'

Dimitri dropped his tone of voice and pointed to himself and Calvin. 'We are errand boys and don't mean you any harm, but the boss is different. He will have no problem sending other guys to hurt you.'

'Fine,' she told them tiredly. 'I'll see if I can find it. Now, I have things to do.' She closed the door and leaned against it with a hand on her chest.

'Two weeks, Gabrielle.' Calvin said and hit the door.

They knew way too much already and what exactly was she supposed to do about someone else's debt? But if she found the money, would she be able to get it back? How? It was not as if banks understood personal dilemmas.

'They said half a million?' Charles asked in shock.

'That's what they said.'

'Do you know what kind of business this was?'

'I know nothing. I don't know what they did, who they knew, where they went... so this is all I have.' She showed him the paper.

'Let me make a copy and write their details down. Perhaps I can discover something. I know some people—'

'Daddy, you are not to get yourself in trouble because of two pathetic people.'

'I am not thinking trouble at all; I am thinking keeping you out of it and solving this mystery.' He perused the paper. 'It's written well, and I don't like it that they threatened you. Do you know what this Calvin and Dimitri do?'

'No, they work for someone I know nothing about; but I have a fantastic description for you.' She told him about almost too quiet Dimitri and lard-head Calvin.

He pursed his lips. 'You're serious he made a pass at you.'

'Why would I lie about a disturbed man like that?'

Unexpectedly, Charles burst into laughter. 'Well, imagine dating and marrying that.'

She stared at him, crinkling her nose and forehead, then, she too saw the comical picture; a man in a neon tuxedo, walking down the aisle to some Country and Western tune. Hair greased down, gold tooth sparkling, a pair of pointy white cowboy boots peeping from the bottom of his pants, and a huge ruffle barely covering his hairy chest. She also laughed.

Jonathan stuck his head in the office. Whatever they were laughing about must really be funny because his father did not often laugh like that. As for the sound she was making, it made him smile and think of fun. 'Am I interrupting?'

'No, come in.' Charles motioned and became serious. 'It's all right, sweetheart, I promise I will look into it.'

'Thank you.' She walked away from the window. 'Hello, Jonathan.'

'Gabrielle,' he nodded.

She did not know why, but Jonathan came across as a confused man. Sometimes, he was like this. What was this? Strange and moody, and at other times, he was open and funny, as if he had forgotten about something that infuriated him.

Gabrielle made a pit stop at Amy's desk. She was friendly and supportive, and a comfortable relationship was developing between them. Subsequently, every time she needed advice concerning Tammy, she asked Amy, as she had two children of her own and was a down-to-earth mom.

CHAPTER SIX

'Jonathan,' Amelia made a scene when he went to pick her up from the theatre Sunday evening. She had been trying how long for him to come watch her again, as he usually only made the first and last performance, so this little surprise pleased her a great deal. She did not like his disinterest in the limelight much, because she needed him on her arm.

It had taken her a while to find him, she was not about to scare him off, but did he have to be so stubborn? Presently, he was an absolute brick wall about the subject; she had to take it slow until he came around. Then, she would be in the news more, being gorgeous, alongside one of the best-looking men in town, not to mention just about richest. Well, he would be one day, when he took over from Charles.

'You did well.' He told her and leaning over, brushed her lips lightly.

She grabbed his shirt and kept his mouth against hers a moment longer, just long enough for a photographer to get his shot. 'Thank you Jonathan, I enjoy pleasing people.'

'Are you ready?' The less time he spent here, the better.

They went to Melrose Arch since she wanted to be seen yet again. He could not open a magazine or newspaper where a picture or article did not mention her and she thought she needed to chase after flashbulbs.

Dinner was a long dreary affair, he was tired but she ran on batteries. He thought he was going to start yawning in public, because she was determined to stay out as long as she could endure. She forgot that he went to work at eight, while she usually slept until eleven.

They went to her place, as they did most times, and he was so tired that he fell asleep on the sofa while she made coffee. She had offered him a drink but he thought that sleep and alcohol did not sound like good partners, as he still had to drive home.

'Darling,' she called huskily.

He opened his eyes and saw her in a sexy pink negligee. 'Sorry,' sitting up, he reached for the coffee.

'You are tired.' She said. 'I've never known you to pass on beautiful nightclothes that simply scream to be taken off.'

He gave her a crooked smile. 'Yes,' he eyed the pink froth surrounding her. 'It's very nice, but I have been extremely busy.'

'Drink your coffee, and maybe you should stay.' She slipped onto the sofa beside him, ran a hand down his leg, and reached for her own cup.

When they finally made it to the bedroom, he would swear he had swallowed lead. He could barely move, felt as if his body belonged to someone else, and his reactions although all there and on cue, were merely so because she was in control.

When he opened his eyes, he saw it was four in the morning. Tiredly, he climbed out of bed, got dressed and went home. There, he took a shower and discovered that he could not sleep.

He walked around the place, going into all the rooms, wondering why he had bought a double-storey house. Then he recalled why he had acquired the property. His financial advisor had told him that it was a wise investment and he knew this to be true. In the last year, the value had gone up by forty percent. It was still too large; he needed to fill it with something.

He went into the gym, did a workout, took another shower, and looked at the time. Could not possibly go to sleep now, so he got ready for work. Getting there early, he sat in his car, just watching people drive into the underground parking.

He saw Gabrielle arrive and studied her as she got out of the car. She looked flustered, and leaning forward, rested her forehead against the car.

Getting out, he walked over. 'Morning, Gabrielle. Are you all right?'

She glanced at him. 'Just tired. Tammy is teething, so she doesn't always sleep when she should.'

'Which means, neither do you.' He looked into the car. 'Naturally, she's having the time of her life now.' He said with a grin as he saw the little girl fast asleep.

'Yes, babies are very selfish.' She smiled wanly. 'I wish we had beds around here.'

'Interesting you say that. If you are really that tired, come up to my office. I have a sofa-bed, and it has never been used. I got it a while back thinking that I would, but never have. Even if I'm not there, you can just go in.'

Definitely odd. 'Thank you, but I think I'm okay.'

'Do you know where my office is?'

Clearly, he realised that she was not taking his offer altogether seriously. 'I have an idea.'

'I mean it. Come rest when you need to. And you should not drive around if you are so tired.' He was one to talk. Yesterday, he had felt just like this. He got the stroller ready and then watched as she took the sleeping baby out. He enjoyed watching her; she was a good mother, very loving, with a soft touch and voice.

Tammy decided that she was not standing for being disturbed, so she opened her mouth and lungs as soon as she felt her back in the flat position. Gabrielle tried her best, but even that was not good enough.

'Let me.' Jonathan suggested and took her from Gabrielle. 'Hey, my baby,' he cooed. 'What is making you so unhappy today?'

Tammy hiccupped, sobbed softly, and started talking in her baby language. Both Jonathan and Gabrielle stared; she was complaining.

'I think she missed you.' Gabrielle suggested. A weekend was probably a long time for a baby not to see someone she liked, and she liked Jonathan a lot.

'That is adorable.' He said with a pleased grin. 'Okay, I'll take her up.'

That morning, they got many interesting looks, but none more interested as when Paul caught sight of them from across the other lift. He sighed. He had to get rid of the crush he had on Gabrielle, because she was never going to look at him as she was doing at Jonathan right now.

'I'm serious about resting,' Jonathan told her as they were in the lift again. She had told him to take the other because he was going up and she down, but he ignored her. Climbing out on her floor, he studied her pale face. 'Are you also skipping food?'

'I'm fine.' She didn't like it when he paid her too much attention. It made her feel peculiar, breathless, and shy.

Then, for he did not know what reason, he leaned over and kissed her cheek. The contact turned her pink, and as she caught her breath, her gaze flew to his. He knew instantly that something unusual had just happened. His heart started a drumbeat against his ribs, and he too felt as if his breath was being knocked out. All he wanted to do was push her against the wall, press his body against hers, and kiss her properly.

'Thank you Jonathan, you are kind.' She did a stupid thing too. Raising her hand, she placed it on his face and with a finger smoothed one eyebrow. Then returning to her senses, she let go, and went to work.

He stood there, unable to move, basking in the rush her touch had caused.

'There you are,' Paul said as Jonathan walked into his office. 'Where were you?'

'Helping Gabrielle, Tammy isn't sleeping so she's tired.' Jonathan dropped his laptop on the desk, removed his jacket and went to the window. 'I don't understand why she doesn't get help; it's not as if they can't afford it.'

Paul decided to veer the conversation in another direction. 'So, did you see Amelia this weekend?'

'Yes, even went to the show again, but how many times does she think I can watch it? I'm not saying she's bad, because she's not, but it's very boring. And I can't stand all that attention.'

'What on earth were you thinking when you started dating her anyway? That comes with the territory.'

'And it displeases me a great deal.'

'Oh yes, why I'm here. Leroy Granger.'

'Daddy,' a deep furrow stretched across Gabrielle's forehead. 'Please tell me you will not get involved in this.'

'Not if I can help it, but I definitely want to remove you and Tammy from danger because heaven knows what your father was doing with those low lives. The verdict about the money is this. No one knows what happened to it, except that Charlotte withdrew it all. Obviously, she was afraid you might change your mind and do something else. Could they have spent it?'

'They had it four weeks. I don't think it's possible to spend it all, even for a drug addict. And they didn't buy anything.'

'Where does one stash a bag like that? Because you cannot walk out of a bank with that amount of cash in your pockets,'

'The problem is that boss. How do I pay him? Because they promised to return, and will keep coming back until I do something. But if you can't find it through the right channels, could they?'

'You never know. These people have connections and often know more than everyone else.'

'Then I hope they find it and keep it because I don't want to see them again.'

'Yes, the less you know of those people, the better.' Charles placed a hand on his chest. 'I swear your father gives me heartburn, even after he's gone. Sorry,'

'Don't apologise to me, I have sleepless nights trying to figure out what he was into. For Tammy's sake, I hope we resolve this quickly. Now I also know how mom felt when she chose to lie to me, because I might have to do the same with Tammy. Poor mom,'

'Eleanor was a grand lady but Malcolm's parents did not approve and were not moved that I stood firmly by her. In fact, they used to look down their noses, and did nothing to stop her from leaving.'

'Did they both die before I was born?'

'A couple of years after. Your grandfather was diagnosed with cancer, and your grandmother became exhausted with it all. He died when you were two, and she six months later, and Malcolm began an unmatched spending spree. He had been reckless before hence why your mother could not deal with it, but when they passed on, he went mad.'

'If we can't find the money, what do you think those people will do?'

'You are not to concern yourself about this any longer.'

'Dad, what the hell are you doing?' Jonathan stormed into Charles' office.

'What are you referring to?' Charles asked.

'Why am I getting calls from the financial department checking if all the paperwork is ready for the money you are borrowing?'

'The attorney told me to do it this way. I wanted to pay through Knight Industries, even from my personal account but he said it would be frowned upon. One can't give money to the Russian mafia without someone becoming suspicious.' Charles removed his jacket.

An incredulous look appeared on Jonathan's face. 'You're joking...'

'No joke, I have to pay them half a million.'

Jonathan sank into the chair, absolute horror on his face. 'Dad, please tell me you are not involved with the underworld.'

'Oh, no,' Charles tugged at his tie. 'Do you feel hot? It's an unfortunate business but I have to take care of it. If I don't...' Charles sat down heavily. 'I'm not feeling well. Hope the doctor isn't right.'

'Right about what?' Jonathan asked concerned.

'He says my heart has some problems.' Charles smiled ruefully.

'And you think it's funny. What did he tell you to do?'

'Just take it slow as there isn't much to be done. Anyway,' Charles dismissed with a hand. 'It's all sorted. I've already spoken to the bank manager, everything is legal. I just have to speak to the police—'

'The police?' Jonathan stuttered in shock.

'Don't worry, I'm not a criminal, and neither is Knight Industries.'

'Can you tell me what this is about?'

Charles placed a hand on his chest then gazed at Jonathan; a young man who stood on his own two feet and no man could be prouder than he was of his son, but those two little girls... what chance would they have if something happened to him? Damn it, he had forgotten to change his will, he wanted to leave Gabrielle some means so she could look after herself and her sister. 'I think you must call the ambulance, I'm not feeling well at all.'

'Oh lord,' Jonathan rushed around the desk and pulled the tie off Charles, unbuttoned the shirt and grabbed the phone at the same time. 'Amy, get anyone you need to, dad is having a heart attack.'

CHAPTER SEVEN

'Are you okay?' Paul asked as he dropped onto the chair beside Jonathan.

'Not fantastic, but obviously much better than he is.'

'How is your mom dealing with it?'

'Not too badly, because she knew about his heart problems,' Jonathan said sharply. 'I'm so upset with them. Apparently, it wasn't necessary to mention it to me, and both had been preparing... What about me, didn't I need to prepare?'

'Well, you know how strange parents are.' Paul leaned back and was quiet for a few minutes. 'Does Gabrielle know?'

'And how would I explain her to my mother?'

'She has a baby—'

'Which she shouldn't have.' Jonathan said irritated. 'I'm sorry, but right now, we are important. Besides, what difference does it make if Tammy is here? She'll never remember any of this.'

'I didn't think Tammy needed to be here for herself, but your dad will want to see her. Actually, I was thinking more about Gabrielle.'

'Of course you were,' Jonathan told him furiously. 'If something happens to him, you are free to do as you wish—'

'Stop,' Paul cut him short. 'I know you are distressed but don't start on nonsense.'

'Nonsense, you say? I almost hear the racing heart.'

"Funny, you have described yourself rather well." Paul wanted to tell him then he pointed. 'So much for you thinking Gabrielle unimportant; evidently, Amy thinks otherwise.'

Jonathan turned. When Gabrielle saw him, she passed the stroller over to Amy and held out her hands. She looked pale, scared and sort of ended in an embrace, squashed against him.

'Oh Jonathan,' her eyes shone unhappily. 'What— how did it happen?'

'He wasn't feeling well, and then—' Thinking about this unexplainable relationship upset him, but without warning, he felt like crying on her shoulder. He pressed closer into her, letting her warm body and fresh scent comfort him.

'Are you not allowed to see him?'

'Mother is in there.' He always wondered about her reactions every time his mother's name came up. Was there not supposed to be a twitch, a jump, a guilty look when her lover's wife was mentioned? But no, nothing, and here she was, as if she had a right, totally unfazed. 'It doesn't look good at all but they are running some tests, even if he is still unconscious.'

'Did something upset him? Did he have a shock, or eat something he shouldn't have?'

'We were talking. Although,' Jonathan said with realisation. 'We were discussing a peculiar subject.'

'And what was that?'

'He was telling me some strange story about paying the Russian mafia off.'

Gabrielle went paler and closed her eyes, but the tears still squeezed through.

Now, he was the one comforting her, and there was that confusing resentment again. She mixed him up. He did not know what he felt, or how to feel when in her presence.

'I told him to leave it.' She rested her head against his shoulder as soft sobs left her.

'Do you know something about that?'

Amelia came around the corner, like an apparition. 'Jonathan,' she stared at the scene before her, not liking it at all. Now who the hell was that in his arms?

Jonathan let Gabrielle go and turned to Amelia. 'Thank you for coming, but you didn't have to. How did you find out?'

'I heard it on the radio and knew you needed me.'

'Gabrielle,' he realised he had not finished the conversation. 'I still want to talk to you. But I'll let you know.'

Gabrielle went to sit beside Paul.

Automatically, he placed an arm about her shoulders. 'Are you okay?'

She nodded, but her eyes were full of tears. 'What if he dies?'

'Let's not go there.'

Charles came to, but everyone knew, him included, that he would not live much longer. So he started calling everyone in, one at a time.

'Jonathan,' he said. 'I'm sorry, but I am going to burden you with some things. Knight Industries is fine, and I know you will be a good leader; I'm not concerned there. What bothers me are the personal things. Of course, your mother is taken care of, but she is going to need companionship. See that you visit her regularly.'

'Yes dad, I will not just leave her in that large house and forget.'

'My anxiety is for Gabrielle and Tammy. I don't know if she ever told you—'

'Dad, I know what's going on but for the life of me, I never dreamt that you would cheat on mom. And,' he said angrily, as he stuck a hand into his hair. 'You have not only a young lover in distress but also a baby who...' he took a deep breath. 'Will never know her father.'

Charles' heart was the problem, not his head, so he stared at Jonathan, suddenly realising how his relationship with Gabrielle had been misconstrued. This also meant that she had not said a word, which was definitely best; the fewer people knew she was related to Malcolm, the better. The last thing he wanted was for more creeps to turn up, because Malcolm had cut quite a path through all financial institutions in the city, legal and illegal, so keeping Gabrielle and Tammy hidden was of paramount importance. Which reminded him again, she had to leave that flat.

'Don't worry, I will look after Tammy, after all she is my sister. And I promise I'll keep an eye on Gabrielle too.' Jonathan made an irritated sound. 'But why, dad? She's so young.'

Charles could not take his eyes off his son, suddenly seeing something he had not noticed before. 'Do you like Gabrielle?'

'Like...' he looked puzzled. 'I think I do, despite the fact that—'

Charles waved a hand. 'We already know this.' Now here was an opportunity but an opportunity for what? 'And yes, you must look after them both. Would you mind letting Gabrielle in, I want to see her.'

By a fortunate coincidence, Barbara was down in the doctor's office when Jonathan came out and told Gabrielle to go in. He eyed her with that mixture of confusion he could not explain. He wanted to dislike her, but found he could not, not completely.

Charles lifted a hand to her face as she stood against the bed. 'You know, to be a biological father is one thing, but to be one by choice, something else. I'm guessing this is what adoptive parents feel. I can't tell the difference.'

'Oh daddy,' the tears rolled down her face. 'You are breaking my heart, just like mommy did. I wanted you to be here always, to see me raise Tammy. I'm going to be sad for the rest of my life without you and I don't think my heart can be mended.'

'No sweetheart, you will get over it and remember me fondly.' He wiped her tears. 'Tell me something, are you friends with Jonathan and Paul?'

'Not really friends. Jonathan helps me every day with Tammy after work, and Paul sometimes. They are a bit strange, but also quite funny.'

'How strange?'

'They have this obsession I don't understand.'

'And what's that?'

'Ever since I met them they want to know all sorts of things regarding Tammy's father. What am I supposed to tell them? He's my father too, so I dodge the conversation. I think I drive them insane.'

Charles smiled, beginning to see the picture the two young idiots had in their minds. 'Which one of the two do you like best?'

'Paul is a joker. But lately I get the feeling he doesn't really want to be around me.'

'Why?'

'I don't know. I don't really understand either of them.'

'But you do like Jonathan,'

Unconsciously, a pink tinge crept across her face. 'He's very helpful and Tammy loves him to bits. She cries on Mondays when she sees him, because she missed him over the weekend. I think he's starting to love her too. It's all a little dangerous because if we ever leave—'

'No Gabrielle,' he interrupted as sternly as he possibly could. 'You must never leave. Promise me that you will not go anywhere.'

'But daddy—'

'No buts, it's too dangerous. Promise me.'

'Okay daddy.'

He caressed her face. 'That's my girl. Now, will you tell Paul to come see me?'

Paul stood awkwardly in the room. He had always admired Charles, ever since Jonathan had dragged him almost kicking and screaming to spend a weekend at home when they were sixteen, and thought they knew everything. Throughout the subsequent years, he could see Charles' influence on his life, as much as it was on Jonathan's.

'If ever there was a good friend, you are it. You have always looked out for Jonathan and I thank you for never encouraging him into the stupid things I see so many young men get involved in.'

'Well,' Paul smiled mischievously. 'I think we are a good match because he has done the same for me. I won't say we are perfect, but we have managed to stay out of trouble, and jail.'

'Thank God for that. Paul, I need to ask you something.'

'Sure, anything.'

'Where do you see this relationship of Jonathan's going?'

'You mean Amelia?'

'Yes. Is there a future? What I actually mean is, does Jonathan love her and is it a good future for him?'

'Uncle Charles, shouldn't you be asking him?'

'Humour me I'm a dying old man.'

Paul made an incongruous sound. Charles old? Never, but okay, they couldn't do anything about the dying. 'No, he does not enjoy that world at all. He likes her but she's—'

'I know what she is; I have friends who dated her before.' Charles made a face. 'Does he love her, or want to marry her?'

'Oh no,' Paul said quickly. 'I know she was trying to get herself engaged a while back, but—'

'I get the picture. Now for the real question, do you like Gabrielle?'

'Sure, she's a lovely girl, regardless—'

'That she has my child.' Charles smiled faintly; poor fools, both of them. 'Did you know that Gabrielle has been talking of moving?'

'But...' Paul's face fell. 'Jonathan— He loves his sister so much, she can't go.'

'No, she can't. Given time, do you suppose Jonathan could love Gabrielle?'

Any man could love Gabrielle. She was gorgeous, sweet, smart, and such a good mother. Paul fixed his gaze squarely on the man he thought of as a father. 'Uncle Charles, he is already half in love with her, he just doesn't realise it because he is too busy being mad at her for being your mistress.'

Charles took two deep breaths. 'And from the looks of things, so are you. Why are you taking a backseat?'

'Because it's him she wants.'

'Are you sure of this?'

'Oh I see everything they are not aware of. The looks, the blushes, the sighs, and all disguised under caring for Tammy. I have never seen Jonathan look at a woman the way he does at her. And it's not just a physical thing, it's much, much more, something he himself doesn't understand.'

'This is the best news I could get right now. I wanted to do something special for Gabrielle, but this... It's beyond perfect. Because Jonathan is like me, wouldn't you say?'

Paul nodded, that they were. In fact, they were the best example of what a father and son should be. They liked each other, respected the other's opinion above everyone else's, and had always enjoyed the other's company. Except for Gabrielle and everything pertaining to her life, he did not think there was a secret between them.

'Yes,' Charles smiled pleased. 'Now, I want you to help me get them together.'

'But, she's your—'

'Not for much longer.' Charles swallowed a painful breath. 'Only thing is; we need a catalyst to push them together because that little girl is very stubborn, and she has put it into her head that she does not want or need to love anyone else. However, she has a huge heart and is trying to fill it up with all things Tammy only.' Charles became pensive for a few seconds. 'Please give me your word of honour that you will not disclose our conversation, especially not to those two. But of course, it will be at your discretion.'

Charles could have thought of worse, and considering it, Paul realised that it wasn't such a bad idea. If Jonathan married, Amelia would leave him alone, or wouldn't she? At least she couldn't marry him. He sighed, trying to let go of Gabrielle from his fantasies. If ever there had been a smidgen of possibility, by doing this, he would be waving it goodbye. 'I give you my word.'

'Good man.' They spoke for a while; discussing this and that then finally, Charles told him. 'Now, will you go outside and see if Barbara is there?'

Charles was comfortable but definitely not well. His heart rate kept dropping and no one could do a thing about it. The doctors started talking pacemaker and for a day, there was hope. He asked to see them all again, and all said the farewells they could bear. Then he went into surgery, and even before they made the first incision, the heart attacks began, then, multiplied and his weakened body simply could not withstand the shock. None saw him alive again.

The one person she could most relate to was Jonathan, for both, even if he was not aware of it were Charles' children. Surprisingly, he seemed to feel the same.

Everyone was grieving but only Gabrielle truly understood what he was going through. During the day he called her up to his office or met her in the cafeteria. He liked how she sat silently drinking tea as he reminisced. She smiled and nodded but sometimes had trouble controlling the tears, so he reached across the table or desk and patted her hand.

He had not moved office, as the company had not yet appointed him officially and although he liked the things his father had collected, he felt peculiar around them. He was in two minds; should he remodel, or keep it as a memorial? He would ask Gabrielle.

She had a distinct knock, so he turned his head at the sound. She did little things that filled him with reassurance, and what he really liked about her, he noticed lately, was that she never complained. If she sat down, she probably could write a list of everything she did not have, all the things both she and Tammy needed, yet it seemed as if it had never occurred to her to ask or whinge, because shockingly, Charles had not made provision for them.

He motioned for her to sit as he was wrapping up a phone call and noticed that she looked exhausted. Tammy must be keeping her up nights again. He watched her sit in the comfortable armchair and lean her head back. Somehow, the conversation dragged a little longer, so when he finished, he could see that she was asleep. Moving around the desk, he went to stand in front of her. 'Gabrielle,' he called. She did not respond.

Leaning towards her, he noticed a few hairs stuck between her lips. Gently, he moved them away. She sighed and he stared at her mouth, feeling something happen inside him. He could not have helped himself if he had tried, which he absolutely didn't want to. Bending, he covered her mouth with his. He was doing nothing but touching her lips, but the rush that went through him was as if someone had plugged him in at the electrical socket.

Becoming a little bolder, he ran the tip of his tongue along her bottom lip. Her mouth opened, wanting more. Lightly, he savoured her maddening fresh sweetness, waiting for the moment when she opened her eyes and possibly slapped him. She did not and he thought that he would rip their clothes to shreds as his body told him that it wanted all of her. Lifting his head from hers, he took a step back, inhaled deeply, passed his hands through his hair, and went to sit behind the desk.

'Gabrielle,' he called. 'Gabrielle.' Nothing. 'Gaby,' he said suddenly, liking the intimate undertone.

She fixed her gaze on him and blushed. 'Sorry,'

'Is Tammy giving you sleepless nights again?'

She nodded, straightened her neck and passed her tongue over her lips.

He grabbed a pen on the desk and almost broke it in half.

She noticed his discomfort. 'Are you all right?'

'Just something on my mind,' he waved a hand above his head. Oh yes, he was trying to imagine what she looked like naked, in his bed. He started coughing to cover up that he was almost hyperventilating.

She got to her feet, went to the bar fridge, took out a bottle of Evian, poured it into a glass, and handed it to him. 'Just drink some.' She said as she patted his shoulder.

The door burst open and in traipsed Amelia dressed to the nines. Seeing Gabrielle's hand on Jonathan's shoulder, she narrowed her eyes. She did not like this little girl one bit. She was too cute, too wholesome, just too something and she wanted her nowhere near Jonathan. 'Darling,' she swept closer.

'Are you okay?'

'Thank you, Gabrielle.' Subconsciously, his hand went up to pat hers. 'I'll speak to you tomorrow.'

It was opening night for who knew what, which he vaguely recalled Amelia mentioning, but he had already forgotten. There was a red carpet, hordes of photographers, she moved as if she were an acrobat, and he had no wish to be there.

They watched something, but he wanted no one to ask him anything about it because he had no idea. His mind had not been there the entire evening, because it was across town, stuck on Gabrielle's mouth. Hell, what had he done? Now that he had felt that, whatever that inexplicable feeling was, he wanted more.

'I don't know,' Amelia was laughing. 'You will have to ask Jonathan.'

'Ask me what?' Heaven knew what she was talking about.

'Is your engagement on the horizon?'

That nonsense again, and of course, Amelia did nothing to discourage the rumours. He would in fact be right if he guessed that she had instigated them. 'I have just lost my father,'

'Yes, of course.'

Amazing, the reporter was more understanding than this incredibly selfish female. Some said entertainers were egotistical; he differed in that opinion because he knew other actors and all were great people. He had even dated another girl who was now in the US, and although she had needed her career more than him, she was still a wonderful person. This one... just about every sentence started with I and ended with me.

CHAPTER EIGHT

Paul eyed him with interest. 'So she's trying to do the whole engagement-marriage thing again. But I'm guessing you are determined not to be sucked in.'

'Sucked in? She is setting traps. I even suspect she would drug and drag me somewhere to go through the ceremony while I'm unconscious.'

'Why don't you break up?' Paul asked curiously.

'Don't think I haven't considered it. There is just one problem, Amelia. She is utterly self-centred and if I do, she is going to create some absurd scene. I have just lost my father; I am not going to be in the papers as some loser kid who is already destroying his father's legacy and present my mother with an idiotic scandal, which will be all her making. I hate being in the papers, even dislike it when it has to do with Knight Industries, and I want to be Heat and People magazine fodder? I wish she would become annoyed over something and break it off. But now I wonder, would that cause any less publicity?'

'I see.' Paul walked away from the desk and went to stare out the window. Perhaps it was true, sometimes things were meant to be. He turned around and fixed his piercing blue gaze on his best friend. 'I think I have a solution.'

'There is music to my ears.'

'As long as you are certain you want out of this thing.'

'Well,' Jonathan said. 'When she's not being a weirdo, she can be a lot of fun.'

Paul rolled his eyes. 'I have heard the sex is incredible. So, you are uncertain if you want completely out, but you are certain you don't want to marry her.'

'She drives me mad already.' Jonathan made a hand gesture past his head. 'I would not be able to stand it afterwards.'

Paul eyed his friend a moment longer. 'It seems to me as if the answer lies in a problem that I happen to have.'

'Oh yes?' Jonathan asked curiously. 'What are you dealing with?'

'Do you remember that money your father borrowed?'

Jonathan furrowed his brow. He had quite forgotten it, and he still had to speak to Gabrielle, as she might know something. 'What about it?'

'I tied things up a week ago. Anyway,' He flicked a hand. 'The person on whose behalf the money was paid is about to receive the first account. Unfortunately, she will not be able to afford the payments.'

'Fantastic.' Jonathan said sarcastically then fixed his gaze on his friend. 'Paul, what the hell are you talking about, and how are these two things connected?'

'They are and you will see how in a moment. And two problems can be solved at one go.' Paul took a breath, now that he had started it he had better do it right.

Jonathan was becoming impatient. 'Who was the money for?'

'Gabrielle.'

Jonathan almost fell off his chair. 'What? As I understood it from dad, it was for the Russian mob or something.'

'Which is true. They were blackmailing Gabrielle, and your father wanted to pay them off, so they would leave her alone.'

'Why the hell would anyone blackmail Gabrielle?'

'Are you blind? Who is your father? Big-shot businessman, respected member of society, married forever, young lover and a baby.' Sometimes he thought Charles had concocted lies on top of secrets because he could not see where the beginning of the ball of yarn was, but that money had been paid to those dubious characters. Paul shrugged. 'The problem lies in that Gabrielle has to repay that money. How can she on her salary and with a child to raise?'

Why Charles had insisted on that had not been immediately clear but he was starting to understand the point. He needed to use it as leverage because if anyone needed a push it would be Gabrielle. Charles had then also told him that if the two could not possibly work it out and build a decent life together, he was to scrap that debt, because he never wanted her to carry that burden.

Paul had sat at his PC, added enough interest to make anyone weep, and worked the stupid thing out over five years. Technically, it was fraud, as he was creating something out of thin air but if anyone audited Knight Industries' finances, they would not be able to find the damn thing, because it did not exist. It was a bizarre idea and he had wondered how this thing could possibly unfold, if at all, or if a chance would ever present itself to carry out a dying man's fanciful wishes. Unsuspectingly, Jonathan himself had given him entry into the brew.

Jonathan's forehead furrowed deeper. 'I still don't get what you're trying to say.'

'Well, I've had time to think about this dilemma and a resolution seems clear.'

'I suppose that's good. What is it?'

'You must marry Gabrielle.'

Had anyone hit Jonathan with a chair over the head, he would not have looked more astonished. He gulped then closed his eyes, to snap them open again. 'Excuse me?' He jumped to his feet. 'How does this solve everything?' He certainly couldn't see it.

Enter the piece de resistance. 'Gabrielle needs someone to carry the load she cannot. She is quite destitute and she has a baby to care for, who needs a father. May I remind you that she is your sister? This way, you can have the say in her life I notice you desperately crave. Imagine if Gabrielle decides to leave, or meets someone and gets married. Don't think it's improbable, you see how men look at her. What if that man wants to adopt Tammy? Then you will have absolutely no say, perhaps not even visiting rights.

'It would just be between Gabrielle, you, and me, and none of us will proclaim it to the world. Gabrielle marries you and you have free access to your little sister. Amelia— tell her, break it off, or use the security of marriage to shield yourself. Bloody hell, don't lie to yourself, you love that child as if she were your own.'

Jonathan was speechless, simply staring at him.

'Okay, I did spring it on you out of the blue, but it does make sense in a twisted kind of way. And now you are prepared for when Gabrielle comes storming in here because I am sending her your way.' Why he had latched onto Charles' wild imagination and come up with this rubbish, he had no clue but it was scaringly accurate. Only thing was, he wanted neither Jonathan nor Gabrielle to become suspicious nor query it, because it was an insane house of cards. 'Oh, by the way, she has been looking sickly. I told her to book herself off and go to the doctor but I think she messed with the medical aid as well because she got all worried about that.

'Think about it, being married is the best weapon against all other hopefuls, especially Amelia. Hell Jonathan, we are almost thirty years old and we have never done anything that is worthwhile. We have never needed anything; in fact, we always get what we want. Can we for once not be self-serving and help two girls who are just about lost?'

Gabrielle wondered why her life went through cycles of crying. Ever since her mother announced she was sick and dying that was all she had done. She lay on her bed feeling miserable, wishing she would fall asleep and never wake up, but if that happened, poor Tammy.

For once, she thought she understood Malcolm and Charlotte. Drugs, whatever kind, probably removed the feeling she had sitting right in the middle of her chest, and the persistent worry that refused to leave her mind.

Dragging herself out of bed, she looked into the cot and passed a soft hand over the small forehead; Tammy was sleeping a little better. She did not like that cough she had picked up at the nursery school. Just one more thing to worry about. She went to the kitchen and made herself tea but never drank it; her throat was closing up out of stress.

Grabbing a magazine, she flicked through it tiredly then stopped on a page. There was her father's house, the one that should have been hers and Tammy's; she couldn't bother to read the article. Malcolm had never written a will, never made provision for anyone in his life. Given, he had not known about her but he knew about Tammy and done nothing for her either; and Gabrielle had lived there over a year. It would not have mattered if she had been there since birth, they would not have gotten anything out of him.

She reached into her handbag, took out the white envelope and stared at the statement. How had this happened? Two hours earlier her heart had dropped to the ground floor when she opened it after they had returned from the doctor. Something must have gone wrong because she had been under the impression that Charles did not mean for this to happen. But whatever her thoughts, here it was in black and white, an account made out to Miss Gabrielle Dunstan.

Barely able to breathe, she called Paul, as the creepy thing had come from his department. He was understanding, became terribly concerned, and gave her one piece of advice; go see Jonathan. He's the boss he'll suggest the best course of action.

She was so tired, she could not do anything about it now, but she did need to go speak to him about this horrible surprise; because if she did not start paying something, someone would come after her and what would she lose? She did not care about anything but Tammy. She could lose everything, but not her little sister, and the first thing to go would be this flat.

She opened a small box and took out a disk then opening the laptop, she slid it into the drive and sinking onto the chair, pressed play.

'Luc,' Gabrielle asked as she lay beside her mother. 'Why are you home so early?'

'I rushed.' Luc said off-camera as he panned over Eleanor's face for a moment and then fixed focus on Gabrielle. 'Have you eaten?'

'Not hungry.'

'I guess my mother is not here, because she will not let you go without food. I brought you some Basler Leckerli,' Luc said. 'They are on the kitchen table.'

'Luc,' Eleanor whispered. 'You are such a good boy. Yes, tell her to eat. Go on darling.'

He held focus on Gabrielle until she was out the room. Then he turned to Eleanor. 'Okay, you can leave your message for Gaby now.'

'My darling,' Eleanor said as she tried to sit up and started speaking slowly. 'Yes, I am beyond sorry I am leaving you so soon. But when you fall in love, become engaged, on your wedding day, or when your first baby is born... You will think of me, and I will be right there with you. I wish I was strong enough to leave you many hours of good advice, but I do know one thing, you will find your own way.' She moved on the bed.

'I am cutting.' Luc said. 'You are very tired.'

'I wanted...' the tears ran down Eleanor's face. 'My darling, I love you so very much.'

Gabrielle paused and placed a hand on the screen, but she couldn't see anything, the tears wouldn't let her.

The evening began in a peculiar manner. Jonathan called and said he was taking her out. Amelia heard something in his voice instantly and unable to put her finger on it, she felt apprehensive; whatever he was about to impart felt like bad news. Perhaps he had eventually tired of her. She wanted to laugh out loud; there was no man who could escape her once she put her mind to it.

'Darling,' she began as she leaned into the velvet seat at the restaurant. 'What is on your mind tonight?'

'It is not a subject to be discussed here.'

She pouted. 'But I am so curious.'

'Be that as it may, you have to wait.'

'Is it a surprise?'

'Quite.'

She could swear he meant to laugh. Maybe he was teasing her and it was going to be something wonderful, so she became impatient with dinner. They eventually left and went to her place, and tonight he was not tired. He was in fact extremely alert, as if something was feeding him an invisible force. She disappeared into the bedroom to change and when she returned he was staring out the window.

She went to him immediately. 'Isn't it a stunning view?' She draped a hand over his shoulder.

'Very nice.' He agreed.

'Darling,' she called huskily. 'What is bothering you?'

He turned around and taking her hand, pulled her to the sofa. 'I have to tell you about something that I need to do.'

She liked the sound of that. In a way, he was asking her permission about something. 'What is it?'

'I have to get married.'

A huge grin spread on her face. 'Oh, darling—'

'No Amelia, you don't understand. I don't mean us; I have to marry someone else.'

She thought her head had just filled with bees because she could hear buzzing. 'Excuse me? Since when does Jonathan Knight have to do anything?' She snapped.

'Well, I have to do this.'

'Why? Who do you have to marry? What is going on?' Now she was scared.

'I have to marry Gabrielle.'

Her eyes narrowed. 'Who the hell is Gabrielle?' Then she recalled. Miss cutie pie? Oh crap, she knew there was a reason why she did not like wholesome girl. 'But... how... why... What about me?'

He gave her an edited explanation about his father's twisted clandestine affairs, and the product thereof.

'But why do you need to marry her?' Her eyes filled with tears. 'This is so horrible for me. Couldn't you just pay her something every month? What is a bit of money for you?'

'This has nothing to do with money but with rights, which I have none. I have to marry her if I want to become my sister's legal guardian. Gabrielle can go anywhere, do anything, make whatever decision she wants.'

'So... so, it's actually not going to be a real marriage?' Her eyes brightened to just as quickly narrow again. 'And once you do whatever you need to do— which is what exactly?'

'I don't know yet, maybe I need to adopt her. I can only look into all of this afterwards.'

'And then you can divorce what's-her-name?'

'Something like that.'

'Okay, this sounds better. So when are you planning to do it?'

'As soon as it can be arranged.'

'Have you asked her already?'

'Not yet. I just need to do it right, to give her no chance of turning me down.'

'You are not going to have a big wedding, are you?'

'Big wedding? No, no, none of that. So, are you okay with this?'

'Not exactly, but I get it. Besides, we can still go out all the time, and,' her hand went to his leg, starting to rub it up and down. 'Ooh,' she made a face. 'Let us pretend this is a movie, a very erotic one, and this is the very last time we will have sex.'

CHAPTER NINE

Jonathan recalled the visit to Amelia as he stared out of his office window. To say that she understood was a big cover-up because she had no patience. This could become a sticky situation if he were not careful. He had steered clear of the money Gabrielle owed, as Amelia was not exactly secrets central and he did not want to provide her with unnecessary ammunition that she could use against anybody.

Swivelling around, he wondered what was taking Gabrielle so long. Only he could solve the predicament, what was she doing? If he did not know better, he would almost think that he was excited about the idea. 'Hell no,' he told himself. What he wanted... he could not put it into words either, because even he did not know.

Unexpectedly, a thought occurred to him. What if Gabrielle wanted a big wedding? He imagined her in a wedding gown; she would look beautiful. He brushed the thought aside; that was not what this was about.

Monday passed extremely slowly and he could not understand why she had not come to see him at all. Before the day was over, he went down to the underground parking. Strange, her car was nowhere. Had she come to work at all, Paul had mentioned that she looked sick.

He dialled a number. 'Amy, do you know if Gabrielle came to work today?'

'She did not, she's at the hospital.'

'What? Why?'

'Tammy—'

He felt something happen to his head, or was it heart? 'What's wrong with her?'

'What is usually wrong with babies who go to nursery schools; she picked up some bug from another child.'

'Where are they?'

Amy gave him the hospital's name. 'I'm guessing you are going there.'

'Of course I'm going. And next time, don't wait for me to ask, just tell me what's going on with the two of them.'

He was annoyed with traffic because he wanted to get there sooner. He asked at reception where he should go and realised at once how problems could develop. Everyone asked if he was the father. 'Yes, damn it,' he agreed. 'I'm the father.'

He found Gabrielle sitting on a chair, under an oxygen tent, leaning forward, her hand and forehead on the bed. 'Gaby,' it just came out of him.

She had not heard him, but realised someone had arrived. 'Jonathan!' Surprised, she disentangled herself from the plastic tent. 'Why are you here?'

'Why wouldn't I be?' He placed a hand on her shoulder; she was as tense as guitar strings.

'Thank you for coming.'

'How is she?'

'Not good.'

'What is it?'

'She's teething, which means her immune system is low, so she caught a cold, which led to bronchitis, and she couldn't breathe.' Her eyes filled with tears. 'I was petrified.'

Jonathan pulled her gently into his arms. 'It's okay, I'm here to help.'

'Thank you.' She wiped her eyes. 'Do you want to see her?'

Jonathan was under the oxygen tent, his hand caressing the sleeping baby girl's face. When she woke up and saw him, she wanted to be up in his arms. He fed her, and cradled her tenderly. Oh, he loved her all right. After she fell asleep again, even if breathing with some difficulty, he studied Gabrielle. She was pale and exhausted.

'Come,' he grabbed her hand, and took her to the coffee shop downstairs. 'Please eat.'

'I'm not hungry—'

'Doesn't matter if you have an appetite or not, you are eating something. How are you supposed to look after her if you are sick? But you don't just look sick, you look worried too. Is something wrong?'

'I am concerned,' she admitted. 'I did a silly thing a while back to save money, I downgraded our medical aid. So now, it's inadequate. Tammy won't be able to stay here longer than two days if she needs to.'

'Yes, we must look at this medical aid of yours. But it doesn't matter,' he stopped as he realised where he was going with the conversation. Should he just announce it or wait for her to ask?

'As time passes, I realise how much like your father you are.'

'Am I supposed to say thank you?' He snapped automatically, upset. He liked being compared to his father, by anyone but Gabrielle.

She stared at him, realising the comparison had displeased him. She leaned back in the chair, tears brimming in her eyes. 'I'm sorry I offended you.' She was exhausted; all she wanted to do was close her eyes and sleep.

He watched the lids bat furiously. 'I apologise I know you meant well. Would you like some fresh air? Hospital smells get to me.'

They walked for about five minutes then he could tell that she was nearing falling over, as he listened to her dragging feet. He led her to a garden bench. When they sat down, she leaned against him tiredly and he placed an arm about her shoulders. She sighed and dropped her head against his neck. When her breath fanned his skin, he thought he would go mad if he did not kiss her.

Pushing her a little away, he pressed his mouth to hers. She parted her lips and he repeated what he had done at the office. He could swear he felt that kiss in his toes, especially when his tongue touched hers. Taking her face in his hands, he kissed her whole face, and through it all, he knew that she was asleep. Then he sat holding her against him for close to thirty minutes.

'Gaby,' he called softly.

She pulled her head up. 'How long have I been asleep?'

'Not long. Do you feel better?'

'A little, thank you.' A smile appeared on her face.

Getting to his feet, he took her hand and placed it on his forearm. 'Let's go see how Tammy is doing.'

As he sat watching the poor baby struggle for breath, he knew that he never wanted to see her in a hospital again. For that to happen, she could not be in that nursery school, but at home with her mother. All she was supposed to do was play, be happy, and grow up.

He glanced at Gabrielle. Being here was killing her; she hated it as much as he did. Paul's idea was much more than that. Now, he just had to wait for her to ask for help because he could not simply blurt out the offer, could not make it sound as if it was a real proposal. Hell no, he had no wish to be married.

'Go home to rest. You have work tomorrow.'

'Look who's talking. You are just about dropping and you tell me to go home.' Smiling, he reached for her, pulled her onto his lap and made her rest her face against his chest. She sat stiffly for a few seconds then slowly relaxed, snuggled closer, and before five minutes passed, was fast asleep. Leaning back into the armchair, he wrapped his arms around her waist, and closed his eyes.

Tammy improved somewhat the next day, had an almost pleasant night, and on the third practically looked like her old self. The doctor kept her one more night and then let her go. Jonathan told Gabrielle to stay home until completing the medication course and that now he was concerned about her returning to the nursery school. He could see she was thinking the same.

He was tempted to suggest that she move into his house and stay home to look after Tammy, but she would never agree. Besides, people would say all sorts of things and he was not going to open a newspaper and be embarrassed or annoyed, or worse, humiliate his mother. One thing he was getting loud and clear; Gabrielle needed to be pushed into requesting help because she was trying to do everything alone.

He got the idea while she was home. Returning to the hospital, he asked for a printout of everything Tammy had needed and used. What Gabrielle did not know was that he had spoken with the doctors and demanded they do the absolute best they could to get that baby out of there as fast as was possible, and paid for all the extras she would not have been able to afford on her current medical aid.

It was not as if Gabrielle had sat in his office every day but for some inexplicable reason, the days started to drag, in fact, becoming extremely boring, so for lack of entertainment, he went to visit Amy on the top floor.

He could see she was concerned about her position, as she had been Charles' PA and now sat helping other executives' PAs. It was true that he had his own secretary but he also knew that there was no one better qualified than Amy in the entire building. After sitting in his father's chair for twenty minutes, he went out again and told her that he had decided to keep her, and promoted his secretary to assistant to the PA.

When he saw the broad smile and sneaky tears, he was glad that he made someone happy that very boring day. Then he returned into his father's office.

At home, he walked around the rooms, imagining Tammy crawling, eventually stumbling in her unsteady steps and finally running through all of them. He smiled contentment. When he reached his bedroom, a peculiar thought occurred to him. Where was Gabrielle supposed to sleep, here? The idea made his heart rate accelerate and his body told him that it liked the suggestion very much but that was not about to happen, because Gabrielle would never agree. Besides, this was a business transaction, so what were these odd notions doing in his head?

Midweek, he drove to Gabrielle's flat, not only to see Tammy but also to speed things up. He rang the bell and waited.

'Jonathan,' she was surprised. 'Why are you here?'

'I have some bad news.' He said as he waited for her to slide the chain off. He looked around quickly; it was cute, comfortable and very neat.

'What bad news?' She swallowed dryly.

'I went to the hospital to pick up the account, as I wanted to check with the medical aid. You were right there are things they don't cover.'

She fixed her gaze on him. 'How much do I have to pay in?'

'Nine thousand,'

She turned pale, fell onto the sofa and a trembling hand went to her temple. 'I don't have that.'

'It doesn't matter. I told you that I would take care of it.'

'Do you believe in seasons of trouble?' She asked unexpectedly.

He regarded her with interest. 'What do you mean?'

'It's as if the entire world is conspiring against me. I have debt, responsibilities, things that never existed before. And I don't mean that I didn't expect things to change with Tammy, I mean that it is all upside down.'

Then she did something strange. She started rattling off in French then jumped to Italian, when she thought that she had run out of good sentences she moved into German, and for good measure, she finished with a few words he had no clue what language it might be. He stared at her. 'What on earth? I think I recognised some of it, but that last bit...'

'It's Romansh. I was born in Switzerland and we speak all those there. I have not been long in South Africa.'

He recalled his father talking about Switzerland all of his life, some holidays spent there during his teenage years and often sensing that Charles had secrets. Once or twice, he had tried to find out what he did, but Charles had always brushed it aside. 'Why did you come here?' But why wouldn't she have come to be near her child's father?

An extremely sad look appeared on her face. 'I... my...' she couldn't get the words out. Just thinking about her mother reminded her of the good life they had once possessed. How she had loved arriving home to the smell of Anna's biscuits, how carefree she and Luc had been, how they laughed and teased each other when they went for walks, those videos they spent hours on...

'Is that when you fell pregnant?' He sat beside her.

What misunderstandings could do, but she couldn't tell the truth either. 'You have no idea in how much financial trouble I am.'

Hell, it had taken her long enough to get here. 'Then tell me, but it doesn't matter, we'll sort it out.'

She stood up, went to her handbag, took out the envelope, and handed it to him. 'Even this?'

Taking the statement, he looked at her face. She was paper white. 'This is a lot of money. What did you need it for?'

A strange look appeared on her face. 'If you saw who asked for it, you would laugh your head off, but they were asking for their boss, who is as dangerous as you can get. I didn't want your father involved in this but he would not listen, as he was afraid for both my life and Tammy's.'

Jonathan nodded. 'You can't afford these payments.' He said as he perused over the statement again. 'And with the hospital—'

'So you do see the crisis I am in.'

'Have you any ideas how to repay any of this?'

'I could become a teacher but would I make more than I do now? Not a chance. I know languages so I suppose I could teach those, but I'm just starting out, how many people could I have in a few months? Tourism is a possibility but again, where do I start? Then there is...' she wondered how well she would fare as a stripper. She had done ballroom dancing, so she probably could adapt the moves. How about prostitution? She shivered as she imagined strange men pawing her. 'Let's not go there. The only other thing I thought of is if you lend me the money and I pay you back. If you did, I would be working for you for the rest of my life.'

'Would working for me be so bad?'

She looked at him searchingly. 'Does that mean that you would consider it? I have to tell you though; I can offer nothing as collateral.'

'Then what if I told you that you could be completely debt-free? That you would not have to worry about money anymore? That Tammy would be safe, healthy and looked after, having everything she needed. That you could look after her and be safe as well.'

A small laugh escaped her. 'What is this, a genie is going to grant me three wishes?'

'No, I'm making you an offer.' He got to his feet and went to stand before her.

'You are going to sell us into slavery, aren't you? But I don't think we are worth much on the black market right now, I've lost weight and Tammy...' She attempted a smile but suddenly, his semblance spoke of different things. 'Sorry, I get silly when I'm nervous. What is this offer?' She asked curiously.

'Marry me.'

She was certain a stupid look had just made a pit stop on her face. 'What?'

'Marry me. Think about the benefits; you will be safe, Tammy too. I'll settle everything, and you don't have to worry about money ever again.'

'Are you insane?'

'Not yet, I don't think.'

'But... you have a girlfriend.' She went to sit down and looked up. 'Why?'

'I told you, I want to help, and this is the best way I know how.'

She said nothing for a couple of minutes, her mind turning the idea upside down, inside out, and back again. Finally, she asked. 'You do all that, what do I do?'

'Nothing, just say yes. We get married and all this will be behind you.'

'No,' she stood up and went to him. 'There is something you want out of this. No one gives that much away without an ulterior motive. So Jonathan, what is it?'

'Why does there have to be an ulterior motive?'

'Because that is how people are.'

'I need a wife. Someone I can have beside me at all these things I need to do, go to, represent— it's endless. I don't have time to go-a-courting.'

'What about your girlfriend?'

'Quite unsuitable, and Amelia does not need me, you and Tammy do. Say yes, it's a fantastic deal.'

'Deal?' She was speechless for a second. 'Talk about the black market, you are the one bidding on us.'

'Gabrielle,' good grief, but she had a wild imagination. 'It's just an offer to help.'

'You are going to take something away from me, aren't you?'

'No.' He wanted to reach out and remove that worry crease from across her brow, but it didn't seem appropriate.

'I want to do this. And I'm not trying to take anything from you.'

'Will you put that in writing?' As she said that, she recalled that stupid paper Charlotte had made her sign. How did she go from carefree to all of this?

'If you wish. Are you agreeing then?'

Another thought occurred to her and she coloured. 'Are you presuming this to be a real marriage? What I mean is—' she felt embarrassed. 'Do you expect me to sleep with you?'

'I don't, unless you want to.'

She made a quick gesture. 'Don't you feel anything real? Just like that, if I want to. I'm guessing you think of the subject as plain sex, not even lovemaking.'

'Whatever you call it it's still the same thing.'

'It is not, there is a huge difference.'

'If you say so,' he was starting to wonder if he wanted to participate in this madness, because what else was it? 'Now, will you agree to marry me?'

She fixed her gaze on him, everything was already wrong. How could he ask and she agree? 'I never imagined that I would be proposed to in this way.' Unwillingly, her eyes filled with tears. 'What is it they say, those who don't have, crawl, and what is it I'm doing? I think you are off your mind to want to do this, and I— I'm sure I am more than that for considering it. But for Tammy...'

He closed the gap between them and raising his hands to her face, wiped the tears away. 'Please don't be frightened because I don't expect anything, and I promise that I will not hurt you.'

Whatever his reasoning, she still had to make him see sense. 'What about when you meet someone you really want to marry?'

'Me, marry,' he scratched his head. 'I can't see it happening, except for now, of course. Do you say yes?'

Something told her to say no, but something else, something so deep she was not even aware was there, yelled that she should say yes. 'Just tell me what I must do.' And right there, she felt that world-crushing hand grab her heart and throw her against the wall.

He wanted to kiss her but thought better of it. Besides, she was awake and he was certain that she would not welcome his advances. The idea that he could only kiss her when she was asleep made him feel as if she were two people. The thing was; he had to marry this one to get to the other one. This was Gabrielle, but he wanted Gaby. He shook himself mentally. What the hell were all these thoughts?

CHAPTER TEN

Jonathan encouraged her to think carefully about what type of ceremony she liked because he did not mind if she wanted a bit of a celebration. Besides, he pointed out; he was taking this marriage seriously, she was not to think that he planned to divorce her for some mindless reason. If Amelia heard him, she would cause an instant scandal because she was keeping quiet on the belief of the exact opposite of what he had just said.

Gabrielle stared at him, realising that he meant it, while still sensing an awful trade taking place.

She chose a sleek pearl gown and picked the Michelangelo in Sandton Square for the ceremony and reception, as there would not be a long list of guests, not from her side anyway. Jonathan knew half of Johannesburg; it was up to him how many people he wanted there.

Then, he took her home to have dinner with his mother. She had met Barbara at the hospital, but also thought both Jonathan's and Paul's behaviour peculiar, and during dinner, she realised that she was right in suspecting that they had done something.

Interestingly, Barbara did not discuss Tammy and she had a feeling Jonathan had asked her not to, but Barbara did not hide her surprise that they were getting married, because she had believed that Gabrielle was Paul's girlfriend. Gabrielle glanced at Jonathan, unable to comprehend why they had encouraged the idea. Definitely weird.

They made all the arrangements and she gave notice on the flat. Then he told her to go over to the house so she could see what she wished to do there, pick rooms, decorate Tammy's, whatever she wanted. When she did, she liked the house very much and thought that she would probably end up having a good time there.

He surprised her further, by asking where she would like to go on honeymoon. She stared at him, wondering what he was on about again. He told her that he had spoken to Amy, was giving her time off work - as he wasn't going to be there either - and asked her to look after Tammy while they were away, just so they had some time to learn a few things about each other.

Gabrielle felt like crying when she thought that neither Eleanor nor Charles would be there. She had hoped that he walked her down the aisle when the day came... Bizarre, instead, she was doing it with his son.

The small ceremony and reception were enjoyable, as he drew on the charm that was in fact infectious. He teased and joked, and was very polite and considerate towards her, even when he kissed her, though she had a déjà vu moment as she imagined that he meant to kiss her quite differently. She realised then that a strange detail had escaped her. Their first night was to be spent at the Michelangelo, and there would be no Tammy. As she understood it, he meant for the marriage to look real.

She thought she would start hyperventilating even before they went up. He acted as if nothing was amiss; she tried to follow suit. One thing was odd; he danced with her as if he enjoyed it.

'Are you tired?' He asked when they finally made it upstairs.

She nodded. 'Quite.' He had danced with her like a maniac, what did he expect? And it was better to be tired than to be worrying about heavens knew what.

'Then go have your bath, shower and go to bed.'

He was trying to get rid of her to do something. She was past thinking that he was weird. Her gaze swept around the room. 'Where are you sleeping?'

'Don't worry about me, the sofa looks comfortable enough.'

She wondered where he was when she returned to the bedroom because he wasn't in it. Curious as to what he was up to, she decided to wait for him on the sofa, perhaps to discuss this bizarre thing they had just gone through. Regardless, she needed to thank him for what he was doing; it was no small thing in anyone's book.

He had needed to occupy his time and mind, gone to the lobby to get her flowers, but on his return, she was sleeping on the sofa. After finding a vase, he went to take a shower.

He did what was becoming a ritual, but this time, she was in her cute silk pyjamas and he had to restrain himself from sliding his hands under the fabric to touch her skin. He kept them on her face as he deepened the kiss that was sending him into a crazy place. How could an unconscious woman do this to him? He felt fire all over his body and he could not think what it was about her kisses that drove him wild. There was so much pleasure in her fresh and sweet mouth that he thought he would pass out.

'Gaby,' he called.

'Huh,' she sat up slowly.

'Looks like you were already dreaming.'

She gave him a sleepy smile and nodded. 'I think you were in it.'

'What was I doing?'

She blushed and got to her feet. 'Where did you go?'

'It's not important, go to bed.'

Although tired, her mind could not stop going over things. This was the oddest situation. Here she was in a room, with a man, who was her husband, and they were not in the same bed. She did not like the idea of starting a marriage like that, with a chasm already between them.

Then again, this was not a real marriage. Had she just given up all chance of happiness when she said yes to this?

One arm went to the other pillow and found something. Picking it up, she turned it over in her hands, trying to see in the dark, but all she knew was that it was a smallish box tied with a large ribbon. Switching the light on was out of the question as he might be asleep, but she was curious. She slid out of bed and went into the bathroom.

Sitting on the closed toilet seat, she pulled the white organza ribbon from the earth coloured box, opened it, and looked inside. There lay a beautiful white gold bracelet with four charms. She studied them, trying to see what he meant by them, or if they had any significance whatsoever. There was an angel, a baby, a shoe, and a heart. Except for the baby, she had no clue what the others meant.

Switching the light off, she walked out of the bathroom, stood a moment adjusting her eyes to the darkness, and called, 'Jonathan.' Getting no response, she walked over to the sofa, sat against his chest, half-draped herself over him, placed a hand on his face, leaned over, and kissed his cheek. 'Thank you.' She told him softly then got to her feet and returned to bed.

Now, he could not close his eyes. When her body had made contact with his bare torso as her top rode up, he thought his skin would ignite, every nerve ending becoming aware of her. His heart pumped crazily, and it took some control not to reach out and pull her down to him. Who would have imagined? His little bride was quite the aphrodisiac, a love goddess of the night.

They flew to a game reserve and being on *honeymoon* people did not intrude. They went on safari, had fantastic meals, walked around, but above all, they spent time alone in their baobab tree-house, which had a breathtaking view of the watering hole from the overhanging wooden veranda.

He heard about her life in Switzerland, that she had been happy, and that her mother's death had initiated the chain reaction that brought her to South Africa. She spoke about university and explained that she had graduated from Wits, although most of her studies had been done in Zurich.

In turn, he told her how he and Paul became friends, some childhood adventures, holidays he remembered spending in Switzerland, realising also that one of the houses he recalled well was the one she called home. Then, he mentioned how he had always wanted to follow in his father's footsteps. When he said that, a bizarre idea crossed his mind. Had his need to emulate Charles been so intense that he had also needed to take his mistress? That was a sick and depressing thought.

Gabrielle noticed his furrowing brow. 'May I ask something personal?'

'Sure,'

'Why didn't you marry your girlfriend? I'm quite certain she was willing.' She really wanted to know because she had seen pictures of them and that woman wanted Jonathan. Helping her out of a financial bind did not make sense because he could have wiped the debt clean and she would have spent the rest of her life repaying him. As for the reason he gave for needing a wife. He lied. Nothing was a have to for him. Unlike her, he was free to do whatever he wanted. She did not understand it.

He considered his answer. 'Willingness— no, Amelia did not lack that. I just saw this as both urgent and important. She doesn't need me, you and Tammy do.'

That wasn't all of it but it was his offer for now. She shrugged, perhaps one day he would tell her.

'What's your secret?' He asked the following day as they sat on the loungers on the veranda.

'What kind of secret are you referring to?'

'That one thing that is truly annoying. Like biting your nails when you watch horror movies, or smoking when you have failed at something.'

'There are two and both have to do with slumber.' She leaned comfortably into the chair. 'I sleepwalk. I'll do all sorts of things and then not remember. My mom was adamant I tell people I spent time with about it; in case they needed to help me or found me in the middle of the night.'

'Did you ever do something dangerous?'

'Once, before we moved to Zurich. I was eight, walked out of the house and went up a hill. Rescue services came out, but I had gone to sleep in a cave. I was very scared, especially when I woke up and started walking around, completely lost. But they found me, after I was certain a wolf meant to eat me. Afterwards, mom locked all outside doors as soon as I entered the house so she could hide the keys where I wouldn't find them.'

'Does it just happen?'

'Mom always said it seemed to get worse when I was stressed, such as during exams.'

'Makes sense and you are right, I should know. You really don't remember?'

'I even have conversations and do things, just don't ask me in the morning. I think I haven't done it in a while, I'm hoping I've outgrown it.'

'You said there were two things, what's the other one?'

'I'm also a heavy sleeper. You almost have to detonate a bomb to get me up.'

'Heavy all the time?' He was fascinated.

'That's the funny thing. You make a racket and I can't hear it, but drop a feather... I swear I'm tuned in to whispers. What's yours? Is it bad, funny, or strange?' She turned sideways on the lounger.

He was starting to understand how those kisses had happened. Gazing at her, he wished he could run a finger along her silhouette. They had been out to the small elephant herd earlier and she had burnt a little, her skin glowed with health. Yes, she was quite lovely without makeup. His eyes went to her lips; what elixir ran in her veins that a mere glance made him breathless? 'My secret,' he moved off the disturbing ideas. 'I may be allergic or intolerant to alcohol, because funny things happen when I drink.'

'Such as?' She asked curiously.

'I forget everything.'

'Isn't that what happens to everybody?'

'When they get drunk.'

'But I have seen you drink.'

'I can drink but as soon as I exceed a certain limit something happens in my brain. Whatever I do following that it's wiped clean by the time I wake up. It feels like amnesia.'

'Does it matter if you do or don't recall incidental details?' She tilted her head back and closed her eyes.

'Are you tired?'

'Yes,' she said softly, opened an eye and looked at him. His gaze made her feel shy. 'Do you mind if I take a nap.' She had never been too body-conscious; understanding that she had been blessed with what people called 'normal' but she thought was a stupid way for media and fashion to pit women against each other because everyone was normal. Nonetheless, now she wore long enough pant legs, no low cuts, and nothing revealing. Gratefully, each had their own bedroom.

He wished to say no because he was enjoying their chat but of course he agreed that she should rest. So he didn't get to tell her that there was a part B to his alcohol problem, and that that was in fact the strangest bit. Also leaning back, he threw her one last glance. Talk about gorgeous.

She did not have things that could be called sexy, but heavens did he feel sexed up when she walked around in her cute night clothes. When he compared her to Amelia, he didn't get it. Amelia was quite the sex kitten, who liked pieces of fabric that simply revealed all, left nothing to the imagination, and got the responses she was bent on. Gabrielle— He hadn't seen her naked yet, but he could imagine. Everything was in proportion and so mysteriously enticing that he was undergoing some problems.

It was a crazy thing. This was not a real marriage, Gabrielle was not in love with him, and heaven forbid that he should be with her, yet, something was happening. He could only call it lust, but only he felt it, so there was no chance it would be satisfied anytime soon.

On their penultimate day, management announced that there was to be a farewell dinner and requested guests dress appropriately. Jonathan imagined Gabrielle had not considered formal attire for the bush; he could not wait to see how she solved that little predicament.

He decided to shower first, so he could leave the bathroom free for her female routine; then went to laze about on the veranda. When he heard her walking about, he decided to go peek at what she had found to wear. Her back was turned and he gulped right there.

She had a black alter-neck dress on and her entire back was bare. All he wanted to do was run his hands over those shoulder blades and skin. Her hair was in a ponytail and as it flicked about, he thought he would become hypnotized. Then, she turned around— the plunging neckline to her navel sent his eyes rushing to her chest, wanting to make certain nothing was visible. Hell, he felt upset imagining the other men gawking at her. His hand went up, and clearing his throat, he asked casually. 'How do you women wear that?'

She smiled, grabbed the edge, and showed him. 'It's called double-sided tape.'

That was interesting, but had to be a Gabrielle thing because most women he knew were not that modest. They would have worn it as is, in fact, even making sure a wardrobe malfunction happened often. So, she liked to be cautiously daring. The thought made him smile.

'Do I look all right?'

'Very nice,' he noticed that she had a touch of make-up, just enough in all the right places. No, no man could resist what he was looking at. 'Are you ready?'

'Almost,' she smiled and started looking for something. It was her shoes. When she found them, she lifted the skirt to her knees and climbed into them.

All he knew was that he did not want to leave the tree-house. What he wanted— he wanted to take that dress off. His pulse raced, and as if ordained by some torture fiend, she went to him, stood so close that he thought he would levitate, and straightened his collar and tie. Then said let's go, not even aware that he could barely move.

He ate something, and it was delicious, but he hoped there was no quiz at the end of the evening because he could not recall what it was. His senses were being annihilated by her proximity and when his eyes followed that bare line from neck to stomach, he felt faint. What in the hell had he gotten himself into? How would he survive being this close every day and not being able to touch her?

Then she did another crazy thing. When music started playing, she grabbed his hand and dragged him to the dance floor. When his fingertips touched that velvety heaven, he realised one thing. From now on, he was going to compare every other woman's skin to hers. He tried to put Amelia in his head, but simultaneously kept pushing her out. As he held Gabrielle possessively against his chest, he wanted so much more than what he had agreed to, and wanted to tear up that ridiculous contract they had drawn up. It was solely between the two of them but he knew that she was expecting him to keep to his side of the bargain.

As payback for what she put him through, he plied her with wine while he purposefully stayed away from it. He could see that she was travelling in a haze by the end of the evening because when they walked back to their tree-house, she was giggling, quite unable to climb in a straight line.

She disappeared into the bathroom and he imagined that she would take forever, but no, she was out in ten minutes. He went and took just as long, because for once, he did not want her to fall asleep. But when he reappeared, it was already too late. She lay on the sofa, arms above her head, out like a candle. He went to her, craving one of those mind-blowing kisses.

Unexpectedly, he felt guilty. Guilty that he had made her drink too much but especially guilty that he was about to take advantage of her. He leaned over to wake her but she looked so peaceful, he decided to leave her where she was. Grabbing the light throw to cover her, a movement caught his eye.

CHAPTER ELEVEN

The spider ran across the sofa and stopped on her leg, fangs at the ready for the next thing that dared disturb it. Recognition froze him, a black button; if either of them moved, it would bite, and it would not be pleasant. Reaching for one of the cushions at lightning speed, he removed the cover slip and grabbed the nuisance, but not before the arachnid sank its fangs into the calf. Flipping the fabric over, he dropped it onto the coffee table.

It took Gabrielle ten seconds to sit up startled. 'Oww, what...?'

'A spider bit you, and is in there.' He pointed. 'Don't move, so you won't spread the venom.' He grabbed the phone and dialled. 'Yes, a spider just bit my wife. I did, it's a black button. Do you have treatment here? Where's the nearest hospital? Okay, bring me ice and get a doctor.'

She held her leg. 'It's burning.'

'I know.' He sat beside her. 'Gabrielle, I'm not trying to frighten you, but it is going to hurt like hell.' He grabbed some cushions and propped her a little up. 'Let's see if we can contain the venom.'

Next, he perceived an even bigger problem developing. She had imbibed quite a bit of wine and that was never a good mixture with this type of neurotoxin venom. Alcohol tended to confuse the symptoms, and the doctors would have quite a task trying to separate and recognise reactions.

Someone knocked and walked in with a bag of ice. 'You do realise that she is not going to be well at all in a while.'

'Yes, I had a run-in with one of those before.' Jonathan pointed to the folded pillowcase. 'The culprit is in there.'

'I'll take it away and release it later. The doctor lives just on the other side of the hill, so he will be here shortly. In the meantime, I suggest you bring her down to the office, we have a bed there for emergencies.'

'I don't feel well,' Gabrielle complained.

He went to her, sat down, and ran a hand over her face. 'I know,' he told her softly, just as he always did Tammy. 'Hang in there.' That was when she threw her arms around him and started sobbing. He felt helpless, because nothing he said would take away what was about to happen. Why in hell's name did he see her as deserving of his meanness? He felt like crying too. Then picking her up into his arms, he held her tightly to his chest as he went down the stairs and all the way to the office.

She started going through all the symptoms that followed this delightful spider bite. She was in pain, had cramps, her chest felt tight, started sweating, and her temperature rose. She hadn't before with the wine, but now, she sounded drunk, as she couldn't formulate words.

The doctor arrived, gave her an anti-venom shot, and told him that it would be best to take her to the local hospital, as she seemed to be developing a breathing problem. Jonathan weighed their options but feared more complications. He was not one to watch people suffer and Gabrielle was having no picnic. He called helicopter services and asked for a paramedic to accompany them as they flew home. At least there, they were close to home, and she could receive the required treatment.

She didn't arrive a moment too soon, her pulse rate started climbing and the blood pressure shot up; to complicate matters, she became nauseous and started vomiting.

He called his mother, Paul and Amy, and told them. Within the hour, all three were there, all becoming as concerned as he was.

'How is Tammy?' Jonathan asked tiredly when he eventually sat down.

'She is such a good baby.' Amy smiled. 'Roger is crazy about her, so is Brian and Jenny.' Her husband and kids. 'I didn't think I should have brought her out in the night air.'

'Yes, you did right.' Jonathan agreed. 'I just missed her.'

'Whose baby is she?' Barbara asked unexpectedly.

Paul and Jonathan glanced at each other. Why had they not thought that Barbara would eventually become curious?

Jonathan said the only thing he wanted people to believe from now on. 'Mine.'

'I have been a grandmother for months and you tell me now?' Barbara stared at him, as if uncertain that he was her child. 'And Jonathan, honestly, I would have thought that you knew better, but at least you are taking care of your responsibilities. And for goodness sake, is it too much to ask to let me know your wife and child?'

Amy sat quietly furrowing her brow. What on earth? Then again, Gabrielle also said Tammy was hers. Perhaps they had more in common than even they realised.

Gabrielle went through fifteen hours of delirium as the symptoms subsided and increased at will, and then she fell into a calm sleep. When she woke up, she had a swollen leg and an ugly rash she did not like, but the doctor assured her that it would clear up, and that one day she would not even remember that she had been bitten. Presently, she had to walk, because her leg muscles had been affected by the venom.

'Please tell me that you have been home,' she said as he entered the room.

'Yes, I went to take our things, shower and change. How are you feeling?'

'Much better, thanks. The doctor says I can leave tomorrow morning. He just wants to keep me overnight to make sure my blood pressure doesn't skyrocket again. I'm supposed to become mobile.' She threw the bed-covers aside and lifted the good leg, when she tried to move the other, she realised what the doctor had meant. 'It feels dead.'

Jonathan helped her down. She couldn't stand properly, so he held her against him, with an arm around her waist. No, he had not known what he had agreed to. Her mere presence was intoxicating him. 'How far are they expecting you to walk?'

'No marathons yet.' She smiled up at him.

'Then, you would really kill yourself.'

'As if I asked for this,'

'No, it was my fault.'

'How do you figure that?' She asked curiously.

'If I had left the cover alone, it might not have bitten you.'

'Or, it might have crawled onto my face and given me quite the look. Things happen, stop blaming yourself.'

Jonathan discovered that people liked Gabrielle. Everyone wanted to help her, all offering to spend from minutes to hours with her at home, so they could fetch and carry for her. Not that she needed it, the servants were there, and they were just as willing. For a couple of weeks, the house had people coming and going during the day, and of course among them was Paul.

Paul had started thinking that he had been a fool to agree to Charles' matchmaking adventure, because he liked Gabrielle a whole lot. She was beautiful, charming, and quite the innocent, which was unexpected considering circumstances. She was never mean, extremely charitable, and just plain fun to be around, and he could not find enough reasons to visit her, but stark reality brought him straight back to earth. He enjoyed good conversations with her and now knew a few things that Jonathan might not, and not least of which, was that she took her marriage vows seriously.

Because of Gabrielle's immobility, Jonathan hired a nanny to look after Tammy and he witnessed how the little girl thrived with individual attention. He liked to sit in her cute room; Gabrielle had the decorators create a garden in greens and yellows and he always felt joy and peace in the pretty atmosphere. He loved to play with her, to tickle and hear her baby laughter, to bathe and feed her, to plain do all the things that dads were supposed to do. And when she fell asleep in his arms, his heart ached for all the babies who did not have what she had. She was his little girl, and he could not love her more if he tried.

Thankfully, Gabrielle recovered fully and now he saw that she too was having a good time looking after Tammy. The three of them had a daily ritual that he enjoyed tremendously; they shared the evening meal. He liked watching Gabrielle feed Tammy, because usually, both ended up quite messy, and he laughed aloud when he saw carrot or pumpkin in her hair.

One afternoon, he arrived home earlier than usual and wondered where they were, as the house was extremely quiet, then realised that he could hear them making happy sounds. He found them in the pool; Gabrielle was teaching Tammy how to swim. However, when she saw him, Tammy wanted out of the water immediately.

Gabrielle wrapped Tammy in a towel, handed her to him, and started drying herself with another. She was wearing a pair of shorts, but suddenly, she tugged and grabbed as the elastic snapped. She pulled them off and threw them onto the deckchair.

The afternoon sun bounced off her skin, wrapping her in a soft glow and Jonathan could not help but swallow his Adam's apple a couple of times. Then she turned, and gave him a gentle smile. He wondered if she knew what a look from her did to a man because it was not merely her body that enticed but the way her eyes sparkled. All he wanted was to walk over and kiss her. Goodness, he had almost forgotten those hidden kisses he had stolen and he wanted more.

They usually sat for a while in the lounge after one of them put Tammy to bed, and tonight, Gabrielle went, but after thirty minutes, he wondered what was taking her so long.

Going to investigate, he found them fast asleep in the rocking chair. Obviously, cavorting in the pool had tired them out. Gently, he took Tammy from her arms and put her down in the cot. Next, he turned to Gabrielle. Finally, his chance.

She moaned softly as his tongue explored the delicious wonders, then, something he did not expect happened. Her hands went up to his face, cupping it. He thought she was awake and straightened his back but there she sat, fast asleep. He decided to test this secret dance further.

Reaching for her hands, he pulled her to her feet, picked her into his arms, and let her lean snugly against his chest. He stood there a moment, then went into her room and dropped her carefully onto the bed. Sitting beside her, he caressed her face, and covered her mouth with his again.

This was not the same kiss; something was changing. She was giving as much as she was getting and was quite insistent. He delighted in her responses but this wasn't right. He would prefer it if she opened her eyes and looked at him, because he always got a thrill when their eyes locked. 'Gaby,' he called softly.

She turned from him and he knew the moment was lost, that was all he would get tonight. He felt frustrated, wanting to climb into that bed and take her clothes off, to run his hands and mouth all over her body.

'Darling,' Amelia purred. 'How is the little marriage of convenience going?'

'Good, Gabrielle is not a difficult person so she is always busy, and Tammy is having the time of her life. Have you ever seen her?'

'At the hospital but not too closely.' She made a gesture. 'You are a good man, Jonathan. I don't know anyone else who would do such a thing. Does your mother know?'

'No, and that is how we will keep it. In fact, I have started telling everyone that Tammy is mine.'

'What the hell for?' She furrowed her brows.

'Because I want no one thinking that I have no rights to her. Besides, she knows that I am her daddy now.'

Amelia did not like this one bit. Kids made people do funny things, crazy things, and if he loved the little brat this much already, he would not just up for anyone. She had to make certain she kept his interest here, so his eyes would not be tempted to stray to the mother. A disturbing thought flashed in her mind and she made a face at the vivid images, simply loathing the possibility thereof. 'Do you sleep with your wife?'

'No,' his response was instantaneous and he noticed that the truth upset him because he was dying to. He realised that he had agreed to a bunch of things Gabrielle had written down, but he detested that list now.

Amelia studied him for a second, not liking how that no had come out. Oh, she knew this, little Miss wholesome spelt danger and she had already observed how both he and Paul ran after her.

Paul! She could tell he liked Gabrielle a whole lot, had to encourage him more. Besides, he too knew this was not a real marriage so he would most likely not sweat buckets while pursuing her. 'What is this story about your *wife* being in the hospital?' She asked, but wasn't really interested in the answer.

'A spider bit her. Quite a nasty little creature—'

'Darling,' she cut him off, done talking about things she cared nothing about. 'Thank you for coming to see me, because I have missed you terribly.' Her hand went to his shoulder, squeezed gently then slid along his torso. Leaning in, her lips started a trail of kisses from his temple to his chin then unbuttoning the shirt, her mouth covered just about every inch of chest. Undoing the belt, she pulled his pants off and sat on his lap.

Jonathan closed his eyes, giving himself over to Amelia's attention, but in his head, he imagined what it would feel like if Gabrielle were the one sitting on him. His body reacted instantly, knowing that it would be pure bliss to have Gabrielle love him willingly. Love? Odd thought! One did not need that confusing emotion to get pleasure, and that he got from Amelia.

'Jonathan,' she was calling now. 'Touch me.'

He opened his eyes and saw her bare chest, so he reached out and placed his hands on her breasts.

'What's wrong?' She murmured as she leaned against him.

'I'm tired. We have been in endless meetings, there is a problem I need to solve, and I'm moving to dad's office tomorrow.'

'It's finally official? This is so fantastic!'

He smiled; she made it sound as if he had won the lead role in a brilliant movie. He glanced at his watch, wondering what Gabrielle and Tammy were doing. He had told her that he would not be home for dinner, but now that he was here... The strangest thought crossed his mind; what if Gabrielle found someone else? His gut wanted to explode at the thought of another man touching her. She couldn't, the very notion made him crazy.

He gazed at Amelia. What about her? He found the possibility distasteful but oddly, he felt no jealousy... Was he jealous of his wife? Would she be if she discovered that he still came around?

Gabrielle had a point, an excellent one in fact. If he liked Amelia as much as he purported, he would have found ways to overlook all her little flaws, and even seen it possible to marry her. Instead, he had chosen a convoluted proposal to pursue, thus avoiding enmeshing himself in this life. So what exactly was he doing here?

'Are you actually present?'

'Sorry but I told you everything is rough. I can't concentrate.'

'Not even on a little loving?' Her hands went down to his shorts.

All at once, he felt terrible, so his hands went there too and grabbed hers. He saw Gabrielle's face on their wedding day while he pledged to keep true to her. It was a pretence marriage but he could try to make those words mean something, but hell, he was already practically committing adultery. 'I have to go.' Lifting her off his lap, he put her down on her feet then rising pulled his pants on and grabbed his shirt.

Ten seconds later, he could not believe that he had said no to sex. "Damn," he swore, a suspicion confirmed. He had known Gabrielle's kisses had done something to him, he didn't want to touch Amelia, he wanted to touch her. Not just touch, he wanted... he wanted to love her. "Crap, I'm falling in love with my wife." Now here was a pretty muddle. He could not remember what else he told Amelia and what her response had been, what he did know was that he wanted to be home.

For weeks, he fought tooth and nail. He pulled his wedding band off, stayed at the office late, went out with Paul, visited friends, went to a couple of clubs, and drank a little too much. He tried to flirt and be flirted with but felt dreadful and hated it. Then he picked up women, trying to erase whatever Gabrielle had inadvertently imprinted into him.

Poor females; some, he left at the door, others, he simply waved goodbye in front of their buildings, as for the rest— he made it as far as the lounge and then some inexplicable thing came over him, forcing him to apologise and leave. He despised what was happening.

To complicate matters, he started dreaming about Gabrielle, not just any dreams, but deeply erotic ones, so when he saw her in the mornings, it was a living hell. Now, what did he do? He had to stop fighting this thing and do something.

The idea snuck up on him; he had to do something big, something that would overwhelm Gabrielle and make her fall in love. She had to because she would not simply do things for the sake of doing them. She believed in love and real feelings. He needed to woo her.

A zealous watch began, as he searched for clues and signs as to what she liked, wanted, and needed; desiring to impress her with his astuteness, thoughtfulness, and care. Anything involving Tammy touched her heart, but she was aware of his love for the baby, so seeing him with gifts was a usual occurrence. Then part two of the idea struck him.

CHAPTER TWELVE

Gabrielle sensed his enthusiasm as soon as they sat down to dinner and asked why he was so happy. Almost bursting, he wanted to reveal all, but decided to wait until she returned from putting Tammy to bed. She was right, expectation was winding him up.

'Okay, I'm here.' She smiled as she entered the lounge.

He wondered why it had taken him so long to realise how insanely nuts he was about her. She was absolutely the most gorgeous woman he had ever seen and he wanted—the things he wanted! He no longer cared whose mistress she had been, or perhaps he had never really minded because he had always wanted her. He grabbed an envelope from the table and placed it in her hands. 'I wrote you a letter. Do you want to read it, or must I tell you what's in it?'

She gave a little laugh. 'Goodness, Jonathan, you are excited. But you went to the trouble of writing it, so I think I should read it.' She opened the envelope, took out the single sheet of paper, and began reading. It was written in his neatest script and he started by thanking her for having entered his life. Then her eyes caught sight of two words. Her eyes flew up to look at him. 'What is this?'

'I want to have a paternity test done so Tammy can be registered as my child.'

She was certain stupidity had plastered itself on her face. 'What... why?'

'Because she needs a father and I want to be able to do more, and to have the right to do it.'

Gabrielle stared at him, her mind going into that figuring out place she tended to overuse. She sat down and glanced at the letter again, instinctively knowing this was some trick. 'Explain it to me.' She certainly didn't understand what he was getting at.

He could tell her that he was trying to impress her, that he loved Tammy, or that he believed the little girl should have her rightful name. All would be true. 'We are a couple and we have a child.' He thought he would start with that.

'We are not a couple, and we, do not have a child.' She told him pointedly. 'Although I get it that you feel so inclined, and I thank you for it, Tammy is not your responsibility.'

That annoyed him. She was his little sister, and he wanted to provide for everything she would ever need. 'Of course she is.'

Gabrielle folded her arms. 'How do you figure, because you buy her stuff?'

She was treading on dangerous ground. 'I don't buy her stuff; I give her gifts because I love her.'

She leaned back on the sofa. 'You are hiding something, just as when you proposed. And a paternity test—' she stopped there, utterly confused. 'What are you doing?'

'I want to...' what did he say? That he wanted all the privileges fathers were meant to have, that he never wanted to lose her, or that he wanted to prove how much he cared for her mother? 'I want to be her father, now that she doesn't have one anymore.'

'Now that she doesn't have one,' she repeated nervously. Had he discovered the truth on his own or been set upon it by someone? If he had, did this mean he did not care whom they were related to? 'What do you know of her father?'

'That he was a great man, a wonderful father, and a good husband, regardless. That he was smart, funny, and loving. And she should be proud of her surname.'

Gabrielle made a face, everything he had said did not describe Malcolm Barker-Hayden. 'Jonathan, who are you talking about?'

'Tammy's father, my father. Gabrielle, I know she is my sister, but I think this is best. We can always tell her about him later on. My DNA should be close enough to his for it to match hers. I'm sure we can get away with telling everyone that she is my daughter.'

Gabrielle felt as if the ceiling had detached itself and landed squarely on her head. 'Excuse me?'

'Don't be embarrassed, it's just one of those things that cannot be undone. So you had an affair with my father, I disliked it a great deal in the beginning, but I'm over it. Let me become my sister's father and we can be a family.'

Two things happened simultaneously. First, an incredible fear filled her. Under no circumstances could she let him pursue this avenue because the minute he discovered Tammy was not related to him... Well, she didn't know what would happen but she guessed that it would not be good. The second was a deep disappointment, and she felt as if she were about to have some type of attack. She jumped to her feet. 'So, we finally have the true reason why you married me. How long have you known this?'

'Sort of since the beginning—'

An absurd anger filled her as she pointed a finger. 'Oh my God, you wanted power over me. You want to control me, and the fool that I am, walked right in, blinded by your manipulating capabilities. You can just forget it.' She tore the letter in half. 'Why didn't you tell me this from the beginning? Why did you pretend that you cared? And another thing, I'll have you know that Tammy—' she stopped. If she revealed the truth, would everything revert to how it had been before this circus? Where would Tammy be without his support? Where would she be? Owing him a lot of money, under his thumb, and possibly, in grave danger.

'Tammy is what?' He asked equally angry. 'I can't wait to hear it. Stop being selfish, you are not the only parent she deserves. She is as much my blood as she is yours, so I think we have equal rights.'

'Does everybody know that she is your father's child?' That wasn't how she meant to ask but there it was.

'Paul and Amelia do. Amy might, and my mother— Well, I lied to her and have been telling everyone that Tammy is mine; to uncomplicate things.'

She almost laughed at that, uncomplicate things indeed! 'No, you assumed that anything you decided was fine, that you didn't have to consult me, or ask anything. Now, I want to know. Did you want to take her away from me,' she stopped as her eyes filled with tears and her breath caught, the idea hurting deeply. 'Were you planning to get rid of me once you were her father?'

He was upset, as nothing was going according to plan, so he didn't measure his words very well. 'It did cross my mind.' Then was instantly sorry he had said that nonsense.

Her eyes refilled. 'As I said before, the world likes to conspire against people. This is not the first time my heart has been broken by those I care about, so why should you have considered my feelings. You are Jonathan Knight, who can do whatever he wants.' She turned around and ran out of the room.

'Crap.' He sank onto a couch angrily. How had this happened? Why didn't she want him as Tammy's father? Could it be that she didn't see this union as permanent and meant to leave? The thought sent him into a rage and he didn't know which he disliked more. Losing Tammy or losing her. He stormed to his room.

He couldn't sleep, trying to figure out where he had gone wrong but eventually closed his eyes. It was the middle of the night when he awoke to a mournful sound.

Getting out of bed, he followed it until he stopped outside Tammy's room. Opening the door a fraction, he saw Gabrielle in the rocking chair with her.

She was sobbing, Tammy gurgled. He leaned against the wall, not understanding. Did he go in? What did he say, what did he ask, where did they stand? He looked at her again, she looked sad. Then he recalled. Earlier, she mentioned being hurt by the people she cared about, so he understood perfectly well that she meant him too. She did care, but he had somehow messed it all up.

He jumped up in bed again and glanced at the time, certain he had heard someone enter the room. Turning his head, he saw a silhouette standing by the window, holding one of the curtains. 'Gabrielle, what are you doing?'

'I think we should change them to green.' She held out the curtain to him.

Considering it was dark, he wondered how she had come to the conclusion that green would look good in the bedroom. He switched the light on, got out of bed and went to her. 'Green you say, maybe with pink flowers.'

There was a glazed look in her eyes so he waved a hand in front of her face. No response, she was sleepwalking. 'Come Gaby,' he told her softly, took her hand, and led her back to her room. There, he kissed her gently and put her back into bed.

He found her hiding in the study the following morning, and while he didn't want to bother her, he needed to tell her something before going to work. 'Good morning, Gabrielle.'

'Morning,' she didn't look up.

'Okay, you don't want me to do this, although I would like to. So let us leave it alone until you trust me enough and ask me out of your own free will.'

She looked at him. 'Do you mean that?'

He took a step closer. 'I get it that we are not friends, that there are things I know nothing about, that you don't believe or trust me completely, but I swear that I did not want to take her away or upset you like this.'

'But you did marry me to get to her.' Accusation flashed in her eyes again.

'Partly,'

'What was the other part?'

How would she react if he told her that he had already been falling in love with her back then and that he had simply not realised it, which was why he had not seen the idea as completely crazy. That he knew now with certainty that he could never have anything meaningful with Amelia. That he was trying to win her heart. 'I think we must leave the damn thing alone.'

'As you wish,' she knew he had not told her everything and she dreaded to imagine what other weird reasons had prompted him to do this.

'Okay, moving on. Off the topic now, may I ask a favour?'

'Of course,'

'Next Friday, we are having a dinner and dance to celebrate my instatement as Knight Industries' CEO. I would like you to be there, so can I ask you to get something beautiful to wear? Don't worry about money; it's already in your account.'

She felt hot with shame at that moment because she felt like a kept woman. She did nothing for him and he had all these desires to do things to make their life better. Except that he had shocked her senseless with last night's surprise, it was in fact a brilliant idea, if they were a real couple, and if Tammy were related to him as he imagined, but none of that was real. 'Thank you and I will try to make you proud.'

He wanted to tell her that she didn't have to try because she simply did, but he was already late. 'See you this evening then.' He wanted to kiss her, but she would probably murder him with the letter opener on the spot.

Fear had spoken not logic because if facts were as Jonathan imagined, it would have been right to have him declared Tammy's father. It was also typical of him, to simply go all the way, not even consider adoption first.

Feeling that she should make proper amends, she decided to go to Knight Industries. Meeting someone on his own turf spoke of contrition and humility. She wanted him to understand that she was repentant about her outburst.

She chatted with Amy for a few minutes, as she waited for him to return from somewhere in the building, but when Amy became busy, she went to wait in the office. Minutes later, she heard Paul's voice outside the door.

'So she freaked out?'

'Completely,' Jonathan said.

'Maybe you surprised her.' Paul offered.

'I guess I did. But it was more than that, she was scared.'

'Considering how the relationship began, it is possible she does not trust you to have so much power so quickly. Think about it, would you have married her if you didn't know about Tammy?'

'Of course not,' Jonathan admitted and sighed. 'I just wanted to make sure Tammy stayed in my life, that I can look after her, that I have a say—'

The office door burst open, out she waltzed, glared at him, and stormed down the passage.

'Gabrielle,' he ran after her. Of all the inopportune moments when he opened his mouth to merely state old facts.

'As you said, let's leave it.'

'Gabrielle,'

She reached the lift and smacked the button. It opened immediately. 'It's fine, it's done, and I don't want to hear anything else.' She closed the door on his face and started the downward descent.

'Not even that I love you?' He mumbled.

For a week, neither said much to the other, both busy dealing with their feelings as to what had taken place, both also having had a glimpse into the other's temper. It was not as if they believed that they would not run into personality clashes, character disagreements, and contradictory behaviour, but things were changing, emotions were blurring, and expectations were shifting.

She had been ruminating over her reaction and the answer was beginning to bother her. Yes, she had been frightened of Jonathan finding out that he had no blood ties to Tammy, not because she wanted to hide it forever, but because she was so very unsure about his response. To suddenly discover that she had used non-disclosure might upset him in ways she didn't know, and she could not chance being kicked out, because, where would they go, what would she do again?

The second reason bothered her more. She had known there were no feelings involved from either side so why did his reason for this malarkey bother her so deeply, because she could not think about it without getting the nastiest sensation right in the middle of her chest. Perhaps she was developing some condition she was not yet aware of.

Friday morning, he found her in the study again. She seemed to take refuge in there when troubled and he wondered what it was she did there apart from reading, because sometimes he was sure he could hear her talking to someone. 'Gabrielle, I apologise for last week, for upsetting you; it was not my intention.'

She looked up from the PC. 'I know you didn't mean it how I understood it. And I too am sorry.' she made a gesture.

'Don't think about it anymore. Are you ready for this dinner?'

Here she sat, making some things important when he ran a company that employed thousands, had huge responsibilities, and ploughed through quite a few headaches over it all. 'Is there something I need to know, do, say?'

'No,' he smiled. 'You must just enjoy it.'

'I'm guessing your mother will also be there.'

He shrugged. 'I am never certain as she didn't always participate in these things when dad was alive either. In the last two years, she has done better, and she did attend the yearly Christmas ball. There are things about my family I should tell you about, unfortunately, I don't have time now. We will use the weekends for that.'

Talking and playing with Tammy was all he could use weekends for, so was he willing to live like this indefinitely, without a real family, a real wife? Why oh why had she agreed to this craziness? She furrowed her brows, wondering what secrets he could possibly reveal about his mother.

CHAPTER THIRTEEN

Jonathan played a little in Tammy's room. She tended to become clingy when she saw him dressed up, knowing that he was going somewhere without her. Esther, the nanny, hovered around, so when it was almost time to leave, he made sure Tammy had something interesting to do, otherwise she would yell her head off. After seeing that she was enthralled with SpongeBob, he went to wait for Gabrielle in the lounge.

Hearing the heels as she rushed a little across the landing, he went to the hall to give her a hand on the last step, but when he saw her, he was the one who needed the hand.

She looked stunning in the cream strapless shift dress delicately gathered on one side of her waist, moulding her curves, her shoulders enticingly bare. She had a pair of loopy white gold earrings and his bracelet on. He was pleased that she had considered it worth the evening, as he had not seen her wear it before and wondered if she didn't like it. In her hand was the prettiest clutch bag covered in dainty silk flowers.

Most women had nothing on his little Gabrielle and he did not think merely in terms of looks. There was a sweet innocence about her that endeared her to just about everybody. He already knew that he was going to be upset at the male population; they were going to ogle her.

The moment he saw all the fancy gowns most women chose, he realised Gabrielle was underdressed, yet, she looked the best. The insane photographer couldn't stop clicking his irritating camera, he felt like punching him, and a couple other men too.

Then, he became exceedingly annoyed. As he looked across the hall, he saw Paul with Amelia. Why was she here? She would have been if he was not married, but he did not like it that she was present, and now, practically not invited. But he could not deny it; she looked magnificent in her red gown and cascading golden tresses.

Involuntarily, he glanced at Gabrielle's hair. She had beautiful natural light brown hair, and tonight, she had slicked it all back into a ponytail, showing her perfect bone structure. He wanted to trace that line, to run his fingers across those brows, to taste her lips.

'Darling,' Amelia greeted theatrically and came over to kiss him.

Gabrielle exhaled deeply. Goodness, but she disliked this woman, and she did not often do another person. She was phony, plastic, and pretentious, and when she registered how Amelia's eyes just about swallowed Jonathan whole, she liked her even less. Then she wanted to laugh when Miss bright-lights greeted her as if she were the bump on the road, which she obviously was in Amelia's highway to fame and fortune.

Gabrielle wished she had been there to hear how Jonathan presented his little dilemma, wondering if Amelia had cried, if she had thrown a tantrum, or if she had tried to put up a fight. She might have done all three but Jonathan had obviously not been moved because he believed in this more. Although it had been a demented decision, it told her something about him that she liked very much. Family came above everything else.

As she thought about family, she saw Jonathan's mother, who must have decided that supporting her son was worth the effort. Barbara was a grand lady, very regal and there was authority when she spoke. She smiled at Gabrielle warmly and took her hand, a gesture that seemed to please Jonathan, because although she could tell that he loved his mother madly, he always looked nervous around her.

Paul. She was aware that he liked her more than he should, but at least he was funny and smart, and because she liked him too, she did not intent to encourage him in any way, and if possible, veer his attention in another direction. Sometime during the evening, he asked Jonathan if he had his permission to dance with her. It infuriated her that those two, although modern men, sometimes behaved in old-fashioned ways. As if she could not make the simple decision of dancing with someone other than her husband.

Paul held her with a firm grip as they twirled a few times and Gabrielle realised why he had dragged her onto the dance floor. There slithered red python all over Jonathan. She stiffened, unable to understand why that woman's artificiality made her blood boil.

'What's wrong?' Paul asked, but following her gaze, saw instantly. 'Don't worry she is not getting what she's looking for.'

'And what is she looking for?'

'Unfortunately for her, Jonathan has made other arrangements.' He gazed at her pointedly.

'You mean she wanted to marry him.'

'It was quite the dedicated quest.'

Gabrielle felt heat rise in her face. So, Jonathan's other reason for marrying her; in fact a weak cover-up so he could keep Amelia at arm's length but still pursue his affair. Now, how many other little insane reasons had he used? Weird and amoral. What was that? Amelia's hand travelled up Jonathan's thigh as she leaned into him. Never in Gabrielle's life did she feel like hurting another human being as much as she did then.

'Well,' Paul said, interpreting her reaction. 'I wondered how long it would take.'

'Shameless. And in his mother's presence,' she exhaled. 'I think I'm overheating.'

Paul chuckled. 'Love can be quite upsetting.'

'What?' She returned her focus to him.

'It's written all over your face. You are in love with Jonathan, and this little episode of daytime soap opera is driving you nuts with jealousy.'

'Me, love Jonathan?' She made a sound. 'Except for Tammy, I don't want to love anyone.'

'Is it?' Paul smiled. 'Then you have a problem already. Because it seems that here,' he pointed to her chest and then her head. 'And here are not in complete agreement.'

She stared at him for a second then dropped her head despondently. 'Ignorance is so much better. I didn't want to see or know about any of these things. And now to think about them together— Why did you bring her?' she asked unhappily.

'I didn't ask her, met her outside as I arrived.'

'Wasn't there someone you could have asked?'

'I didn't have time to think about it.'

She noticed the sad eyes. 'I'm sorry. And I can't say it would have been any different even if we had not done this mad thing, but here we are.'

'I know.' This was why he had fulfilled Charles' wish, because as much as he desired it otherwise, he had known it from the first moment they had set eyes on each other as the one glanced up and the other down over that balcony at Knight Industries. Looking towards their table, he noticed Jonathan's discomfort. Fine, he had to end this silliness. Leaning over, he kissed Gabrielle's cheek. 'I'm learning how to deal with you as only a friend.'

'Thank you.' She told him shyly. Then as she lifted her face, there stood her husband.

Paul pretended surprise. 'Your wife is quite the mover.' If he didn't watch it, Jonathan would move his face.

Jonathan inhaled deeply as soon as he wrapped his arms around Gabrielle, loving the way their bodies moulded together and her hair filled him with a fresh fragrance, which he liked very much. As he spun her around, he imagined taking a shower with her. They would laugh and tease each other and then he would gently push her against the wall and make love to her. Afterwards, he would take her to their bed and love her again. He felt quite light-headed at the idea.

Amelia was upset when Paul sat beside her. 'What is happening?' She flicked a hand at the dancing pair and her pitch went up a notch. 'He said it was for convenience.'

'Please lower your voice,' Paul suggested as he glanced towards Barbara.

A dark look appeared on Amelia's face. 'He lied to me, didn't he?'

'I don't think he did. He just didn't know himself that he was in love with her.'

'Love!' She almost exploded. 'You mean it's the whole thing, not just a distraction?'

'Oh no, Gabrielle will never be that for him.' She wasn't that to anyone.

She pouted and narrowed her eyes. 'This is so unfair to me, all the time I spent nurturing him—'

Paul interrupted her. 'He's not a tree, Amelia. Besides, there are a lot of men who find you very attractive.'

She fixed her gaze on him. 'Why didn't you chase her? You seem to like her a whole lot too, which I don't get anyway.'

'It's a little late for that. They are married and I will get over it, and if not, I will hide it well and continue being their friend. You see, one should not mess with love, and that is what those two have, they are just not sure of it yet.'

Displeasure plastered itself on her face. 'I understand contracts. The one he and I made may have been only verbal but this is not what I agreed to. I knew she was trouble the first moment I laid eyes on her, look at her. Do you know if they are sleeping together?'

'How am I supposed to know that?'

'You are his best friend and he tells you practically everything. Can she dance?' Amelia asked as she watched Gabrielle move on the floor with professional agility.

'Yes,' Paul nodded. 'Quite well actually, she took ballroom dancing.'

'I cannot bear this dreadful display.' Amelia complained and grabbed her satin purse off the table. 'She lies, he lies. Take me home! I need to rethink this backstabbing story.'

Gabrielle was near seething because she did not like what she had witnessed at that table. Unless she was a doctor or nurse, no woman had any business touching an inch on him. The fact that he walked away, got him a reprieve and as he drew her closer, she found herself letting go as his masculine scent enveloped her. It made her feel safe, and she wondered if this was what Tammy experienced when he held her because he had a strong but gentle touch.

When they got home, after bidding Esther goodnight, she went straight to the coffee, not tired at all, yet she had just about danced the night away. They drank in silence, as if there was nothing to say. When finished, which was almost simultaneously, both got to their feet and stood centimetres from each other.

Reaching out, he pulled her to him. 'Thank you for tonight, it was a wonderful evening.' He kissed her softly then gazed at her. The first time with her awake, better take it slow, in case she rejected his advances. She didn't. Her eyes were wide, full of mystery, so he kissed her again, unhurriedly, giving her time to respond. She did. She was sweet, soft, pliable, making his heart sing as he felt desire unfurl. Covering her face and neck with tiny kisses, he pushed her gently onto the sofa.

Falling to his knees, he kissed her forehead then travelled slowly to her eyes, forcing them shut. Her breath was quick and hot, but her hands stayed calm, going to his neck, where her fingers began a tender exploration. Those night assignations could be buried, he loved this. 'Tell me you like it.' He begged against her face as he pecked her nose then returned to her mouth and gently slipped his tongue into its secrets.

Like it, she had never known anything like it and she never wanted him to stop.

He wriggled himself out of the jacket, unbuttoned his shirt, and drew her closer. 'Tell me you want me, just as I want you.'

She couldn't reply, for she had not known that she could desire someone this intensely. She had imagined herself in control, able to dictate what she thought and felt... her body trembled and shook with cravings, passion tumbled out, and she wanted— she wanted him.

He invaded her mouth again, savouring her taste, as one hand went under the skirt to remove her shoes and then ran from ankle to hip. A finger went to where her knees touched, and began drawing little infinities on the inside of her leg.

'Jonathan,' she whispered, her eyes filled with wonder, yet feeling so terribly shy.

'Do you understand that my selfish ways are over? That you are my priority; that I want to make you happy?' He pecked at her lips.

She did not comprehend why he imagined himself so because since meeting him, he had never been that. She would label him weird and confused but also attentive and caring. She just did not know him well enough to discern what she could trust him with.

He watched her face as she figured things out and wondered if she was comparing him to his father. The thought upset him. When it came to loving Gabrielle, he did not want to be compared to or compete with anyone.

As if seeing inside his head, she placed a hand on his face. 'You are wonderful.' She could tell he wanted to take this all the way to the bedroom now. Lowering her eyes self-consciously, she readjusted the dress.

'Da... Da...' Both heard a baby voice call.

Jonathan glanced at the coffee table. There stood the hand-piece of Tammy's intercom. 'What is she saying?' He asked and ran a finger across her brow, down her nose, and past her lips.

'She's calling you, calling you daddy.'

Jonathan fixed his eyes on her. 'Do you mind?'

Gabrielle shook her head. She did not mind, in fact, liking it more than she could explain but he wouldn't understand any of it because of her outburst over that letter.

'Da...' Tammy continued and started complaining, which would become a wail if someone did not respond soon.

Jonathan gazed at Gabrielle. She was feeling awkward and uncertain, and in that mood, she was done for the evening. It was fascinating how he could read her. 'Let me go see what her majesty requires.' He said with a crooked grin as he rose to his feet, but before walking away, he bent over, brushed his lips across her neck and shoulders and then left the room.

Given the respite, she disappeared quickly. Was she mental? What in heaven's name was she playing at? Because although this little rendezvous had been wonderful, it would not be all he would expect next time. She felt something squeeze inside her as she imagined more... So far, neither was doing particularly well with their contract.

She recalled that little agreement they had sat down to discuss, write, and sign. They had already broken it a couple of times, especially Jonathan. He had agreed not to expect any physical contact from her but look at it; his mind and body could not get out of that place. She had agreed— what was it again? He had not demanded much from her, except that he had asked her to be a good wife to him.

What was a good wife supposed to do apart from dressing pretty and following her husband to public functions? She didn't think that withholding sex was a good wifely practice.

He hungered for her, gazing in her direction expectantly, hoping she made a decision, and then the move to his room. The physical need was driving him insane, but it was much more than that. Sometimes, when her guard was down, he got glimpses of what he imagined she was truly like. She was approachable, open, and often revealed a surprising sense of fun. It made him sad trying to imagine what had moved into her heart to conceal it so well most of the time.

Now that she had a faint idea what lovemaking might be like, she wanted her husband with a maddening intensity. Yet, she never created the opportunities to make it happen, because how could she? She didn't know how she knew, but she suspected that he sometimes stood outside her room in the middle of the night, wishing her to be a proper wife. She wanted to be that, and more, but she was petrified. What if he denounced them and kicked them out? Should she confess that she had almost stolen her sister, that she was a hypocrite, and that she was no one's mother any more than he was a brother?

CHAPTER FOURTEEN

She heard the front-gate bell ring and knew that Peter had answered it. He was very good at getting rid of nonsensical people as they often had odd characters asking for all sorts of things. The bell rang again, and then it became an annoying long drone. Whoever was outside was persistent, or a pest. She was not surprised when Peter appeared in the study.

'Madam, there is a man at the gate who insists on seeing you. I have told him to go away, but he refuses. He says he absolutely has to see you.'

'Does he have a name?'

'He says it's Dimitri. At least it sounded like that to me. Must be Russian or something but he sounds quite South African.'

She did not like the sound of that. 'You did right, don't let him in; I'll go to the gate to hear what he's looking for.' If it was whom she thought, she did not want him in the house.

She walked down the driveway, arrived at the closed gate and didn't see anyone, at least not at first. Leaning against the tree in the shade, he was invisible. Why was he here?

'Hey Gabrielle, I like your digs.' He said straight away and pointed to the house.

'I thought you agreed not to bother me.'

'No bother, but some things have transpired and I thought I should warn you. I'm here as a friend.'

'Okay, so what has happened?'

'Did you know that Charlotte had family?' He asked.

Gabrielle shook her head. 'What does that have to do with me?'

'Well, you see, there is something they know and are looking for.'

'Is this about the missing money again? You know I don't have it.'

Dimitri glanced at the house. 'Maybe you don't have that one, but you do have money.'

'This is my husband's house, what you see here belongs to him, not me.'

'Look,' he said. 'I'm not the one after it, they are. I just thought I'd come tell you so you can be prepared. You are a decent girl and I'm not bad all the time.'

It was possible he was telling the truth. 'Who are these people?'

'The one is Charlotte's husband. She was not divorced so that makes whatever she left his. He knows about the money she got from Malcolm's daughter, so he's searching for you. And the other one is her father. Those two don't see eye to eye but have decided to partner up until they find the money and split it.'

What was she supposed to say to this? 'What can I do?'

'Oh, wait, that is not the bad part. They know there is a baby—'

Gabrielle grabbed the gate. 'What do you mean?'

'They say it's theirs. The husband swears he's the father.'

'No,' a sick feeling filled her. 'She is my sister. She looks just like me. She is not his—'

'I know, because I saw Malcolm and her together all the time, and this trash was not around, but he can make your life very unpleasant. He could go to the welfare services and they might take the baby from you while all this is being sorted out. It could take months, years, and she will be somewhere without you.'

That could never happen; this baby was her blood. She felt weak, her mouth dry and bitter. Here was the world sorting her out again, making sure she reaped her reward because of her meanness towards Jonathan. 'What do you suggest?' She could not believe she was asking him. 'What I mean is— what must I do to get rid of them?'

'The baby is an excuse because two men are not interested in a child, unless they are paedophiles—'

'Stop!' She shivered with fright and disgust. 'They are not getting their hands on her. So I am guessing the next best thing is money. How much do they want?'

'That I'm not sure about but it will be at least a couple hundred thousand.'

Gabrielle turned pale. 'Where must I find that?'

Dimitri gazed towards the house again. 'Your husband is rich. It's not all that much for him.'

'What is it people assume out there in the world, that because someone worked hard and built something, now he must just give it all away? This came from people who used their talents and minds, and now some good-for-nothings come along and just take a piece of it? I don't think so.'

'Anything you believe, they don't care. They want money and they are going to get it. I came to warn you, now you do what you must. Either pay them, hand the baby over, or ask your husband.'

She was so upset she could barely think. 'It was kind of you to do so but can I ask? What do you want?'

He gave her an inscrutable look. 'Right now nothing, but I may need your help sometime in the future, or your husband's. One never knows.'

Heavens, this could become quite the disaster, and getting Jonathan embroiled in it was not her plan. 'Where are these men and how are they hoping to find me?'

'I'm guessing you don't read newspapers often. You are a pretty girl; your picture is a regular feature. Just a while back, you wore a stunning beige dress. All women aspire to be as stylish as you are.' He grinned.

She could not imagine why. "Jonathan must hate it." She knew how much he disliked publicity, which made her think that that was probably another reason why he had not wanted to marry Amelia. She grabbed her thoughts together. 'Please tell me they will not come here.'

The grin widened. 'Gabrielle, I know you are Malcolm's daughter, they don't. They also have no clue what you look like and are looking for a girl with the Barker-Hayden surname, which you never were, so you see, you are still okay for now. Before they do become clever and come intrude in your life, I suggest you go see them. If you do, it will circumvent them finding you and discovering things that are none of their business. I arrange the meeting, you hear what they want, and then figure out what to do.'

'Is any of this true?'

He became serious. 'This is no joke and I would not waste your time with nonsense.'

How was it possible she was considering becoming mixed up with this man? Right now, he was the best friend she had because she refused to involve Jonathan in her troubles. She felt ill, where was she supposed to go find so much money to satisfy two extortionists? Oh heck, there was that conspiring world again.

'Jonathan,' she began as she sat on the sofa. 'I'd like to work again.' She could not think of any other way to make money quickly, so this was the next best thing. Would probably need to work five years to make a couple hundred thousand but at least she would be trying.

'Why,' he asked curiously. 'Are you bored?'

She would not say bored but she lacked stimulation. She loved looking after Tammy but Esther was always around. The study was filled with wonderful books and she enjoyed reading but she could not read the whole day. She used the gym often and was in great shape; if she used it any more she might be able to enter bodybuilding competitions. There was the PC and she communicated with Anna and Luc in Switzerland almost daily but she also needed to see other people. Occasionally, she went out with Tammy. Shopping... how many of everything did anyone need? She liked the servants and she imagined that they liked her too but she could not chat to them incessantly.

'Do you mean back to the office?'

'Maybe,' she said unconvincingly.

'You don't look all that excited about it. What is it you would really like to do?'

She was good with languages so perhaps translating, interpreting, a tourist centre, or teaching, giving private lessons... How much could she make from any of those? What she really wanted to do— she wanted to continue her studies but becoming a student would make her even less money, because she would be spending it.

Jonathan watched her face, seeing all sorts of ideas fly in and out of that smart head of hers; she wanted something but was not going to be forthright. It always disappointed him when she did that because all he wished was for her to tell him what she wanted and he would do his best to give it to her. He loved seeing her expression when he found something she liked, wanted, or needed.

'What is the quickest way to make lots of money?'

'How much is lots of money?'

She stared at him, realising she had said it aloud, and he, who never let anything slide, was going to say something in three seconds.

'What's going on? You need, want, whatever money for something. What is it?'

Not even torture would make her tell him. 'I was just thinking.'

'That's true.' He fixed his gaze on her. 'But you are thinking for a reason. What do you want?'

'Nothing,' she stood up. "Say goodnight and disappear." Because when he looked at her like that, she felt funny, sometimes weepy, and wanted to tell him everything. Lately, he did this all the time, just sat looking at her, very... She didn't want to label it.

Rising so quickly that he startled her, he reached for her wrist and pulled her to him. 'If you don't tell me,' he dropped his tone, turning it into a caress. 'I am going to kiss you until you do, but if you refuse, I'm taking you to my room,' he grinned wickedly.

She was sure her heart was in her throat because it beat wildly there. 'It was a simple question.'

'It was not.' He brought her a few centimetres closer. 'Tell me.'

She passed her tongue over dry lips. 'I need to— Tammy—'

'Do you know what I love about you? The fact that you are so weird. Gorgeous girl, but utterly confused, and in this smart head of yours,' he cupped her face. 'There are birds' nests. Gaby, my darling, what do you want?'

She took a faltering breath. If she didn't know any better, she would swear he was talking as if he truly loved her; and had he just called her Gaby? She closed her eyes, basking in fuzzy feeling. But it was a trick because he had said that he was going to make her talk. 'Please forget I said anything.'

'You are not getting away that easy.' Without warning, he swept her up into his arms, and with purposeful steps walked out the lounge, through the hall, up the stairs, and into his room. There, he dropped her onto the bed and half fell over her, making sure she couldn't escape.

Her heart threatened to jump out of her chest. 'Can we talk?'

'No,' he said and covered her mouth with his. She opened hers instantly. Loving her compliance, he engulfed them in a kiss that was pure ecstasy.

'Stop,' she begged breathlessly, knowing that she had to get away.

'What do you want me to do to you?' He asked close to her mouth.

Naturally, he was going on the assumption that she had had sex but it was a subject she had never given much attention to, simply because no one had ever attracted her enough to date. Back in Zurich there had been a few interested boys but she had found them— well, boyish.

Jonathan. He made her thirst and hunger, something that started close to her heart and ended in the very core of her. Her body loved his proximity, his scent, his taste, his voice. The things she could say and all would be absolute heaven.

'I need to confess something.' He ran a hand over her chest, feeling the wondrous curves.

Good, if they talked he might leave all this well alone because she just wanted him, more than she should, she was certain. 'Yes, Jonathan.' She encouraged.

'Haven't you realised it yet? I'm in love with you. I need you, I think about you all the time. Damn that contract, I want you.'

She already knew this and couldn't explain how very happy it made her feel to hear it. 'Oh, Jonathan,' she closed her eyes, trying not to see the expectant look in his.

'Don't you feel anything for me?'

The word feel had nothing on what was happening to her but she had to detour him. Neither could be thinking about this. 'How is Amelia, have you seen her lately?'

The last two times Amelia had called in the evening, Jonathan had just about lost his temper. She didn't know what they had discussed, but it appeared as if Jonathan had ended the relationship. However, Amelia was clingy, and lately, Gabrielle felt as if she was stalking Jonathan. He seemed very displeased about the whole set-up.

He knew what she was doing because he was exceedingly aware of her reactions, and somewhere at the back of everything she used as a front, she was in love with him too. But something— something was preventing the relationship from moving forward. He needed to find out what that was because she would not be so compliant with her kisses if she didn't feel. Now, what the hell was this money business?

His concentration broken, she scooted herself off the bed and sat in the armchair. 'I really need to know—'

'How much do you need to make whatever is upsetting you go away?'

'I'm not taking money from you.'

'Why not, you are my wife.'

She shifted in the seat uncomfortably. 'I want to do this on my own.'

'I can see that.' He snapped. 'You want to do everything alone but you cannot go through life on your own.'

'Why not, it causes the least problems and pain to others.'

He stared at her. 'Don't ever think that you are a burden on me. I told you minutes ago that I love you, and I mean it. I love you. I love Tammy. She loves me and I think that you either already do, or want to, but have too many strange things going on in your head and refuse to let go.'

It was her turn to stare. He could read her really well, but no, she could not tell him.

'Okay,' he said. 'Just give me a figure so when this problem is over you might actually allow yourself to feel something.'

That made her burn with shame. 'I am not asking for money, I just want to know how to make some, really quickly.'

'This is what I'm going to do. Tomorrow, I am transferring some funds into your accounts. What you do with it is up to you.'

'No, I can't—'

'You can, and you will use it for whatever you need. As for work, you don't have to. Unless you find something you really want to do and enjoy, and going back to the office is not it.' He fixed his gaze on her and lifted his brows pointedly, but she didn't understand what he meant. Sighing, he told her. 'This is my room, or do you want to make it our room?'

A red blanket spread under her skin. She got to her feet and was going to say something but he turned his back and disappeared into the bathroom.

She lay in bed worrying. Again, he was doing things for her and she— what did she do? Nothing, she never did anything. All she did was take from him. She did not see this as a fair relationship.

Barbara invited her to afternoon tea; she and Tammy went. Gabrielle was enchanted by the part of the house she got to see, as it was exactly the type of place she loved exploring, and when she saw the library, she lost her heart because it was even more impressive than her father's. She wondered about that house sometimes but had no idea if she was supposed to try to do something about it, at least for Tammy's sake.

Gabrielle saw how Barbara came across as intimidating because of her grand way of walking and speaking but once one went past that, she was a woman with a large trove of experiences and a good heart.

Of course, she wanted to know how she met Jonathan, how their relationship developed and all sorts of other things. Gabrielle tried not to lie and stuck to the most plausible explanations when she did.

Barbara liked Tammy, the little girl seemed to like her pearls a whole lot too, and Gabrielle thought it looked rather interesting to see such a magnificent woman sitting with a child on her lap.

'Perhaps when you have a boy he will look like Jonathan. This cutie pie is all you.' Barbara told her with a smile. 'We need children around here. And I pray that the sadness that befell me will not affect you.'

'Couldn't you have more after Jonathan?'

Barbara shook her head. 'I struggled to fall pregnant before Jonathan, had four miscarriages. After Jonathan, I had another three, the last one being twins. I always lost them late in the second trimester, but the twins were eight months. So all in all, I lost eight children. It broke my heart and I fell into a depression that lasted years and became a recluse. Which is why still today, I don't like to leave the house unnecessarily.'

Gabrielle nodded, understanding many things. Why Charles had always been alone, why he had never considered cheating on or leaving her, why he had thought of her as his own daughter. He too had missed having more children. 'I'm so sorry.' For some unknown reason and if she had thought about it she would not have done it, Gabrielle automatically reached out for Barbara, hugged her tightly and said some idiotic thing. 'I hope your grandchildren will make you very happy and bring you great joy.'

'Thank you honey, I'm sure they will.' Barbara smiled as she dropped a kiss on top of Tammy's head. 'She is so good; you are doing a splendid job.'

Gabrielle laughed. 'You have not seen how she carries on when she is tired, or when she doesn't want to eat her vegetables. And if we are busy with something and Jonathan appears, it is the end of whatever we were doing.'

Barbara smiled. 'Jonathan a father, quite the contradiction. I never expected him to marry until well into his forties, but I am thrilled that he has become so calm and happy. And of course I can tell that he is absolutely crazy about you.'

Gabrielle blushed furiously. If only Barbara knew what went on in their house.

CHAPTER FIFTEEN

'Hello,' Jonathan greeted as he saw her sitting behind the desk in the study. He would love to kiss her, but she looked very serious. Instead, he sat opposite her.

'I did something today.' She announced. 'I went to see a lawyer.'

'Gabrielle...'

The look on his face tore a path right through her heart. 'Oh, no, that's not why.' She told him quickly. 'And I apologise for my meanness before. You were right, but I'm rash and don't always think before I'm supposed to do something. I went to ask about adoption procedures.

'We'll go this way, as I can't think about the poor baby being prodded, poked and pricked for blood tests.' She lied right there. 'And I feel we don't have to lie.' If only she could stop. 'I'm not sure how everything works yet but there will be papers and interviews, at home and work. But the lawyer said there should be no problems, as I am also a stay-at-home mom, and apparently, they really like that.'

After the initial shock, as he imagined her trying to divorce him, he sat back and watched her as she explained a few more things. Certain as he did that if anyone needed a picture of love for a dictionary, his would be perfect. Crazy, jealous, smitten, whatever anyone wanted to call it, he felt it. He dreamt of her, his body hungered for her, his mind needed her, and his heart loved her.

She tried to avert his gaze. It read her too well and she often felt as if she were bare. It was true that she did not want to love him, but she did. With a furious intensity, and lately, he also made her heart race, just as he was doing now. 'As I said, sorry for before.' She got up from the chair and walked around the desk, on her way somewhere.

He reached out and pulled her onto his lap. 'Thank you, my darling.' Wrapping his arms around her, he flicked the hair away and dropped a gentle kiss on her neck then swept up slowly until reaching the earlobe. Taking it into his mouth, he twirled his tongue around. Feeling her tremble, he tugged a little with his teeth then drawing a short line with his tongue straight across, stopped on her mouth, touching it softly. She sighed and parted her lips. His tongue went in slowly. Moaning, she offered hers and buried her fingers into his hair. One of his hands went under the skirt, travelled from knee to hip and found the top of her lace panties. Sliding his index finger just under the top elastic, he ran it across her tummy, feeling how her skin reacted to his touch.

Realising where his hand was, she felt faint, wishing it somewhere else. If she encouraged more he would want everything, and that she could not do, but just a little. She cupped his face and kissed him.

Sometimes, he would swear she did not know what she did because she was a fascinating paradox; right now, her kisses were a strange mixture of pure eroticism and an adorable innocence. Experimentally, he slid his finger further.

She came to her senses, grabbed his hand and lifted herself off his lap. 'Jonathan,'

He also arose and gazed into her eyes, which were full of passion and desire. Yet, under everything she wanted, there was that look, the one that screamed unspoken fear, and for that very reason, he did not want to give up. 'Yes, my darling,' he told her softly, covered her mouth with his, and pushed her against the desk, sitting her on it. With the left hand, he grasped the back of her neck and the right went to her back, bringing her to him, as he pushed himself between her legs.

This was as dangerous as it could get and she did not need experience to understand where he was taking it. Her body simply reacted to his and this position was sure to yield the desired response. Stiffening, she willed herself to fight against nature itself.

Her reaction was like oil to a flame. Hell, he wanted to break her, the primordial hunter instinct telling him to do it then deal with the consequences after. But this was Gabrielle, the woman he would die for; all that macho stuff could only lead to resentment, and who knew what else. He relented and released her, to follow where she would lead, if anywhere. There she sat primly, refusing to let her body feel anything and shut her brain down so she would not think.

'I get it,' he snapped. 'You will not give in, let go, capitulate, surrender, whatever you want to name it, wanting to do this on your own terms, but those stink. I'm almost certain that you love me, because if you didn't, none of this would be happening. People say actions speak louder than words, I see it, because you are utterly confused. Whatever you are hiding, cannot, will not, ever make me stop loving you. I want you and you know it, but I will never take you against your wishes. How the hell did you conceive Tammy? What am I doing wrong? What did my father do right? Were the two of you high on something? Fine, we revert to your contract.' No, he could not fathom his little wife; she looked shocked.

Once again, her selfishness shone bright, only taking, never giving anything in return, because every time these little encounters occurred, she goaded him on then retracted her steps. She was such a charlatan.

From the expression on her face, he would guess that she felt downright guilty that she had allowed another man to touch her intimately. He was upset. He did not want her to evoke anything from the past, even if the man was his father.

She stared after him as he walked out, took the deepest breath she was able to, and sank weakly into the armchair.

Something woke him up and turning in bed, he heard running water. He lay there a few seconds, trying to recall if he had forgotten to turn off the shower. Jumping out of bed, he went to the bathroom. He stared, all the taps ran at full-force and vapour rose to the ceiling.

He stopped in front of the steamed up shower; Gabrielle was inside. Now who took showers at three in the morning? 'Did something happen to yours?' He asked as he closed the taps on the basins. She neither answered nor moved, her hands against the wall, water cascading over her.

Perhaps she was upset over the study episode and was ignoring him. Whatever the reason, she would be out soon enough. But twenty minutes later, she was still in there. He jumped out of bed and went to check again, she had not moved. 'Gabrielle,' he called but received no response. It dawned on him; she might be sleepwalking.

Opening the shower door, he realised instantly that she had played with the taps, was now standing under cold water and it would be an absolute miracle if she did not get sick. He climbed in and turned the thing to hot. Holding her against his chest, he let the steaming water envelop them in heat, rubbing her arms and face, wanting to see than blue tinge leave her skin.

When pink covered her body, he grabbed a bath sheet, wrapped her in it, and towel-dried the hair. Lifting her into his arms, he felt the wild shivers. With no idea how long she had been under the cold water, he also knew not to wake her, had always heard that about sleepwalking.

Grabbing a plush throw, he enfolded her and made her lie in bed while he ran to dry himself. Then climbing into bed, he pulled her into his arms, adoring how they fit together. If only she chose to be here willingly. Entwining his feet and legs with hers, he started massaging her exposed shoulder, arm, and back, and slowly drifted off to sleep.

'Jonathan,' she called in a throaty voice.

He opened his eyes and saw her beautiful but confused hazel ones regarding him. 'Good morning. How are you feeling?'

'I don't know. Why am I here?'

'Do you remember anything about last night?'

Except for that insane episode in the study, she had no clue. Heat spread beneath the skin. 'Did I do something bad?'

'We made wild passionate love.'

All colour drained from her face. It could not be. He would not be this calm, with no questions, or without demands for explanations.

He watched her reaction with interest. He had said that sentence to some women, when neither was sure what they had done the previous night. Usually, it did end up like that, but not today. There was that horrible look that he was starting to dislike intensely.

'Liar.'

Definitely interesting, but he was not going to worry about it now. His hand went to her face. 'You sleepwalked into my bathroom, turned all the taps on, and climbed into the shower. Heaven knows how long you stood under the cold water until I woke up. I wrapped you in that because you were iced, and that is why I made you sleep here, so I could keep you warm.'

She sat up, pulling the throw closer. 'I was hoping I didn't do that anymore. Most people stop sleepwalking as adults, and I hadn't for some years.'

He realised she was not aware that this was not the first time she was doing it in this house. 'Is there a trigger? Like migraines.'

'Although it's not proven, they say stress and anxiety are usually the main culprits.'

Of course it would be those two because he saw them all over her face just about every day. If only she told him what made her feel that way. 'Maybe you should go see someone.'

'You mean a professional?'

'If you want to,' he got out of bed, went to his closet, looked at her, and smiled.

'What's funny?'

'Not funny, nice. It feels right to see you sitting there.' He threw himself across the bed, landing with his head on her lap. Reaching out, he pulled her head down. It was a gorgeous kiss because everything was out of alignment. Then he recalled what he had told her the previous day. 'Sorry, forgot about the contract. But one day soon, it will be more than kisses we share in the morning. I promise you now; I am going to wear you out until you finally acknowledge that you love me.'

Gabrielle sneezed, thankful for the interruption, she did not want to talk about all that other stuff.

Jonathan was right, she did need someone to talk to, but she was going to see if having a friend first helped more. There were three things she stressed constantly about: Charlotte's relatives, what Dimitri had implied - she wanted him nowhere near Jonathan, Charles' entanglement in that mess was quite enough - and lastly, Jonathan himself. Subterfuge blended with fear was turning her into a paranoid wreck and it was manifesting in sleepwalking all over again.

Amy was always happy to see her, and enjoyed sharing the funny news from the office. She loved working for Jonathan and Gabrielle could tell that some hero worship was going on.

'Although I miss you,' Amy said. 'I'm glad you are having a nice time being married and a mom.'

Gabrielle dropped her gaze and turned her face, as if the pretty table in the corner was forthcoming with some answers.

'Okay, happy, but not altogether happy,' Amy said astutely. 'Come; tell me, you know it's going nowhere.'

'What do you know about Jonathan and my situation?'

As it turned out, Amy had a lot of background information from Charles' time. She was uncertain why the marriage had happened, as there had been no inkling from either side for anyone to think that it would, but one thing she knew for sure, Jonathan was in love. After hearing several off-the-chest things, Amy asked. 'I can see that most of this is under control, what are you really trying to tell me?'

'I am scared. There is too much stuff going on and I don't know how to deal with it.'

'I get it that both of you went into this marriage with unorthodox reasons but now have feelings for each other. Just explain what the actual trouble is, because I'm not quite seeing it.'

'It's a ludicrous situation.' She explained about Jonathan's and Paul's delusional belief, mentioned the lawyer and that she had started the adoption. Then she explained how petrified she became about the suggested paternity test. 'I threw such a tantrum out of fear, accusing him of all sorts of things. Do you think he only wants Tammy?'

'That man would jump in front of a train for you, and I tell you, you will give him the thrill of his life when you two finally happen.' Amy leaned in now. 'But how, why, what in heaven's name... why do they think Tammy is Charles'?'

'I don't know how they concluded this. I suppose it could look like that, as I never spoke of my father, so how would they know? I don't know if Jonathan ever met him but let's hope not because that man was a disaster. Forever getting involved with suspicious characters, borrowing money, wasting what wasn't his, just doing unacceptable things, as you well know, so this is where we stand. Jonathan believes Tammy is his sister, and loves her like a daughter. What if when he discovers that I misled him, it changes the way he feels about her?'

Amy regarded her. 'I have a few crazy suggestions for you. Go to a doctor, ask him to remove impediment, do it yourself— Dear lord, I'm corrupting you. Jonathan will never know the difference, unless you want to pick some guy off the street.'

'That is gross. As for the other ideas—they are all weird.'

'And I'm flabbergasted that this could actually be a predicament. I say tell him the truth and go from there.'

They stayed another hour discussing the new problem, Charlotte's relatives. Amy became concerned and suggested she go see the lawyer again to find legal protection for all of them. The Russian mob was not to be trifled with even if Dimitri said he did not want anything. He was not to be trusted under any circumstances and Gabrielle was never to see him alone. If possible, Gabrielle should tell Jonathan, because he knew people and he could provide the security she needed, before she needed it.

Gabrielle did feel better; and agreed with Amy that she could not take chances with criminally minded people, especially when they were greedy and did not understand what the right thing was. Likewise, she needed to sort out this crisis before if became something else, and if she could keep Jonathan out of it, the better.

'This place is beautiful and a good investment but I so wish Jonathan would agree to move back home. Would you have a problem with that?' Barbara asked a few minutes after arriving at the house.

Gabrielle decided to be truthful. 'I don't know, I haven't thought about it.'

Barbara smiled. 'One day. Now, for the reason why I am here. Jonathan's thirtieth is just around the corner, any ideas?'

Gabrielle felt like a fool. Her head was so full of junk, she had forgotten about the upcoming milestone. 'I apologise, but I have none. Do you want to do something, and what has he had before?'

'Everything: away, at home, at some hotel and in the bush. That year a spider bit him. It was dreadful, which is why, he was beside himself when you were also bitten. Perhaps we should give a ball.' Barbara looked around. 'It's a little small here for that but we can do it at the house. What do I have all that space for? But you tell me. Dig around for ideas and let me know.'

Barbara stayed until dinner and Jonathan was very pleased when he found her there, becoming even more pleased when he realised that she liked Gabrielle and Tammy a whole lot. Not only did this demonstrate that she was coming out of her shell and finding things to do again but he also needed allies in breaking down his wife's defences.

Driving home after dropping his mother off, he imagined Gabrielle would have retired by the time he got back, but no, she was curled up on the sofa in the lounge, obviously intending to wait for him. 'Gaby,' he called softly.

She sat up, opened her eyes, and looked at him. 'It's going bad.'

'What is?'

'They want to take her— I can't let them.' Getting to her feet, she rattled in French. 'Je lui dis... J'ecrire la liste. Je suis si fatigue.' Then she turned and ran out of the room.

What could she possibly mean? Then rising to his feet, he too went to bed.

Opening his eyes, he glanced at the time, sure that he had heard Gabrielle calling him. Had he dreamt it?

'Jonathan,'

There it was, loud and clear. Turning, he saw her silhouette in the doorway. He flicked the light on. She was clenching a cloth in her hand. 'What's wrong?'

'I've hurt myself.' She took a few steps towards him.

He caught her as she fell, and gently dropped her on the bed. Undoing the kitchen cloth from her hand, he felt half-faint himself when he saw all the blood. She must have used a knife or something equally sharp because she had a cut across the left palm. 'Gaby, please wake up.' He patted her face and smoothed her hair back. He needed to look at the wound properly because she might need stitches.

She moved and opened her eyes. 'Huh...'

'What were you doing that you hurt yourself like this?'

She looked at her hand, seeing the blood that would not stop. 'I was making a sandwich and the knife slipped.' Her eyes filled with tears.

He pulled her to her feet and wiped the tears tenderly. 'Were you awake or sleepwalking?' This story was starting to concern him.

'Awake, I just looked away a second,'

'Let's wash it out.'

They stood in the bathroom in front of the basin, washing out her hand. Then he told her to make a fist to see if the blood-flow would stop. She was pale and he made her sit on the chair as he sat on the closed toilet seat. He reached out and pulled her towards him, so she could rest her head against his chest. 'What am I going to do with you? You can't be left alone at night; and perhaps not even during the day.'

She felt lightheaded, nauseous, and the sound of his voice was lulling her into a dreamlike state. 'I'm tired.'

'Let me see first,' he took her hand and opened the fist. The bleeding was slowing down but he still could not see how deep the cut was. He searched for the first aid kit and there he sat bandaging her hand. 'That will do until we get ourselves to emergency—'

'Not now, I need to lie down.' She told him and walked out of the bathroom.

He was startled when he got back to bed. There she lay on the other pillow, her left hand out, as she obviously didn't want to hurt it further. Smiling, he climbed in, scooted himself over, and placed an arm over her. Sleep—what was that when she was this close? Her proximity was something that excited him no end as she always smelled as if she had dipped herself in some faint fruit juice. His body tightened and wanted all sorts of things. Sadly, they were nowhere near that, but unable to help himself, he nuzzled her shoulder.

He awoke again, with her pressed against his back, crying. He flicked the light on and turned to look at her. 'Is it hurting very badly?'

She nodded and lifted her bandaged hand. 'It stings,'

'That's because your nerve-endings have just realised that they have been separated from their pals on the other side.' He took her hand and kissed the two exposed fingertips.

'Are you kissing it better?' She tried to smile.

'Do you want painkillers, or go to the hospital?'

She shook her head, wiped the tears, and whispered. 'In the morning, and stop believing in fairytales, the kissing doesn't work.'

'Of course it works.' He pulled her closer, the silky pyjamas shifting sensually between their skins.

'It's bleeding.' She showed him how blood was seeping through the bandage. 'And I accept your offer of drugs.'

He rushed to the bathroom and brought the first-aid kit and a glass of water to the bed. Finding the painkillers, he placed two in her hand. Then, gently, he unravelled the old bandage, proceeded to wipe the cut dry, and bound a new one. 'Sure you don't want to go to the hospital now?'

'I should go to bed—'

He made a face and pointed. 'What's this then? And you may need me to change that thing a couple more times.' He climbed back into bed and enfolded her carefully so the hand could stay out. 'How does it feel?'

'Nice,'

He laughed. 'I meant the hand.'

'Very sore, I don't think I'll be able to sleep.'

'There are other things we can do before those pills take effect.'

'Such as what in the middle of the night, miniature golf?'

'Not what I had in mind.' He pressed himself closer and pecked the exposed shoulder, then as she half-turned, he kissed her mouth, one hand going to her chest, which rose and fell as he fanned the fire within. Then he remembered... but she hadn't said a word either way, so to hell with the contract.

She cried out.

'There is a moment killer; every movement you make is going to hurt. Lie still and let's talk.' He made a face, which she saw and he knew wanted to ask. 'I have never said that to a woman before.' He made himself comfortable and watched her do the same. 'Can we leave the light on or do you prefer it off?'

It depended on what they were going to discuss. He tended to ask odd questions and she had the bad habit of blushing, so off was probably advisable. She also didn't want him to think that she was hiding things. Whom was she kidding? He already knew that she did.

He wondered if she was aware that just about every thought ran past her face, and there was that mind of hers doing funny figuring-outs. 'Gaby,' he said softly and flicked some hair away from her face. 'Why don't you want to love me? I want to love you until we are both crazy, and I already do, except for the sex. Well,' he gave her a gorgeous grin. 'But it won't be sex with us; it will be the most beautiful lovemaking. So when my darling, when will you give in to my complete love?'

She had known that he was going to ask this type of mad question. Of all her decisions, being in this bed, right now, had to top the list as absolutely idiotic. Why had she let it go this far, to tease and entice him to such an extent that he kept wanting more? What in heaven's name was she trying to do? Drive him over the edge and then blame him for not sticking to their agreement? Did she not realise that she was going to be right there the day that happened, and that no matter her protestations, he was eventually not going to listen? Had she become a fool to not see that she was making it excruciatingly difficult for herself too?

'Do you like my kisses?'

She didn't want to. She didn't want to feel anything but when he looked at her like that and made her feel like this... Her eyes filled with tears and she hoped he thought it was the wound's fault.

He saw them and knew they had nothing to do with the hand. What in blazes scared her so? 'I am still waiting for a response. Men like to be told that they are fantastic.'

Here was her chance, to either make or break him; but she should consider carefully what she was about to do because whichever path she chose there would be consequences, and she had only herself to blame for the spot she had gotten herself into. She loved being close to him, and secretly hoped that one day she clean forgot to fight him off and he did much more than kissing. 'Yes.' There it was, decided. She had better not complain next time. 'It's almost morning, you have to sleep.'

'It's Saturday morning.' He started running his hand up her bare arm, knowing that he was being a beast, but he needed her to admit that she wanted him, to make her crave for him. She closed her eyes with pleasure, sighed softly, and fell asleep. Seemingly, this worked well with the pills at numbing the pain. He lay there just gazing at her. How he loved her.

Severe pain awoke her and carefully she reached for his face. He was always handsome, but sleep lent him a vulnerability that went straight to her heart. She loved him and wished for all the things he promised. Everything he could be for Tammy. Everything he wanted her to be for him. But first there was something she had to take care of.

'Gaby,' he said sleepily, opened an eye, and taking her hand from his face kissed it. 'Can you dress yourself or must I help you?'

For a second she could not understand why she should get dressed. Then making a movement, she winced.

'Yep, that hand must be throbbing right about now.'

CHAPTER SIXTEEN

It did not help much that she was sitting on a park bench. Public or not, she felt exposed, unsafe, and very nervous. She had waited until Monday to call Dimitri and asked him what was happening with Charlotte's relatives. He told her he was not sure but that they should meet anyway so he could tell her some new things. So here she sat, waiting for him to show up.

'Gabrielle,' he called behind her.

She jumped a little, as she had not heard him approach. He was a decent-looking man, and she noticed that his clothes were of superior quality. He had a good pair of jeans on, a well-cut shirt, and leather shoes. He could pass for anyone's friend, but she imagined this type of acquaintance did not require the standard shaking of hands. 'Dimitri,'

He sat on the bench, slid his arm across the back and stared straight ahead. 'What happened to your hand?'

She didn't exactly want to turn this into anything resembling a friendship, but equally, she did not want to antagonise him and lose her link to the men who gave her sleepless nights. 'It's nothing serious; I injured myself and needed four stitches. But I'm well, thank you, and you?' Politeness cost nothing.

'Very busy, but I'm okay.'

'Where is Calvin?' She asked and couldn't help but shiver at lard-head's image.

He noticed. 'Trust me, Calvin is not as bad as he appears, but I'm doing this on my own. My business associates,' he said somewhat mockingly. 'Don't know about those two yet, and I want to keep it that way. I told them that I would help them privately, that they don't need my boss' help. Besides, the boss always wants a cut of everything, so they do know that they can score higher if they are on their own.'

She breathed deeply. Of course, he would do his boss in if he could; were these people not well known for backstabbing each other? 'What is going on with Charlotte's people?'

He turned to gaze at her. 'You have luck on your side. The father is in hospital, so the husband is waiting until he gets out.'

'What is wrong with the man?'

He made a gesture. 'What always happens to heavy smokers. It must be emphysema because his breathing is not all that hot.'

'Have you been to see him?'

'No, he breathes like that all the time, sounds terrible. This is why they chase after money, because they never have any. They smoke it, drink it, snort it, whatever their weakness.'

Naturally, he was one of those who knew exactly how to exploit weaknesses. 'What kind of business are you into?'

He smiled, understanding her train of thought. 'If I can avoid it, I don't get involved in that stuff. My boss has a bunch of strip-clubs and quite a few shares in a couple of casinos. I run one where we do loans from, which is how I met your father. It's very profitable and we don't ask as many questions as banks do.'

'What did my father borrow money for?' She still recalled the money he had wrangled from her for some pharmaceutical investment.

'He wasn't too good with information, but I think it was to help pay off a huge debt I once heard him talk about. Do you know what he told us he was using as collateral?'

She knew it was going to be some absurdity. 'No.'

'You,'

'How do you mean?' Surely, he did not mean it the way it sounded.

'He said you were good for it. I did a financial check and learnt that you were; which is how I learnt you did not have your father's surname.'

This also explained how Malcolm and Charlotte discovered how much money she had.

'But those two reached higher than they should have, so now, there you have it.'

'Do you know anything about the man who killed them?'

'I have a few ideas. Do you want me to do something about it?'

What would he expect from her then? Besides, whether the murders were solved or not, nothing in her life would change. 'The police are investigating, I will wait.'

'You are never going to know anything like that, as there isn't enough evidence to incriminate anybody. What I would like to know is if it was because of the money, and if he has it.'

She was tempted to tell him about her father's last words, that money had indeed been the reason for their demise, but no one was supposed to know that she had been there. 'I needed that money for my little sister.'

'But your husband can provide.'

She dropped her head. 'But I would feel better if I contributed to her upbringing, as she's not really his responsibility.'

'I know Jonathan Knight, Paul and some of their friends, they have been at Red Bare a few times; decent guys overall. Haven't seen Jonathan in a while though,' looking at her, he grinned. 'Why would he need entertainment, he has you.'

She blushed, embarrassed. 'So you say they are quiet, but what about when the old man comes out of hospital?'

'Don't worry, I'll find out what they are concocting. What I do know is that they are going to make it expensive.'

'I told you before, I don't have money.'

'Of course you do, your husband just gave you some a while back.'

Her head shot up, now recalling Jonathan telling her that he would transfer some into her accounts. 'How do you know that? I haven't even looked...' She was upset now. Who did this man think he was to go snooping into her private affairs?

'Two million,'

'What?'

'Your husband must love you a whole lot because he deposited two million into your accounts. It was split three ways, between a fixed-deposit, some off-shore - earning fantastic returns. He's very smart that one. And the rest is at your daily disposal.'

Her heart dropped all the way to her feet. Of course Jonathan loved her; she saw it every day in how he wanted to fix things, so he could not possibly imagine that his giving character might have created a worse danger. Because now, all sorts of people knew that she had it and most were smart enough to find ways to extract it from her. Never mind those men, Dimitri was probably after it. She felt quite ill.

'I see from your expression that you did not know. Well, it's there. As I said, some can't be touched but the rest would make those two very happy. You must make them sign, as my boss did.' He smiled. 'But Mr Knight should not have worried about that; I would not have let them hurt you. If it was today,' he fixed his gaze on her. 'Maybe as Calvin suggested that day we came to find you, I too would have made a different plan about that blasted money.'

What was written on her forehead that men wanted to buy her? Even Jonathan was in on this humiliating practice.

She hated it. Perhaps he was slightly different because he had not started with intentions towards her, merely thought of using the debt as an excuse to get to Tammy; and had wanted to evade Amelia's clingy arms, greedy hands, and celebrity syndrome. Still, it felt abhorrent to think that she had somehow traded rights to her little sister. When, oh when could she rid herself of the dreadful feelings she carried around? 'Do you have any idea how long the man will be out of commission?'

'He's in a state hospital; they will kick him out as soon as they can.'

'How do you know all these things? It's not as if banks give their information away.'

'I have many customers, including bank managers. Funnily enough, it's not they who give me that kind of information. People talk when they need things. All I do is mention a name, and within days, I know what I want to know.'

She wondered how information equated money. Then again, there were many things she knew nothing about. Now, she was both glad and upset that Charlotte's people were taking their time. Glad, because she had time to think and work out a plan, but this dragging out just stressed her more. She noticed Dimitri was watching her. 'What?'

'I would like to know what happened with the baby. I mean, how did you get her?'

What was the use of pretending? He already knew most of it, telling him the truth was doubtless irrelevant.

'So they signed the baby over to you?'

Gabrielle nodded. 'Unbelievable, but they did. They were never interested in her, just the money. I felt terrible about it, and sometimes still do, because it felt as if I was buying her, but it wasn't like that. I simply wanted to save her from them.'

'Do you still have this paper?' He asked curiously.

'Yes, and although my suspicions turned out as I dreaded, I still feel guilty. So I pretend to be my little sister's mother.'

He reached out and squeezed her shoulder. 'I deal with this type of thing every day.'

She did not understand what he meant.

He smiled. 'Doing the wrong thing for the right reason. Anyway, let's leave all this well alone. Have you ever been to a strip-club?'

'No.'

'As I was saying, sometimes, one does wrong things for the right reasons. Some of the girls are pretty smart too; a few are even university students.'

'I understand about people having to make choices, and considering I don't know everyone's circumstances, I can hardly judge why people do what they do.' She wondered about her own situation. If Jonathan had not married her, what would she have been willing to do?

'I like this about you. A good person who doesn't tell others how bad they are.'

She guessed it was a compliment. 'Do you think I should set up a meeting with the husband? A sort of divide and conquer strategy.'

'No!' He told her vehemently. 'Wait until I get back to you again because you do not want to get involved with that man on your own.'

'Is there something wrong with him?'

'There are different levels of bad, and he is top of the range. He has been in jail four times, one of those for killing two men.'

She shivered, that certainly put a different perspective on things. She studied Dimitri. In a strange way, he was protecting her from those men. Yet, he would make money off her if given the opportunity. There were very odd people in the world.

'I would like to ask you to dinner—'

She cut him short. 'No, I can't.'

'And I'd say your husband would commit a few crimes if he found out. I know I would if some man was trying to put the moves on my wife. Like I said before, he's a decent guy and you are a good person, I should not mess with that.'

'Thank you.' This business was making her very nervous.

'Finally, the big thirty is creeping up.' Paul said as he walked into Jonathan's office. 'How do you feel?'

'Not much different than I did last year.'

'How is Tammy?'

Jonathan grinned. 'Cute, naughty, and adorable. We play now. Not too long of an attention span yet but I love making her laugh.'

'So you are not sorry about your decision.'

'Sorry? No, I'll never regret it.'

'Does this include Gabrielle?'

Jonathan took a deep breath and fixed his eyes on Paul. 'Tell me something, why did you concoct this particular marriage plan?'

'I don't really know.' Paul excused.

'Be honest. Did you at any stage think that I was in love with her?' Jonathan asked curiously.

'I may have thought that it looked like that.'

'You were right, because I am.'

'I know this, but why don't you look completely happy?'

'You do recall that we do not have a real marriage.' Jonathan made a gesture.

'I wondered about that, but I'm guessing you would like to change it. Have you started courting, wooing— doing all the stuff women need?'

'I'd call it badgering.' A faint smile touched Jonathan's lips. 'If I were her I don't know how I would have survived this long. But there is something that prevents her from letting this thing happen. It's either very important or very scary because she never forgets it. I wish I knew the secrets that she keeps but she won't let me in. So I'm breaking her down, a little at a time.'

'If she's putting up such a fight—' Paul hesitated. 'What if it's something she fears will make you stop loving her?'

Jonathan made a pfft sound. 'What could she possibly tell me that would make me stop loving her?'

'You feel that strongly.'

'I'd have my skin flayed for her.'

"Well, Amelia, your goose is truly cooked now." As it happened – and he was not about to divulge – Amelia was trying to convince him to put the moves on Gabrielle. Almost tempted by the idea and indeed curious, he had begun this conversation to find out where the two stood.

Sure, something was up with Gabrielle, but whatever she did or did not want to acknowledge, she was in love with Jonathan, which was why he no longer visited regularly. As for Jonathan— he was head over heels; perhaps Charles' little matchmaking exercise had now reached the halfway mark. 'That's great, but not the flaying. And you have no idea what it is?'

'None whatsoever. I beg her to tell me, but she gets all sad and teary eyed and plainly refuses.'

'Are you sure you're in love, not just in lust because you haven't—'

'It's love. I know it because I never felt it before.' Jonathan swivelled in his chair. 'She is in my head, my heart, my dreams— I have no idea if you have ever loved a woman, but it's right here.' He grabbed his chest. 'It hurts like hell.'

'How's her hand?' Paul pointed to his own hand.

'Healing; she worries me sometimes.'

'I can see that.' Paul pointed to the frown on Jonathan's forehead. 'Is she clumsy?'

'No, she sleepwalks.'

'Really,' Paul was intrigued.

'She tells me the weirdest things when she does that. It always sounds as if she's talking in code and seems to be concerned about someone all the time.'

'What does she say?'

'Things like; watch out, it's all bad, they are not doing that. It seems *they* are always after *her*. Often, she says it all in French. We can have entire conversations, but the next day she recalls nothing.'

'Then have you tried asking her sleepwalking self what she's so concerned about? And why she won't let the relationship develop?'

'Funny you mention it; I was considering doing just that. Maybe then I'll be able to communicate better. It just feels sneaky.'

Paul glanced at a catalogue on Jonathan's desk and pointed. 'Have you picked a costume, and do you know what Gabrielle is planning?'

'I know nothing about hers but I know what I want. Why my mother wants to do this is a mystery, and in a few weeks, I'm apparently not allowed at the house. Don't know what that's about, but she calls Gabrielle a hundred times a day.' Jonathan smiled.

Paul returned the smile. 'That is a lucky strike to have your mother actually become excited about something. Does she like Gabrielle?'

'Very much.'

'Would she still like her if she knew the truth?'

Jonathan's face changed instantly. 'Let's not go there, ever. She is not to know anything except that she has a nice daughter-in-law, an adorable grandchild, and a son who is pleased that she has found life interesting once more. She even takes drives to the house on her own, just to visit with Gabrielle and Tammy.'

'I'm glad about that, and you are right, when things like this happen, one should not rock the boat. Talking about rocking boats, I saw Amelia the other day. She's not doing too well.' He made a gesture against his head.

'I'm sorry to hear it. What's going on with her?'

'She is hoping you remember the original idea why you married.'

'Although I am almost Tammy's father officially, as things are, no divorces will be forthcoming.'

'She knows that too but wishes she didn't. Naturally, she cannot understand what you see in Gabrielle. She tells me, repeatedly, how fantastic Amelia is and how very unreasonable you are.'

'Do you see her often?'

Paul shook his head. 'She phones me regularly. Hell, that woman can talk, and everything is about one person. Count your lucky stars because I cannot imagine anyone staying married to that woman.'

'She's very good in bed so that should count for someone.'

Paul laughed. 'I've heard.'

Unexpectedly, they heard a commotion outside. Amy was trying to stop someone from entering the office.

'I don't care, he owes me this much.' Amelia said angrily.

Paul lifted his brows at Jonathan. 'Speak of the devil.'

She burst in. 'Hello darling. Paul.'

Amy stood in the doorway, an apologetic expression on her face.

'We'll be fine.' Jonathan told her with a smile, seeing how she wished to drag the mad woman out of there. 'Hello Amelia, how have you been?'

'Suffering under your horrid lies. You told me this was to be a temporary arrangement.' She arched her perfect brows. 'It feels pretty permanent to me. So, what is your excuse?'

'Just as a matter of interest, how long did you imagine something like this would take?' Jonathan asked curiously.

'Definitely not this long,'

'Then you don't know how the legal system works.'

'Does that mean that we are still on track?' Her eyes glinted happily.

'Sorry Amelia, but what I told you then and what has happened since are two different things.'

'Oh I know this, and I also know that you are infatuated. I'll exercise patience because this thing will run its course and you will tire of her. I mean, what can she offer you?' She went around the desk and placed her hand on his shoulder. 'I know what you like, what you want, what you need. So I came to inform you that my door is still open because don't you imagine that you are the first married man I've been with. This wife story is exasperating but I can deal with it, as long as you pay me some attention too.'

Could he be with this woman again? He never thought about her, unless she crossed his line of vision, and he hardly remembered the sex. 'Amelia,' Jonathan began. 'This may shock you, especially as it comes from me, but I am not planning to cheat on or divorce my wife. I know it's not how it started, but it is where it ended. I love my wife. It's more than that actually; if I can't have her, I want no other woman, and if I have her, I don't need anyone else. Something has happened to me, changed me, and I cannot look at another woman, not even one I used to be intimate with.'

Paul watched his friend quietly. Never in his life would he have thought that he would hear Jonathan say those words, and mean them.

'I think I have been rather unfair towards you,' Jonathan continued. 'Because I should have told you before—'

Amelia's hand went up to silence him. 'Okay, we are officially broken up. So, can I ask for one last thing?'

'Certainly,'

'May I still come to your birthday party? And we will call it our swan song.'

Jonathan studied her. Of course she wanted to be there, she knew it was to be quite the social event. Something told him to say no, but he suppressed it. 'Sure, and you promise no more waltzing in here or phoning me at home.'

'Deal. Paul,' she turned to him. 'Do you have a date for the party already?'

'Huh, no.' He admitted.

'Then you pick me up'

'Okay.' He told her with a crooked smile. The woman was impossible and clearly believed that she was an entire galaxy all on her own.

'Now that that's settled, I feel better. Bye guys.' She waved at them and walked out of the office.

'Wow,' Paul said when they were alone again. 'What a strange creature.'

'Yes,' Jonathan said under his breath. 'And why is it I feel as if she just set me up?'

CHAPTER SEVENTEEN

Tammy crawled like a caterpillar, stood against everything she found, and boldly took steps even when she shouldn't. She was a daring toddler, not afraid of much, and hardly cried when her bottom found the floor in a rush. She promised to be an interesting communicator, having mama and dada down and happily chattered the entire day. Esther would easily give an arm for the little worm, and in turn, she got the best hugs anyone could get from the little whirlwind.

The adoption was going well but Gabrielle was beyond feeling guilty about her deception. Some might reason that it wasn't direct lying, but she felt otherwise. Jonathan adored Tammy, and did so much more than that with her. She knew it, she felt it, and she held it dear in her heart but how did she plan to have a normal relationship if she kept all these secrets between them?

As Barbara requested, she set out to discover what he liked and had figured out that he was into a broad spectrum mythology, with favouritism towards Greek. Barbara grabbed the idea and suggested having a type of temple dance-floor erected in part of the back garden for the occasion.

It was to be a costumed ball, so that removed some secrecy out of celebrations, as Jonathan also needed to find a costume. Two hundred guests were invited; most from Knight Industries, but some were people Barbara had sadly relinquished relationships with, and the rest of the list comprised of neighbours' names.

Gabrielle began her research in the books in the study then went online. She eyed the well-known goddesses with a wary eye, not particularly taken by any. But soon enough one caught her eye. She hoped Jonathan got it and appreciated her ingenuity.

'Yes, Peter,' she said when she realised he was standing in the study.

'Ma'am, the Russian gentleman is back at the gate.'

'I'll go hear what he wants.' She got up from behind the desk, touching the wood panels as she went. This wasn't a grand or old house like her father's or Barbara's, but she enjoyed its modern openness, the wide glass windows, and manicured lawns. But mostly, she liked the little gazebo at the bottom of the garden where she hid when she needed to cry.

That was the contradiction of living with Jonathan. She was as happy as she was sad. Happy because he only wanted their best, tried so very hard to impress her, and plainly loved them. The sadness was all self-inflicted.

Dimitri had decided that under the tree was his favourite spot for waiting, because he was in the same place.

'Hello, Gabrielle.' He looked towards the house. 'You have good servants, they are very careful how they listen and what they say.'

She smiled, knowing he meant Peter. 'Thank you. What brings you by today?'

'Snoop is out of hospital. That's the old man's name. And the other one is Valk. Do you know what it means?'

'Sounds Afrikaans but I can't speak it; I just know the few words and sentences my mother taught me. It sounds like the German word falke, which means falcon, is it close to that?'

'And like him, always alert, waiting to stoop down on the unsuspecting victim.'

'Have you spoken to them?'

'We had a conversation and they have agreed to see you, at my place. I did not think it was appropriate for them to come here.'

'You're right about that.'

'The old man is not well at all, and I think he knows it too. They want to get this thing sorted out so he can spend some of the money, and I'm guessing what he doesn't use, Valk wants.'

'Have they told you how much they are looking for?'

'I lied to them.' He showed his nice teeth. 'They know I can get information on anyone, so they asked about you. I told them that you don't have much anymore. That your inheritance was blown away by your father, which is true whichever way you look at it. They believe me, just haven't said the actual figure.'

'Again, thank you.' She regarded him closely. 'No one does anything for free, so what will I owe you?'

'I told you before, nothing. Sometimes, knowing someone is better than having his money. Believe me when I say that I'm not after yours.'

'Okay, but there is a condition to this agreement.'

He looked at her with interest. 'What might that be?'

'Whatever we agree to is between you and me, not my husband, or Knight Industries.'

He looked pensive for a few seconds then nodded. 'Will you trust me?'

'Perhaps I shouldn't but I'm going with accepting your word. If you break it, you must deal with whatever you feel or happens afterwards.'

He pointed to her. 'You see, that is what I'm talking about. You are that kind of person I respect. I don't meet many of those.'

'Then it will be just between us?'

'Agreed, no husband, and no husband's business.'

'Thank you. When must I meet them?'

He took out a small notebook from his pocket and scribbled on a page. 'The date and address, and I will make sure they are there on time. Don't bring anything then, you are just going to talk to them first. After that, you decide how you pay them.'

'Did you tell them how much I have? Which I really don't because it's Jonathan's.'

'I told them that you only have three-hundred-thousand left. Now, you must be clever and barter down. They are greedy so they might want all of it, but at least it is not a million.'

This sounded like a very dangerous game, but what choice did she have? As long as Jonathan and Knight Industries were not in the picture, she felt vaguely better.

She did not know why but she felt as if her body were going to be under attack at Red Bare, wanting to protect it as much as possible. As she chose her clothes, she put on a pair of baggy jeans, grabbed a top that went all the way to mid-thigh, slipped into her trainers, and did her hair into a plait. Perhaps it was psychological, as she was going where women's bare flesh and curves were highly prized.

She was breathless and frightened when she stopped the car in the adjacent parking lot, so she sat drumming her fingers for a few minutes, hoping the mindless activity calmed her. Peculiar, she also felt breathless and frightened in Jonathan's presence, yet, it was something entirely different. Taking her phone, she dialled the number, doing something she had never done before.

'Gabrielle,' Jonathan answered almost immediately. 'This is such an awesome surprise. Is everything okay?'

'Huh, yes. I just wanted to—'

'Are you missing me, wanting to hear my voice?' He asked astutely. 'My plan is working.' He laughed happily. 'How is our baby?'

'She's fine.' The mere sound of his voice calmed her, but likewise, fed her something else, something that always left her restless, because lately, she felt incomplete. It was as if he had something of hers, and only when he returned it would she be whole again. 'What are you doing?'

'Sitting, staring out the window, loving hearing your voice. But I don't just love your voice; you know that I love all of you, right?'

She stayed silent; loving the feeling he gave her heart.

'Gaby, do you need something?'

'No, I already have so much more than I expected. Thank you, Jonathan.'

'My darling, I want to give you everything.'

'I know. I have to go now.'

'Okay,' he said disappointed. 'But please call me again.'

'I will. Bye.'

'Bye, my love.'

She didn't know what she had expected of a strip-club, but this was not it. She had imagined such places dark, dirty, and creepy. This one was none of those. Bathed in sunlight, the decor was colourful and pleasant, there was a nice carpet on the floor, all the chairs covered in some type velour and there were no half-naked women dancing or gyrating anywhere, might be too early. She stood uncertainly for about twenty seconds and then saw Dimitri. He had obviously been waiting for her.

'Welcome,' he greeted with a smile. 'What do you think?'

'Not what I imagined.' She told him truthfully.

'Yes, I never wanted the same as everyone else. Come to my office.'

'Hey Dimitri,' one man called. 'Are you auditioning today? Take her, she looks fine from where I am.'

It was the strangest thing. Some compliments were rude, crude, or plain unwelcome, and although most women didn't want to hear them, they still did something for their self-esteem and confidence. She never wanted to be mistaken for a stripper and yet those few words somehow validated her femininity.

'She's not a dancer, just a friend.'

'Then I say you have taste.' The man continued.

'It's the place, don't take it too seriously.' Dimitri told her.

'I'm switching off.' Then her inborn curiosity got the better of her. 'You say you have a boss but you keep saying your club, so which is it?'

'Both are correct. This is my place, but I belong to an organisation.'

She thought she heard sarcasm, as if he were deriding the boss.

'I'm not too much of a lackey kind of guy, so it's a type of freelance job.'

'Not exactly what I expected the Russian Mafia, mob, or whatever they call themselves to agree to.'

'Well, you see, there is a reason why I run a different kind of ship. The boss is an old family friend. He sort of learnt under my grandfather and then ran a bit with my father. Pretty much leaves me alone.'

She shrugged. 'What do I know of these things?'

'Sometimes, it's good not to know too much.'

His office surprised her further. It was cosy and well set-out, with lots of books in glass cabinets. She headed for one of the armchairs in front of the desk, but he reached for her arm and guided her to his own chair.

'You sit there, for them to understand that you are conducting this meeting, not the other way around. If you intimidate them a little, they will be more careful about what they say and do.' Looking at her face, he grabbed a cap that lay on a small table. 'Put it on, they must not remember you too well. You do not want them turning up at Knight Industries.'

That could never happen, especially as he said Valk was a dangerous man. The finger of fear gripped her at the very idea of a killer standing in Jonathan's office. 'Do they know my name?' She asked.

'I don't know what they know, so don't say it or give it to them. It is not exactly a social visit.'

Odd, he actually made sense. She plonked the cap on her head and sat down. Leaning back in the chair, she took a deep breath.

'Should I get you something to drink? You look nervous.'

He didn't know the half of it. Her heart rate was already above normal, her palms wet, her mouth dry, and she wondered why she was there. Had she caused all this with one lie? A lie - as Dimitri smartly pointed out - she had committed with good intentions. All she had wanted to do was look after Tammy, to protect her, to love her. 'Water, please.'

Left alone, she glanced around. People had no idea what hid beneath anyone's surface. Beneath Dimitri's there seemed to be a decent man, but beneath hers was a liar and manipulator. She felt like crying.

She focused her gaze on the book spines closest to her. He had some interesting tomes, and quite a few in Russian, which might mean that he spoke the language, or were simply family heirlooms. His desk was neat and a Mont Blanc pen sat regally on a closed file. She turned her attention to the drawers on her left and carefully opened the top one. It was filled with sweet packets, tubes, and wrappers; a sweet-tooth. She closed the drawer, glanced at the door, and opened the second one. A pile of files filled it. She closed that one and turned to her right.

The first drawer was locked. He probably placed personal items, and perhaps even money in there. She opened the second one and closed it immediately again. In there, sat a gun in a holster.

He walked in with bottled water. 'Would you like a glass?'

'No, this is fine.' She said as he gave her the bottle. 'Are they here?'

'Loitering outside. They will come in as soon as they are done talking nonsense to each other.'

'You don't have a lot of patience for some people, do you?'

'There are very silly people in the world, and most lack logic. They do things that make no sense to anyone who has half a brain. I see them here every day, often pretending to be someone else. Those who don't pretend, hide. You have no idea what people tell me. Sometimes, I think I might have been successful as a therapist because I have helped quite a few turn themselves around.'

She wanted to say something, but wasn't sure what. He was a strange mixture of interesting and disreputable with a dash of sharp. But what was he like when he lost his temper? Her mind flew to the gun in the drawer, would he use it then?

'Like I said the other day, you are a nice person and I can tell that you are pretty smart as well. Did you study something?'

'English Literature.'

'Ah,' he smiled and made a sweeping gesture towards the cabinets. 'Then you have already registered all that surrounds you.'

'I see you have Russian novels, do you read the language?'

'Not well, but I force myself now and then. Mentioning reading, I read about your husband's upcoming birthday party in the papers, sounds fun.'

'My mother-in-law wants to do something special.'

'I'm sure you have chosen a fascinating character.' He turned to look at the door. 'No matter, they are here.'

She had not heard anything, but this was his place and evidently, he was tuned into its inherent sounds. She shifted herself upright, took a swig of water, and looked at him. Her heart was pounding. 'Ready.'

'I'll play middleman, so let me start the conversation. That way, they will be a little scared.' He readjusted the cap on her head, bringing it further down onto her eyes.

Never in her life would she have sat down to make up two characters as the two that entered Dimitri's office that morning.

Old man Snoop... He reminded her of an ancient Anthony Quinn, with too much hair on his face, brows and head. He would in fact pass as an excellent caricature of Moses. He entered coughing and what a terrible sound it was. She could not call what he wore clothes, because she couldn't see what they had been, fabric, or colour. His eyes must have been blue, but now... Was he, or was society to blame for this? Her heart filled with compassion for this shadow of a human being.

Valk. Dimitri said dangerous, he looked it. The first thing she noticed about him was that he appeared to have a nervous disposition because his eyes could not stop on anything long enough, so his temper was probably equally attached to a very short tether. He was wearing denims and a black vest, showing off his tattoos, which included a labyrinth on his bald head. She shivered involuntarily; there were some sinister designs on that man. He must have been bulky once because his physique still showed somewhat defined muscles but was now in a deteriorating state. He had a scar on the left side of his face, from above the brow, past the ear, and ending at the chin. Heaven alone knew how he had received that. His eyes were brown, an unusual combination of dark and light.

He made a gesture with his right hand and Gabrielle focused on it. It was as if he were used to twirling something. She wondered what it could be; a cigarette, beads, perhaps a knife, or even a gun. She must never forget where she was and what background these men came from, and that included Dimitri.

He told the men to sit and pulled a third chair closer to Gabrielle. 'Here we are, and we all know why. So gentlemen, have you decided how much you want?'

Talk about preamble. He had clearly decided that he was getting to the point, kick them out as soon as possible, and be done with the nuisances. Strange, that she could read him like that. She was glad he was taking charge because the less she said, the less she exposed herself and showed how nervous and frightened she really was.

'How do I know she's the right *meisie*? *Jy*, you could be pulling the wool over *onse oe*.' Valk spoke in an odd English-Afrikaans mix.

Dimitri touched his own temple. 'Are you empty? You want money, who do you think I would go find to give it to you, my sister?'

Snoop laughed, which lead to coughing, then spitting, and Gabrielle wrinkled her nose as he pulled a handkerchief from his pocket and spat into it. It was dreadful to watch.

'Come, tell us how much you want, and tomorrow she will do the transfer.'

'How much you got?' Valk asked her directly.

She was about to answer but Dimitri cut her short. 'She has two-hundred-thousand.'

'I fout you said three...' Snoop Moses decided to enter negotiations as he showed three fingers.

'And everything is expensive.' Dimitri told him.

'Is she your *flerrie*?' Valk queried. 'Why are you helping her?'

'Listen, talking nonsense is not going to speed things up. Do you want money, and if so how much?'

'What about the baby? I never even seen my granddaughter.'

'*Ja*, where you're hiding that *meisiekind* of mine?'

Gabrielle shifted in the seat. What did she tell these men? To think that the one strange human being was related to Tammy and the other— No, she could not tell them anything. She had to pay them off and see only their backs walking away from her.

Dimitri seemed to be taking his role of leader seriously. 'And which one of you has time for baby-sitting? You are leaving her alone. You,' he pointed to Valk. 'Stop lying, she is not your child, and I can prove it because you were not here when Charlotte fell pregnant. Pollsmoor Prison, was it? I hear it has not moved from the Cape yet. And you,' he turned to Snoop. 'Maybe we can make a plan for you to see her, but nothing else. So, back to the real business, how much do you want?'

'The two-hundred,' Valk said quickly.

'Yes, two-hundred, if I'm giving up the rights to my grandchild.'

'It's settled then, tomorrow, the money will be in your account.' Dimitri said.

'What time?'

'What difference does it make?' There was Dimitri's temper coming to the fore. 'You have waited this long, check the day after, she is busy. I'm assuming you have an account.'

'Can we get it cash?'

'Are you mad? She is not going to cart that around.'

'*Praat sy?*' Valk asked curiously. 'You've done all the chattering, we don't even know if she's alive.'

'What do you want her to say? This is not her daily business, she does not know your kind of life, and she has never met anyone like you. Don't you have eyes in your head? She's a good girl, who has never done anything wrong.'

Did he like to believe nonsense? He was judging the cover, but the inside... What had she unleashed? Because of a lie, she lived in fear and it would never fix itself. It was all a horrible shambles. 'I do speak but Dimitri said all the right things. I'll do the transfer tomorrow.'

'When can I see my granddaughter?' Snoop queried.

'I'll bring her,' she did a quick mental check on everything that went on at home. 'Friday morning.'

'Before you go; you will agree to take that money and never ask for more.' Dimitri grabbed the file sitting on his desk, flicked it open, took four sheets of paper and placed them in front of the men. 'Sign where you see your names.'

'Two for what?' Valk was interested.

'Because she is getting one and I'm getting the other to lock in my safe. You will not change your minds and go bother her again, understand me?'

'What about my granddaughter?'

Gabrielle was becoming anxious about the old man's fixation. She did not want to deny him outright but she could not have Tammy around such a sick person either. He wasn't just sick but in a state of collapse, almost like an ancient ruin one was afraid to be around in case it caved in. How did she explain it to him?

'This is what is going to happen.' Dimitri took over again. 'Once a week, she will come here for two hours. If you are here you see your granddaughter, if not, sorry, you wait another week. That baby cannot be out of the house when you want her to be.' He looked at Gabrielle, waiting for her to concur.

'That is fine, every Friday morning.' She agreed.

Snoop nodded, signed both papers with a flourish, waited for Valk to do his scribble, then both got up and left. Dimitri sat there, so did she, feeling blank.

'Are you okay?' Dimitri asked.

'Do you believe they are going to leave me alone?'

'They'd better. I'm going to sound callous now but this is what I see. The old man is going to see his granddaughter a couple of times and die not too many moons from now, so, no worries there. Valk— He cannot stay out of trouble, and he has made so many enemies, one or two are bound to find him and dispatch him to the other side.'

'You're right, not exactly gooey feelings. But are you serious?'

'Absolutely. That man— how many have come here looking for him. Know what saves him? Prison. He's always in when someone turns up. So we'll see how long this freedom run lasts.'

She got to her feet and offered a hand. 'Thank you, Dimitri. I appreciate everything you are doing for me.'

He shook it warmly then enfolded her in a hug, as he removed the cap from her head. Then without warning, he pressed his lips to hers.

Shock prevented her from pushing him away immediately, so she stood there as he surprised her with a very soft kiss, and she thought of Jonathan. How much she needed him to tell her all the things he did every day and she dismissed as if worth nothing. She could not breathe as she realised how very much she loved him, how much he loved her, how much they had, how much they could have, and how thankful they should be.

'Thank you, Gabrielle.' Dimitri told her. 'And what I told those men, it applies to me too. We are not in the same world, but if ever you need my help, and I mean anything, day or night, my door is always open for you.' He let her go, took a small key from his pocket, unlocked the top drawer, grabbed a business card, and placed it in her hand. 'Even my home address is on it, and I only give those to very particular people.'

CHAPTER EIGHTEEN

Jonathan gazed at her as they sat down to dinner; she looked beautiful in the dusty pink dress. He could not quite put his finger on it but he would swear there was something different about her. 'Have you decided on your costume for the ball?'

'Yes.'

'May I ask what it is or is it a surprise?'

'It's a surprise. How is yours coming along?'

'I would like to surprise you too. Why must we wear masks as well?'

'I don't know that is more a Venetian tradition, but your mother is so into this thing that I decided to say nothing.' She smiled and lifting her eyes, gave him a veiled look from under the thick lashes.

He felt his body tighten, took a sharp breath, and grabbed his water glass.

'Are you okay?'

'Huh, yes.' Goodness, he felt hot.

'Dady,' Tammy called.

'Yes my baby, what is it?'

She showed him the spoon she was playing with and gave him some baby whatevers.

'You are very clever my sweetie.' Let him focus on her so he could calm down. 'What did you do today?'

'I went out to get some things to complete my costume.' After leaving Dimitri's place that was exactly what she had done as she mulled over the day's events.

'May I try guess?'

'Two guesses.' She placed her elbows on the table and clasped her hands, as if the idea amused her.

Good grief, where had the woman been today that some type of transformation had taken place? She had gone from desirable directly to enticing, and he felt as if he were about to die because he couldn't have her. He considered pouring the glass of water down his chest. Instead, he drank some. 'Three guesses, it's the international standard.'

She giggled, shook her head and nodded. 'Okay, three.'

He had never heard her do that; it was gorgeous because it completely transformed her face into happiness, and was the kind of thing he wished he could do with her as they lay in bed every night. 'Considering choice was left wide open to mythology in general, this could be a strenuous exercise.'

'It is, but when you know, it's the kind of thing you say ah-ha to. So, what is your first guess?'

'Before I start, did you pick one of the boys?'

'That's a guess.'

'It is not; I'm merely eliminating a potential waste of time.'

She giggled again. 'You cheat.'

He felt his body tighten further. He had to stop thinking about nights, beds, love, and all such things, so to calm himself, he took another large sip of water and cleared his throat. 'If I get it right will you kiss me?'

She dropped her gaze then raised it again. 'Just guess.' She told him with a smile.

He loved whatever was happening here. 'I'm going with an obvious one first, the goddess of love. Just wouldn't know which you would pick, the Roman Venus, the Greek Aphrodite, the Norse Freyja, as for all the other options, not going to try.'

'I noticed some call her Freya. Anyway, I'll be kind because you are not going to get this. Second guess.'

He regarded her for a silent moment. 'Antiope,'

She furrowed her brow. 'Pray tell, how did you see me as the queen of the Amazons?'

'You are in really good shape, just perhaps a little short.' He gazed at her longingly, how he dreamt of touching every part of her body. He shifted in the seat. 'It's a no then. And you are right; I'll never get it because you have not chosen obvious. You have done something clever and I would have to sit days trying to figure it out, and that is my third guess.'

'Which is actually very good and you are right in that respect, but, you still don't know what it is.' She turned to Tammy, who was banging the spoon on her high-chair. 'Tammy, you will damage daddy's eardrums, not to mention yours.'

That was the first time he heard her refer to him in an inclusive way, as if they were a real family. 'Maybe she wants to be a drummer.'

'Heaven help us, and the neighbours. But I'm going with an electrical kit.'

'Is that less noisy?'

'Not normally, but at least she can plug headphones in and make it silent for everyone else.' Gabrielle took Tammy's plate away, wiped her face, and rising to her feet, picked her up.

'Gabrielle,' Jonathan called.

'Yes,' she turned to look at him properly.

'Where were you when you called me today?'

A blush crept into her face as she recalled Dimitri kissing her and she bit her bottom lip. Then she felt that awful apprehension she detested as she thought about Snoop and Valk.

She looked as guilty as sin right there, and then, that frightened look appeared again. If only she confided in him. 'I love you.'

The words were on the tip of her tongue to be spoken, but refused to come out. 'Goodnight, I'm going straight to bed as I am very tired.'

'Okay, but I would still like to kiss my daughter goodnight.'

Gabrielle walked over and let him take Tammy from her. She should have known that he had something else in mind, because his free arm reached out, grabbed her, brought her up to his chest, and dropping his head, kissed her.

'Go rest, I will take her up. She's not tired, so we'll play a little.'

'Thank you.'

Something was wrong. Jumping out of bed, she rushed to Tammy's room. The cot was empty, the little blanket in the middle of the room, her fluffy bunny upside down. One hand flew to her chest, no, it could not be. She ran to Jonathan's room... she screamed. There he lay, three stab wounds on his chest, blood dripping onto the floor. 'Jonathan, Jonathan!'

'Gabrielle, wake up.' Jonathan called and disentangled himself from her frantic hands.

She sat on his bed, panting and sweating. 'What a nightmare.'

He sat beside her and threw an arm over her shoulders. 'May I ask what the dream was about?'

'I went to Tammy's room and she wasn't there, so I came to yours. It was horrible, you were dead. I'm too upset, I need something,' rising quickly, she almost ran downstairs to the kitchen.

He appeared a few seconds later, glanced at what she was making, pointed, and sat on one of the stools. 'May I have one? Tell me about this dream.'

'It's a dreadful image; I don't want to think about it again.'

'Was I shot?'

'Why do you want to know this?'

'Dreams are fascinating. I dream about you sometimes, actually, often.'

She looked at him. 'I'm sure I'm usually annoying you.'

'Quite the contrary, you are usually pleasing me a great deal.'

She went bright red and mindlessly spooned too much chocolate into the milk.

'You know that you can't stop dreams, right? Do you ever dream about me like that?'

'Like what?'

'Making love to you,'

Now here was a funny question. She never had, but she did dream of him kissing her, even touching her, but never that. Was that because she had not yet in real life? 'No.'

'And of my father?'

'What?' She was truly baffled when he asked that. Then realised what he meant. 'No, never.' And she never wanted to. She shook her head vigorously.

'Then what do you dream about, apart from me dead and Tammy missing.'

'Can we drop this; it's making me uncomfortable.' She pushed a mug in front of him.

He glanced at it. 'We are not going to drink it.'

'Why not?'

'Look at it, it's mud.'

'Stop it, you are confusing me.'

He got to his feet and taking hold of a wrist pulled her to him. Turning the hand over, he kissed the scar, then drew her closer, loving how her pyjamas shifted between their bodies. Slipping his hands underneath, he ran them up her back, pressing her against him. 'The day is coming, that one day when you are going to be mine and I yours.' He told her as he gazed into her eyes. 'Never think of it as just letting go of yourself, but that I too will surrender to you. And, it is okay for you to desire me, to kiss me. Would you like to?'

Like to? She adored the expression on his face, as it was hers alone. His eyes were deep, yet open and welcoming, seeing only her. As for his mouth, she craved it.

'Do it.'

It was as if she were drugged because she could not stop. She pressed her lips to his and threw her arms around his neck. He yielded under the pressure, opening his mouth. Their tongues met and began that secret dance both enjoyed so much and she felt both weak and strong as she dictated the course of that kiss. She trembled, swooned, and moulded herself to him, feeling his need, which matched hers. How she wanted him. Letting go, she told him breathlessly. 'Go to bed, it's a working day tomorrow.'

He decided not to press for anything else, because the very fact that she had kissed him was a step forward. 'Tomorrow is Sunday. Goodnight, my love.'

She was sorry she had agreed to be at Red Bare on Friday. It was Jonathan's birthday, the ball was that evening, and the phones at home had not stopped ringing since early morning.

Most of the calls were from Barbara. It sounded as if total bedlam was in full swing at the house and Gabrielle imagined that it had more to do with Barbara's sudden nerves, now that so many people would be plodding through the property.

After reassuring her for the umpteenth time and promising to go over as soon as she was free, she got Tammy ready and drove away. She pondered about things all the way to the club then realised that she had not bought a gift for Jonathan.

What exactly did one give a man who had just about everything and who had no problem getting whatever took his fancy on a daily basis? How had she forgotten?

She had hoped that only Snoop came to see Tammy, but no, there was Valk as well. He started ranting; calling

Charlotte a whore, slut, lost, good-for-nothing, and spitfire, or something along those lines.

Snoop thought the world of Tammy and pride shone as he pointed out all the clever things she did, but disappointment filled his speech as he noticed that she did not look like Charlotte, or anyone on their side of the family. He stared at the little girl and then at Gabrielle. 'Your father had strong genes to make two of you. But at least it's good genes; you are both pretty and clever.'

Although not minding Snoop too much, even if he was hardly the epitome of health, Gabrielle worried about Valk. He had a puzzling way of staring at her, and it made her skin crawl as she tried to imagine what ran through his head. As for Dimitri...

She was starting to dislike this story of men falling in love with her, and disturbingly, in Dimitri's case, he no longer seemed as dangerous as she had imagined him to be the first time she had seen him standing outside her flat. The opposite was in fact true; he improved every time she saw him.

She wondered what Jonathan would make of what she was doing, where she was and the characters she was involved with. He would probably freak out first, then tell her that she was playing with fire, and then become concerned for her safety. She smiled, liking that she was probably quite right in her assumption of his reactions.

When the two hours were up, she remembered that she had brought a photograph for Snoop, told the men that she would see them the following Friday, and watched them leave.

'May I go to this masked ball I have been hearing and reading about?' Dimitri asked as he watched her getting her things together.

'What?' Caught completely off-guard she was tongue-tied for a second. 'Huh, it's not my house, invitations were sent.' Now why would he want to do such a thing?

'I'm just one person, and I don't want to cause any trouble.'

'Have you even got a costume?'

'As a matter of fact I have two; Perun and Veles. Which should I pick?'

She had merely asked, building stumbling blocks. But he had not one but two costumes to choose from. 'And who are they?'

'The main Russian mythology dudes. You didn't think that we did not have some stuff like that as well, did you?'

'Dimitri, this is hardly appropriate, it's my husband's birthday party—'

'Whom I happen to know. Tell whoever is at the door tonight that I'm a special friend. Tell them to expect Perun, I don't feel like dragging the serpentine Veles around.'

'What's this Perun about?'

'Thunder, lightning, fire, the usual myth god stuff. So, can I go?'

Sighing, she dropped her shoulders resignedly. She would bet anything that if she said no he would still show up. 'Perun you say. I'll tell them.'

'Thank you, it means a lot to me. No funny business, no deals, nothing troublesome.'

She was glad when they were home again; appreciating the safety the house and everything in it afforded them. Esther was on overnight duty, so grabbing her things she got herself over to Barbara.

CHAPTER NINETEEN

She stared in awe when Peter dropped her off. She had been there four days previously and the place had looked like a construction site. Since then, the party company had turned the front garden, and perimeter-wall into an entrance to mount Olympus. She saw what had Barbara so nervous.

The news that such a fantastic thing had been built facing a street had obviously spread like wildfire, and every Tom, Dick, and Harriet was coming around to take pictures. There were cars parked in a long line across the street, and every driver slowed down to a crawl so the occupants could have the closest look, causing an incredible procession.

'Oh dear,' she mumbled.

'I never imagined,' Barbara told her as soon as she saw her. 'What have I done?'

'Life is boring for many people, so this is like Christmas lights,' she smiled, trying to assuage Barbara's misgivings. 'How did they do it?'

'I am not sure but I saw a lot of wood, polystyrene, and cloth. Have you seen that side?' Barbara pointed to the garden.

'Only the dance platform they were busy with when I was here last. Did it come out as you wished it to be?'

'It's quite magnificent.' Barbara drew the drapes aside, as they reached the dining area. 'What do you think?'

'Wow,' Gabrielle stared at the erected acropolis then pointed to the closet column. 'But that doesn't look Greek.'

'If you look closely, you'll notice Roman, Norse, Persian, and Indian columns, statues, bowls, and all sorts of other things. This is a party I imagine we need not concern ourselves with building inspectors telling us that we did not adhere to correct architecture and have massive corruptions in our backyard.'

'No, and it's amazing. You haven't told me about your costume.'

'I thought of Medusa. Then wondered where I'd find that dangerous head, not to mention the tail, and if I had to drag a cement mixer around, just to give it that realistic touch. Though, I don't know how I would have disguised it.'

Gabrielle laughed, feeling happy that Barbara was emerging, as Jonathan wished.

'I wanted to be everything,' Barbara continued. 'But settled on normal, I shall be Hera.'

Gabrielle nodded. 'Very appropriate.'

'I'm not supposed to ask about yours, as I hear you want to surprise us.'

'You spoke to Jonathan.'

'Yesterday. Said you are being very clever and to not enquire.' Barbara smiled. 'Even through the phone I can hear how he loves you.'

Gabrielle dropped her gaze as she felt a rush of desire course through her. It was the craziest thing; ever since Dimitri kissed her, she just had to think of Jonathan and her body went haywire.

They spent hours going upstairs, downstairs, inside and out. They checked things, tasted morsels, smiled, laughed and giggled, Gabrielle enjoying the bonding experience as she had always been close to her mother. She now thought of Amy as her best friend, so if Barbara became her mother figure, she knew that she would have the female voices of reason she needed.

Gabrielle tried to imagine what it had felt like when Barbara went through the trauma of losing eight children, and tears filler her eyes, feeling great compassion for a woman who had agonised endlessly and lost so much, and who now, through some small miracle, was returning to life. She smiled as she compared it to a debutante's coming out.

She had suggested Jonathan take the day off, but he had simply smiled and told her that he could hardly cancel a meeting with Scottish representatives because it was his birthday. She glanced out of windows, turned her head when she heard a car engine, and stormed into the hall twice thinking she heard his muffled male voice. She could barely live inside her skin, as she wanted him to kiss her, to touch her.

'Honey,' Barbara stomped into her daydream. 'He will be here soon enough. I must say, I haven't seen a couple like you two in a while. Then again, when last was I out in the world to know? But what I was saying as you travelled in the clouds. It might be a good idea to take a nap, so you will feel refreshed. I'm going up; do you want to come have a look at the bedrooms?'

'I'd like that very much.'

She lost her heart when the first bedroom door opened and did not retrieve it until they reached Barbara's. Six bedrooms, all beautiful and no one to experience their warmth and comfort, except for Barbara's little paradise.

'See why I wish Jonathan would come home? There they wait, for someone to use and love them.'

'Why did he move out anyway; it's not as if I see you intruding in his life.'

Barbara smiled faintly. 'I never did. What I do think is that he could not handle my depression, although, he loved me through it all. In fact, he was always very protective of me. But in the last three years, he matured, and I'm beginning to think that Charles had something to do with his move.'

'You can't mean that he kicked him out.'

'Oh no,' Barbara said quickly. 'If you knew Charles, you would have noticed how very like him Jonathan is.

And my withdrawing from life threw them into a very close relationship.'

Gabrielle nodded. She had even told Jonathan so, but for some reason, he had not liked the comparison, though, he seemed to like it when other people mentioned that they could see Charles. It was not as if she could see inside his head to understand. 'So you think that he felt the need to go discover his own individuality?'

'Yes, and that is when he bought the house. I don't think he would have done well in an apartment, because he loves space, beautiful things, and books; was quite the reader as a boy. Anyway, enough talk, we need to rest. Pick a room, make it yours, and whenever you need to sleep over that's the one.'

Gabrielle smiled. 'Thank you, I will test them all.'

She settled on the four-poster with the high cupola. When she looked up and saw the Venus de Milo painted in the circle, a gentle smile spread on her face as she slowly drifted off to sleep.

'Just like a princess, only the prince's kiss can awaken her.' Jonathan whispered, his lips touching hers.

'Is it time?' She asked sleepily and gazed into his eyes. He meant to consume her. Without thinking, she grabbed his shirt and pulled him down to her, and let him engulf them in the wettest kiss they had ever shared. Insanely, she returned it, the force making things happen in her body. She pushed him away, before the fire spread out of control.

'You drive me wild, so I keep forgetting the contract.'

'No,' she touched his hand, trying to bring her body under control. 'I'm sorry.'

'We need to get ready for this thing.' He rose to his feet. 'I'm guessing you still don't want me to see your costume.'

'Did you get a mask?' She clambered off the bed, turned her back on him and took a few deep breaths.

'The costume has a sort of mask-helmet thing; it's very grand. I think I should audition for the movies after this.'

That brought Amelia to mind. 'By the way, Amelia is coming.'

'Did you invite her?'

'No, she asked to come.' He pulled her into his arms. 'She and I are done and hopefully this is the last time I'll see her. You are not jealous, are you?'

She snorted, pretending indifference.

'You are.' He laughed happily, 'but I don't want her, I want you.' He kissed her with an overwhelming intensity, softly biting and sucking on her lower lip. Abruptly, he let her go. 'I keep forgetting,'

She needed to tear that stupid thing up because it was annoying hearing him mention it constantly. He was not going to stop doing this, so what difference did it make if it existed or not?

She imagined that he had appropriated himself of his old room to change and shower in, so she took herself to the bathroom in hers. Something had to change, and soon because she could not take the pressure on her senses. Leaning against the shower wall with pangs of desire, she felt her innards continue churning, needing something she did not have. As things were going, she was almost certainly going to become a sex maniac because her body no longer reacted, but completely disintegrated at his touch.

Jonathan called her; whether he needed help was a different thing because he was already dressed when she entered his room. She stopped and studied the costume, uncertain if it was gladiator or warrior. Whatever it was, it was magnificent. The muscled cuirass, or breastplate, sat snugly over the tunic that hugged his toned chest, and the studded pteruges, skirt, dropped from a belt. She glanced at the burnished greaves only tied about the knees. Perhaps he had called her for those, as he would not be able to bend to tie them around his ankles. The plumed helmet that encased his head and almost completely hid his face made him look foreboding.

He took the helmet off and grinned. 'What do you think?'

'What is it exactly?'

'I'm a Spartan Knight.'

She smiled. 'Clever.'

'So, wench, shall thou bind my wrists and assist with mine armour?'

'Not if you call me wench again. I've never liked that word.'

'Damsel then. But should I have tried to say it in Greek?'

She had not known that one could look at a man and wish him naked on the spot. 'Huh,' she said as she realised he was waiting. 'Yes.'

'Yes what, say it in Greek?' He grinned and leaned over her neck. 'I wanted to impress you, seems I succeeded. Should I put the helmet on again?'

She made a phew sound. 'I must stop looking at you.'

'Really,' he searched her face. 'Wow, ancient leather?' He smoothed her hair. 'If you wish, we'll disappear regularly throughout the evening and I will give you as much pleasure as you can handle.'

'Stop talking like this, you have already done something to me.' She told him breathlessly.

Something was definitely happening. 'You undo me.'

'Let's finish this.' She told him as she reached for one of the bracers and waited for him to put his arm up. Somehow, she managed to tie those wraps and straps around his wrists then helped him to figure out how to carry the shield and blade. When he put the helmet on again, she thought she was going to start wheezing. But he was mistaken, it was not the leather that turned her on. It was his proximity, the scent of his skin, what he had awakened and unleashed within her.

A phone call came from home and Gabrielle walked around the house talking to Esther for thirty minutes. Tammy was teething and had developed the habit of clamping her mouth shut and refusing food. Excellent timing, she wanted to be delayed so she could slip downstairs unobserved, to move about incognito and see if Jonathan "discovered" her. Realising she was dealing with home affairs, he and Barbara went down.

There were few instructions to follow, so she got ready quickly. Thinking that some guests must have already arrived, she tiptoed to the end of the passage and eavesdropped for a few seconds. She could hear people's laughter. As it was not a formal or diplomatic party, she doubted her absence alongside Jonathan would cause ripples.

Going as close to the stairway as she would dare, she stole a look from behind a wall. The hall was filling quickly. She went to glance out a window. The dance acropolis was also populated. Excellent, everyone wore masks. She did some final touch-ups, got into her soft lace-up shoes and sneaked carefully down the passage. Jonathan would be hovering near the hall so she circumvented their meeting by finding the back stairs.

'Young lady, what do you think you are doing?'

She turned around and a magnificent costume with gold embellishments greeted her.

'Hello, Gabrielle.'

'How did you know?'

'Who else would come down the back way?'

'Why are you this side?'

'I saw you spying earlier. So, what do you think?' Dimitri did a three-sixty turn.

'I must look into Russian mythology, because you are quite a sight.' She studied the helmet with ram's horns on his head, the beard, and an axe and curly horn hanging from his belt. She pointed to it. 'You are not going to blow it.'

'Not unless I have to call the villagers to a fire-drill. What do you think of Perun's axe? It's sort of like Thor's hammer.'

'Yes, I notice a Norse similarity. Quite the deadly weapon if it was real. But you shouldn't have come.'

He pointed. 'This is an intriguing outfit and I'm not familiar with the character. What mythology is it?'

'Greek, but I'm not revealing who I am just yet.'

'Has your husband seen you?'

'Why do you think I'm hiding?'

'He's going to fall in love all over again.'

'Why did you want to be here?'

'I wanted to see you because I knew you would do something smart. You have not disappointed me. If only we met when you first arrived in South Africa, but Malcolm spoke of you as if you were a child. I think you would have made me a better man.'

'Sorry Dimitri, I am married and I love my husband.'

'I know. May I walk you in?'

Why oh why did these things happen? To use Jonathan's term, why couldn't anyone's life be uncomplicated? She couldn't do anything about that now, but today, she wanted to have fun and be happy, and going in with him would definitely throw Jonathan off track.

'How did you get your hair like that?' Dimitri studied the complicated plaits, knots on top of her head, and cascading black locks.

'It's a wig. I couldn't do this to my own hair.'

'You will catch everyone's eye.' He adjusted his mask.

She smoothed the dress, flicked some hair away, and straightened the mask on her face. 'Ready.'

They walked in through a side door, as she did not want to bump into Jonathan waltzing in on the arm of another man. Besides, it wasn't as if she was supposed to come through the front door. 'Thanks Dimitri, but go mingle. You might meet people you would like to know.'

He smiled. 'Ah, you want your husband to find you. I shall watch the romance from the sidelines.' He let go of her, took a couple of steps back, bowed, and blew her a kiss.

"Oh lord," she thought, also feeling sorry because she could give him nothing. Turning from him immediately, she looked around with interest. There were soldiers, goddesses, and warriors. Apollo, Hermes, Thor, Minerva, Vayu, Indra, Athena, Freya, Osiris... The list was incredible, and she was pleased that most had spent good time on decent transformations.

She noticed a beautiful Persephone and watched her for a few seconds, recognising a certain familiarity. She smiled, walked over, and tapped her on the shoulder.

Amy turned around and stared. 'Yes?'

'Sshh,' Gabrielle said as she lifted the mask. 'You look gorgeous. What's your husband?'

'Gabrielle? Wow. Roger is King Midas.' Amy's eyes were wide with astonishment. 'What is it?'

'You have to guess.'

'Run a competition and no one will get it. I've never seen it. I'm guessing Jonathan hasn't either.'

Gabrielle shook her head. 'Promise you won't give me away.'

'My lips are sealed. I don't know if you know, but Amelia is coming. The crazy woman invited herself.'

Gabrielle nodded. 'Jonathan told me.'

'Are you okay with it? But there is nothing between them anymore.'

'He also told me that.'

'I can't wait to see her, because she will do something insane. But you've been scarce lately.' Amy accused. 'And why don't you answer your phone?'

'I apologise, but I've been so busy—'

'Please tell me you are not mixing yourself with the Russian mafia,'

'Not if I can help it.' Yet, Dimitri was wandering around here tonight.

'So, how are things going between the two of you, have you yet?'

Gabrielle shook her head.

'Just tell him, and it will be amazing.'

'You think so?'

Amy's hand went to her face. 'Sweetie, he loves you so much, Tammy's parentage is not going to matter one iota. This will be the seal, and you will fill each other's heart as you should. Trust me.'

Gabrielle smiled. 'I'm building up the courage. See you later.' Then turning, she went into the next room. There, she ran into two bulky Vikings, Zeus, Neptune, and for some unexplainable reason, two vampires. A grin spread on her face as she caught sight of Antiope.

Moving on, she went towards the entrance, perhaps Jonathan was still around there. She didn't want him to figure out who she was yet, but she did want to tease and tempt him a little. Turning quickly, Barbara stood before her.

'What a beautiful costume, who are you, dear?'

She did not want to give herself away, but how did she not greet the Hostess?

'You like my friend's costume.' Dimitri appeared. 'But she's not telling who she is, you must guess.'

'That is nice.' Barbara studied the stunning blue eyes. 'My daughter-in-law is also into mysteries.'

'Thank you for the invitation ma'am, please excuse us.' Dimitri led Gabrielle through a passage and into a salon. 'Be careful and don't get yourself stuck.'

'Do you know anyone here?'

'Surprisingly, yes,' he grinned. 'I have many rich customers too.'

'What can I say to that, each to his own.'

'This is a saying but you don't believe it. You have very set ideas, and for you it is how it is and there is no deviation. Which is why you will never cheat on your husband, and you expect him not to either. Someone is coming.' Turning, he disappeared out the French door.

She did not manage to make it to the other in time, and there was Jonathan. The very sight of him made her melt. She turned sideways.

'Excuse me,' he said. 'That is an exceptional costume, who may I ask are you?'

She didn't answer, unwilling to give him the prospect of recognising her voice, so she lifted a hand dismissively. Thankfully, someone else entered the room. Registering Jonathan's awareness to the newcomer, she slipped through the French door and plastered herself against the wall outside.

'Paul,' Jonathan greeted and turned to look back at the woman. She was gone. 'So, are you what I think you are?' As he asked, he saw the costume in its entirety and suppressed a laugh. 'Did you choose it yourself?'

'Would I do this to myself willingly?'

'Amelia then, is she here already?'

'Don't you recall? I'm her chauffeur.'

'Is her costume hard to guess?'

'You know her, so take a shot. You would probably hit a bulls-eye.'

Jonathan placed a hand in front of his mouth. 'How are you carrying that half-beast around? And a bare chest, you are becoming bold and daring.'

'Very funny, but the hind legs are attached to my knees so it moves as I walk.'

'How the hell did you drive here?' Jonathan pointed to the centaur rump.

'It's detachable. One of the servants helped me snap the damn thing on.'

'Why did Amelia want you to look like this?'

'I left the thing late so when we went to check the other day there wasn't much to choose from and I had no clue what some of the other costumes were about. Amelia pointed to three: this, Cerberus, and Hydra. No dogs, wolves or lizard dragons for me, thanks, and I would have died if I had to carry a bunch of heads around.'

'You picked right, otherwise, I would either be shooting you with silver bullets or trying to cut one of your heads off.'

'I don't think Cerberus is a werewolf.'

'He's not, it just sounded funny. So, what is she?'

'If you were Amelia and were going to a place where everyone looks fabulous, what in the hell would you do to be even more fantastic?'

'I see.' Jonathan sat down and mindlessly pointed to the other seat.

'Are you paying any attention to this thing? When last did you see a horse's ass on a sofa?'

'Can't you sit at all?' Jonathan burst into laughter. 'Bloody hell, Paul, I tell you, run. And please tell me you are not falling for her.'

'No falling for anything, anywhere, anytime and after tonight I am not planning to see her again. She gives me headaches. What's Gabrielle?' Paul asked curiously, as he moved towards the French doors. Glancing out casually, he noticed the hem of a black dress.

'I don't know, haven't seen her.'

'Amelia is some near-naked creature. It might be a mermaid, I wasn't paying attention.' Paul pointed to the wall as Jonathan glanced at him.

Jonathan rose to his feet immediately. 'Is she bare-chested?'

'Looks like it, and there is hair everywhere.'

'An attention-grabber to the very end,'

'And don't you forget it. Oh, here is the update. She is as mad as hell with you, so she wants to rip Gabrielle to pieces.' Paul went left.

'We will see who rips who.' Jonathan took the right.

'You look good.' Paul said as he stepped outside.

'Apparently I do.' Jonathan grinned.

Startled, Gabrielle turned right to disappear down the garden path. Instead, she walked into Jonathan's chest.

'Not only a mystery but also a spy.' He said with a smile and steadied her.

CHAPTER TWENTY

Clamping the fake piercing blue eyes on his, she placed her right hand above the bracer, ran her fingertips all the way to his shoulder, and felt the sharp shiver race down his arm. He let her go instantly.

'Darling,' Amelia made a beeline for him as she stormed in. 'You look fantastic, and it's Troy all over again. If you had told me I would have been Helen.'

Gabrielle watched the woman for a second. Was Jonathan all that existed for her? Turning quickly, she made it into the haven of night.

Jonathan watched Amelia. It was either mermaid or siren. Paul was right, she was bare-chested, and the bottom half not better covered either. Gabrielle would never do something like that; she would find a way to be cautiously daring. 'Hello, Amelia. How have you been?'

'I don't know why you bother asking, you know I am sad and upset.'

'And I have already apologised for the circumstances, but these are the facts.'

She placed a hand on his shoulder and looked him square in the eyes. 'What is she feeding you because your head is turned. If she were a worthy rival... but no, just some insipid pathetic little girl— I hate her.'

Barbara appeared in the doorway. 'Why are you all in here? The party is outside and people want to dance. Jonathan, have you seen Gabrielle?'

'Not yet. Perhaps she is still upstairs, I'll go check.'

'Let them look,' Amelia said. 'I need to talk to you.'

Jonathan knew he would hear more of the same, he would repeat himself, but it was his fault she was here. 'Five minutes.'

'Ten.' Amelia grabbed the door and almost shoved Barbara and Paul out of the room. 'If you will excuse us,'

He was already annoyed. 'Please remember whose house this is.'

'I'm irritated.' She went to him. 'Tell me again, what are you going to do about us?'

'I'm sorry,' he said patiently. 'But there is no us.'

She stared into his face. 'No, you are not sorry but so I can understand, why?'

'Because I'm in love with her.'

She flipped her long eyelashes upwards. 'You do know that it can change in a moment. How many people say these things and look at them, all separated, with someone else again, so perhaps I must just hang around because the two of you won't work.'

'Gabrielle and I will never leave each other.' He denied heatedly.

'Get real. You are a man, she's a girl, and you are quite insatiable. What,' she flashed half a smile and placing a hand on his shoulder squeezed. 'You think a woman doesn't know? And I've tried bloody hard. If you are determined to go through with this little obsession, let me tell you what is going to happen. Before long she is going to bore you silly, you will realise what we had, appreciate it and want me back. Hell, we were fantastic.'

'Maybe, but that is hardly love, and I love Gabrielle. And if it was as fantastic as you say, why don't I miss it? I never think about you anymore.'

She narrowed her eyes. 'I was wrong, I did not need ten minutes. I'm done here.' Walking away from him, she threw back the door and out she went.

He should have followed his instincts and said no, but he had wanted to— no, he didn't know why he had assented.

Reaching the hall, he noticed interesting costume. Meaning to approach her, he saw a bearded man take her hand and pull her away.

'What did Amelia want?' Paul asked as he walked in.

'To make sure once and for all where we stand, which is nowhere. She is furious.'

'Forget her.' Paul watched a group of laughing people. 'Your marriage has more than one positive outcome; I have never seen your mother so willing to try new things. But what was she thinking when she planned all this? Anyway, it's fabulous and she would make a killing with her awesome ideas.'

'I can't see her wanting to plan parties.'

'No,' Paul agreed. 'Ah, there is Amy.'

'You look good.' Jonathan told her. 'Have you seen Gabrielle?'

Amy pointed. 'Two rooms down that way.'

'What does she look like?' Jonathan asked curiously.

'If you haven't seen her, I'm not allowed to tell. Bye,' she waved and went towards two women who beckoned to her.

Jonathan's attention strayed to mysterious woman as she flitted past and stopped. He was dying to figure out whom she represented because her costume was striking, as she wore no chiton, himation, tunic, toga, or stola, depending on the particular part of the world or era one looked at.

The dress was black, multi-layered, yet sleek, moulding her figure, and when she moved, it sparkled, as if invisible lights went on. Two front slits exposed her black-stockinged legs and ballet lace-up shoes. Above her bust, was a silver border depicting a Greek key, the well-known meander, which repeated on a drooping belt around her hips, upper arms, and on a crown that sat amidst that mass of plaits and knots. The sleeves descended like arum lilies, gracefully following her arms' movements as they attached to her middle fingers with silver rings.

The mask was equally remarkable, a detailed black velvet mould of a classic Greek countenance. It covered her entire face, revealing the striking azure eyes. On her forehead, a row of silver stars glistened, more cascaded down the sides. Interest was propelling him to walk over and ask questions, yet the distinct impression was that she did not wish to be interrogated. As if aware of his eyes, she looked straight at him; in a way that was not to be misinterpreted as casual.

It was more than curiosity now; she was baiting him, intending a very different type of communication. He took two steps in her direction but a crowd entered the area between them and he would never reach her in time if she were planning flight, which she evidently was, because she turned and exited.

'Please do not be taken in by enigmas,' Paul said as he noticed where Jonathan's attention was. 'They can turn into annoying nuisances.'

'You have been around Amelia a while. Has she ever tried to get you into bed?'

'I have never given her the opportunity.'

'There,' Jonathan pointed to the end of the hall. 'Since I am married and looking for my wife, maybe she will tell you who she is.'

'I shall go investigate beautiful vision.'

Jonathan shook his head; perhaps Gabrielle was somewhere outside.

Indeed intrigued, Paul disappeared in the same direction secretive woman had vanished. He did not know as much as Jonathan about mythology, but he knew enough not to appear illiterate. As far as he could tell, that costume did not represent any of the deities he was familiar with.

He obviously guessed right because even as slow as he moved with dragging centaur behind, when he turned a corner, there she stood. 'Hello,' he greeted, but before he could say another word, a bearded man arrived, took her hand, and both disappeared.

'I see you are not being particularly successful either.' Jonathan said beside him.

Paul shrugged and went to join a group of warriors.

Jonathan knew one thing, she was playing hide and seek. The aim seemed to be for him to seek, find, but not speak because when he found her, she dodged and gazed at him very... he could not describe it. The little game almost made him forget that he was searching for Gabrielle a couple of times. Where she was, was anyone's guess and he could not imagine what she was busy with.

He had told Barbara that he wanted no blazing candles on any cake, so she had procured an array of cakes and cupcakes. He wondered if they tasted as good as they looked because they were beautiful and he noticed a couple of people admiring the little masterpieces in awe. When he bit into the triple chocolate wonder, he could not believe mortal hands had baked that. It was truly a food for the gods.

Everyone needed to burn sugar energy away and congregated at the acropolis, the dancing Mecca. He looked around, trying to locate Gabrielle, wanting to dance with her. Then for some reason, Amelia made herself a spokesperson for a moment and told everyone that he had prepared a speech. He glared at her, what the hell?

He went through the duty of thanking everyone for coming out to make his day special and while doing so noticed unidentified lady clasping her hands. An oddly familiar feeling filled him but he could not imagine why. When done, he walked towards her but she turned quickly and went to speak to the band. He wanted to find Gabrielle, and he wanted to find her now. Feeling as if his temper was about to fly over the garden wall, he saw Barbara. 'Where on earth is Gabrielle?'

'Amy told me she came this way.'

'I need to go in for a moment. If you see her, tell her I would like to dance with her.'

'I will.' Barbara smiled, making mental notes to give the band a good referral. Thus far, they had not disappointed, playing a continuous string of excellent music, and everyone seemed to be having a wonderful time.

Barbara exhaled. With Jonathan married to that gorgeous girl, her life was changing and she felt as if she were embarking on an adventure. Looking sideways, she realised who stood beside her. 'Are you having a good time?'

Someone tapped him on the shoulder. Turning, he looked into those strange blue eyes, definitely not real. 'Are you finally going to tell me who you are?'

She remained silent but put her hands out, inviting him to dance.

'I'm flattered but I am waiting for my wife, whom I haven't seen since early evening.'

She didn't change position but instead ran her fingers up his bare arm.

He felt the rush go straight through his flesh. This did not bode well if a stranger's touch did this. 'I'm...' he could not think properly. No, this was very bad.

'I am a damsel in distress,' she whispered and dropped her gaze beseechingly. 'I need a knight to rescue me.'

He smiled, charmed. She certainly was taking the evening seriously. 'Okay, one dance, I'm sure my wife will turn up soon.'

He kept to the proper distance and held her firmly but never tight. She was a good dancer because she never tried to lead, yet she was unquestionably leading him somewhere.

'Do you know this song?' She asked.

He had not been paying attention, but did now. It was Kelly Mueller's Water to a Flame. He had heard it a couple of times as Gabrielle seemed to have an affinity for it. Mysterious woman clearly knew it well too because she had asked as soon as the first key had sounded on the piano. 'Does it have a special meaning for you?' He queried.

'I feel like that every day,' she continued whispering. 'I am not what I seem to be, and need someone to find me, because I am so very afraid.'

He was processing her words when he noticed Paul and Amy arrive. Amy smiled. He turned his attention to the blue eyes again. 'We all feel like that at some point in our lives.'

'But when the true self emerges, many no longer want it.'

Now he knew she was talking something else. Amelia reached the dancing area and he did not like the expression on her face. Bearded man stopped beside Paul, folded his arms, exchanged some sort of greeting, and the two started talking as if they knew each other. Amy had a goofy smile, which was peculiar because she was very particular about women in his life. Every time one went to see him in his office, she hovered around, as if making certain none did anything untoward.

'That is how I feel.' She made a gesture as the chorus began.

There Kelly told the world how very bad she was and how opposites could not possibly survive. It was not coincidence; she was telling him something. Why would a woman try to overwhelm a strange man this way? Unless... unless he was no stranger and there were things she could not verbalise. Unconsciously, he started rubbing her left palm with his thumb.

He gazed at Amy again but she was no longer watching them. Instead, she whispered something in her husband's ear and both made their way to the dance floor. Catching him unawares, mystery woman dropped her face on his shoulder.

It was half-concealed but her scent refused to hide any longer and embedded itself in his brain. He drew her closer. 'Why are you so sad, my darling?'

'I heard what Amelia said.'

'Please don't listen to her.'

'I am sorry I disappoint you, that I hurt you every day—'

Snatching the helmet from his head, he dropped it at his feet then pulled the mask from her face. He gazed into her eyes, now hidden beneath that amazing blue. Sometimes, when she looked at him, as she was doing now, he saw it and felt it, she just had not been able to say the words. But today, she was doing different things, and he was certain those three little words were not far off. An incredible happiness filled him as he cupped her face. 'There are things I wish were already resolved but you make me happy every day. When I get home and see your face, there is nowhere else I want to be.'

'Why do you love me?'

'Because you are you and you fill my heart. I like me when I am with you.'

She plastered herself against him.

'How about going home?' He asked with a smile.

'Would it not be rude?'

'It's almost eleven, we are not breaking any protocols. By the way, you are the most gorgeous deity, but we have not yet been formally introduced.'

'Nyx.' She saw his blank expression. 'I will let you figure it out.'

Wanting to say goodnight to Barbara, one of the servants informed them that she had retired with a serious headache, and requested to not be disturbed, by anyone.

CHAPTER TWENTY-ONE

Jonathan watched bemused as Gabrielle did two things as soon as they arrived home. First, she ran up the stairs to check on Tammy then asked Esther whether she wanted to stay or go. Esther did not live far, so she preferred to go home, as it wasn't too late either. Second, returning downstairs, she went to the drinks cabinet, took out a bottle and brought two flutes over. He regarded her with interest, this was as far from Gabrielle as anyone could get.

She gave him the bottle. 'Today is a special day.'

He glanced at the label; she had chosen the best champagne he had. Charles had brought it from France and told him to drink it at his wedding. That had come and gone and he had forgotten about it. His birthday was as good a celebration as any other. 'It certainly is; what are we celebrating?'

'You, and new things; open it.'

He did, poured the golden liquid into the flutes and handed her one. She must lead this because he had no clue.

She drank half the contents in the flute then pointed to him. 'If you can manage, drink it all. We must finish this bottle.'

'Are we getting drunk?' He asked with a grin. Trust her to do something like this. Get drunk at home, so no one makes fun of you. He swallowed the contents. 'You do realise that as soon as the alcohol hits my brain and I go to sleep I am not going to recall what I did tonight.'

She refilled his flute and drank the remaining half in hers. She felt woozy; sure her bloodstream was already aerated with those bubbles. She swallowed the second flute.

'Since you want me to drink give me the bottle, it will go faster that way.' He quaffed the thing down and made a face. 'Okay, empty. What now, hashish?'

'Sorry I'm doing it like this but...'

'What are you doing?'

Her head felt as if she had stuck it in a fishbowl. 'I think we must change—'

'Gaby, look at me.'

'Can I take this hair and eyes off? I feel strange.'

'Who would imagine that after champagne?' He teased. 'Yes, do that, because I feel as if I have already committed adultery. I'll get out of this get-up too. Leave the dress on, you look beautiful.' He wanted to pull her into his arms but something told him to wait. She was an open book and he loved being able to read her like that. Although the beginning of this chapter felt a little crazy, it also promised to become exciting; he could not wait for the end.

He had clearly not realised that she was going to be quick, because she could hear him struggling with something. Considering he had a load of leather on, he probably needed assistance. She knocked. 'Do you need help?'

He opened the door. 'I do with the buckles on my back.'

'How did you do them earlier?' She asked as she placed her hands on his back and started undoing the straps.

'One of the servants helped me.' He flexed his muscles as the piece fell then feeling her hands still on his back he reached out and pulled her against him. 'I love how you feel against me.' He shook his head. 'Honestly Gabrielle, why did we drink that thing?' Turning around, he put his hands out to her, to undo the straps only her small fingers could reach. 'How men carried all this on the battlefield no one knows.'

'There,' she said as she took the second bracer away. 'How heavy is that?' She pointed to the pteruges he still wore around his waist.

'A couple of kilos. Although, this one is probably not as heavy as the original ones were.' He loosened the belt, dropped it to the floor, and put his arms up so she could pull the tunic over his head.

Without a word, she fell to her knees and undid the straps and buckles on the greaves.

'We have no idea how pleasant it is to wear modern clothing.' He swept the greaves aside with a foot then reaching for her hands, pulled her to her feet. 'Thank you for liberating me. But now,' he dropped his tone of voice. 'Let us continue where we left off at the party. You were telling me something.'

Her gaze dropped shyly as she nodded. 'Amelia—'

'Never mind her, she's full of nonsense. And please take it out of your head that you are an impediment in my life. I have no clue where you got this idea that you hurt me daily.'

'I do, you just don't see it. Why do we always hurt the ones we care about?'

He fixed his gaze on her. 'Rephrase that, and you know exactly what I mean.'

'Why is it so important for you to hear it said that way?'

'Because you never tell me what I want to hear. You tell me how you feel even if I don't like it but it's always the truth. And I keep it all here.' He placed a hand over his heart. 'Tell me.'

She sighed softly. 'Yes Jonathan, I love you.'

'And I love you, adore you and my soul sings at your words.' He lifted a brow. 'But Gaby, you already know that you have me, why go through all this to seduce me?'

Embarrassment filled her. 'I didn't know what else to do. What gave it away?'

'I don't know in how many relationships you've been, but I know a seduction when I see one.'

'I'll bet.' She snapped as she felt a rush of jealousy.

'We can't undo what is but we can start something new. Is that why we drank, because you needed courage?'

As she had told Amy truthfully, she had been working towards this, especially now that her body followed its own course. Her mind had also been in a strange place the entire day, and it had begun with her fretting over his gift, or rather, her neglect of having acquired one, but the final knell was that kiss he had awaken her with at Barbara's house. It had simply consumed her remaining resistance, and it was then she thought of using his alcohol problem to solve hers.

She could no longer fight, she did not want to. Instead, she was going to give their marriage a chance, but for that, she had to accomplish this last deception, because she could not chance him changing his feelings towards Tammy. Say he had fibbed about what he called alcohol amnesia... Had she given him enough? What if it backfired? But she had paid attention where he stopped every time they had something at dinner and she was certain she had given him far too much champagne. Only... when did it kick in? Oh yes, she remembered him telling her; after he fell asleep, and then recall nothing when he woke up. Dear God, when did she become such a schemer?

Jonathan watched as things flew past her face. He could become mesmerised watching her eyes as they flickered through her thoughts. Usually, it all turned negative, as he so often experienced, but tonight, she was not planning on running from anything. In fact, he saw a new light shine in, brighten the place up, and chase away those shadows she lugged around daily. Well then, he was also done talking.

Reaching for her again, he cupped her face and dropped a gentle kiss on the forehead. Slowly, his lips descended to her neck and then moved to her mouth. Stopping there, he barely touched her lips before slipping his tongue in, knowing that she would meet his within seconds, and in sync feel their need swell like an overflowing dam.

Her hands went into his hair, holding and pulling, but never rough, just enough for him to feel the impulses from her fingers, as if she had built static and was now transferring it to him, reminding him that he could never feel anything close to this without her.

Running his hands up her back, he found the criss-cross ribbons, and slowly loosened one at a time. When done, he placed his hands on her shoulders and let the gown fall to the floor. There she stood in alluring black lace and stockings, knocking the breath right out of him. Dropping to his knees, he took her hand and placed it on his shoulder, then lifting one foot, he rested it on his bent knee and carefully undid the satin ribbons; repeating the process on the other side.

Rising to his feet, his hands went to her back, undid the bra, dropped it, and pulled her to him, willing her skin to become part of his. Leading her to the bed, he sat her down and gently pushed her onto her back. Silently taking one leg to his chest at a time, he rolled down the stocking, as if he were handling delicate scrolls.

Every movement he made told her how much he wanted, mirroring hers. Her heart twisted peculiarly, she was a deceiver. 'Jonathan,' her voice squeaked. She inhaled deeply and realised she had done a worse thing, now feeling light-headed.

He lay beside her and propped himself up. 'What is it my love?'

Undoubtedly, she would have to explain later, but that hardly mattered because eventually, he would fall asleep and she would have achieved her objective. She had to if they were to be a couple and a family, right? This was warped, deceptive, dishonest, misleading, and her heart pounded at the lengths she was capable of going. Her mind decided to take over, refusing to stop, screaming that everything was wrong. 'Jonathan,'

'Yes Gaby.'

'I need to tell you with how many people I have been.'

'I don't care, or does it matter to you that I know?' He asked as his fingers began a trail across her stomach.

How had she imagined that it was easy to mislead someone, especially Jonathan, whom she loved? It was because of subterfuge that she had no peace, and she would never attain it unless she fixed this. If she hoped to have a normal life with him, she had to. 'None,'

'Nine.' More than he would have guessed, as he believed she had been just as difficult with everyone before him, which was why he often wondered how she had managed to get herself pregnant.

'Not nine, none, no one.' She turned sideways for a second then back to look at him. Now that she had started, she'd better not stop. 'This is the truth you wanted. I have never been with anyone, and that is why I wouldn't sleep with you, because then you would know that Tammy is not my child. Why I couldn't let you do the paternity test, because she is not related to you either.'

The alcohol was finally taking its toll. He shook his head, trying to hold on. 'I'm not following.'

'Tammy is not my child.' She sat up, grabbed a small cushion, held it against her chest, and dropped her head.

'I thought that's what I heard. Enlighten me.'

'Tammy is my sister and I never had an affair with your father. How could I when he was like a father to me, in fact, more my father than the biological mess I got? I'm sorry for misleading you and letting you continue believing that she was your sister.' Her eyes shone unhappily. 'But how could I imagine that you and Paul had assumed... Only when you requested the paternity test did I understand why you married me, why you were so interested in her, why you wanted us in your life. She was never your sister, still isn't, she's mine, my father's child. But both her parents are dead and I registered her as my own because like you, I too couldn't bear to lose her.' She sighed and reaching for the folded throw wrapped herself before getting up and turning to leave.

'Wait. Sit.' He pointed to the armchair.

She turned around, her pale face streaked with tears. When she sat down, she buried it in her hands. 'What would you have me do? But if you don't want me anymore...'

What the hell? And crap, because he had known she was hiding things, just never anything close to this. Now, even the reason why he married her made no sense. But it never had anyway, because it had been a stupid thing to do. If what she said was true, did he want to kick her out? He looked at her again. Things were starting to add up, but so convoluted, it was an absolute tangle, so where did he begin to unpick this bedlam? 'Tell me something, my father was aware of this?'

She nodded.

'And the money you needed, what was that for?'

'I stupidly signed some papers for my father and he got into trouble with Russians, who came looking for payment after he died. Your father was afraid they might hurt me or Tammy, so he did what any dad would do, and settled it.'

'Then, why did you start getting accounts?'

Gabrielle shook her head. 'I don't know. I never understood that either.'

Jonathan took a deep breath. 'Explain the point of tonight. Why did you want me to sleep with you, and then forget all about it because that was the point, right?'

Tears tumbled down. 'I love you and I want to be your wife, but I didn't want you to discover the truth and then stop loving Tammy. Truth revealed can change how people think and feel. I'm such a liar,' she hiccupped. 'I'm petrified my pretences will destroy you if I stay, or me, if I go. But I love you so much that I wanted to attempt happiness without disclosing the truth— I was wrong, because I can't lie to you anymore.' Jumping to her feet, she ran out the room, across the passage, into hers, pushed the door shut, and throwing herself onto the bed, burst into heart-wrenching sobs.

Jonathan sat there, confused and upset. Hell, he fumed, and in the morning, he was not going to remember this puzzle. Worse, when he returned to lucid, he wouldn't understand anything again. They said to start at the beginning, so perhaps he should do that. He grabbed his phone and dialled a number.

'Hey, why did you leave so early?' Paul asked.

'Are you still there?'

'It's the party of the year, of course I'm still here.'

'Hasn't my mother got out of bed and tried to kick you all out yet?'

'No, I'm sort of in charge.'

'Amelia?'

'She left soon after you and Gabrielle, all huffed up over something.'

'Okay, this is what I want to know. Tell me again why I married Gabrielle?'

'What? Why are you asking me this?'

'I need a refresher course.'

'Did you forget Tammy is your sister?'

Jonathan gritted his teeth. 'Next question. How did Gabrielle's debt come about? I know something is screwy, and I'm damned if I get what's going on. But you on the other hand, I'm certain you know more than me.'

'Why on earth do you want to know this? It's almost one in the morning.'

'I'll tell you why. Tonight, my wife made me drink. Need I explain more?'

'Oh, I see, you're checking with me before you go to sleep, so I can fill you in later. But what difference does it make how the account happened?'

'I've known you long enough to hear that you are hiding something. So I want to know now, and remember tomorrow, because—'

'Because what?'

'My wife told me today, for the very first time that she loves me, but only after she filled me with alcohol.'

'Wow, you two have a really interesting life. But why would she do that?'

'That's why I'm asking you, I have a terrible feeling about this. And now I'm petrified of going to sleep, because when I do—'

'What are you talking about?'

'Paul, if you consider yourself my friend, one who really cares, you will tell me something that can help me, because if you don't, I think I'm going to lose everything.'

'You mean Knight Industries?'

'No, Gabrielle and Tammy.'

'How and why would that happen, you love them.'

'Do I?'

Hearing hopelessness in his best friend's voice, Paul knew he had to help him. 'Okay, then listen carefully. Gabrielle doesn't owe anything; your father took care of that with the Russian mafia or whoever those people were, I merely tied up loose ends with the attorneys. I sent her that account, but it doesn't exist. I needed to make her desperate for your help, and to make you believe that she needed you.'

'Why?'

'First, remember Amelia? It seems she's disappearing rather quickly from your memory, so I would say mission accomplished. Second, because if Gabrielle wasn't stuck between two impossible places and at your mercy, she would not have married you.'

'Explain.'

'You better than me know that Gabrielle cannot be coerced into anything. And truthfully, it was not my original idea; it was your father's.'

'What?' Jonathan sat bolt upright, stunned at this turn of events. 'When?'

'Oh yes, I never told you that was his last request to me. Not just that; he wanted you to love them, to be happy. I had no idea how to get this happening, started thinking it was a silly idea. But then, as if it was meant to be, you provided the opportunity when Amelia began her engagement nonsense.'

'But... why?'

'I know, it's crazy, but that was his last wish. Look, I'm sorry things are messy, but I also thought it would work. And his wish is already half-fulfilled because you were in love with her the moment you looked up and said *talk about angels*. Remember that? I do. I had just told you a joke about angels and she leaned over the wall and you were transfixed.'

'Why would my father do this?'

'I would say because he loved you both a great deal. I know it's insane, because what man involves his son and his mistress this way?'

Jonathan made a face as Gabrielle's sobs reached him. 'What a mess.'

'Where is she?'

'Crying her heart out.' Then he heard another voice. Tammy was obviously picking up on Gabrielle's wailing. 'I have to go, speak to you tomorrow.'

'But— what happened? Did you fight?'

'Heaven knows what I must call it.'

'What now?'

'I don't know. Bye, Paul.'

CHAPTER TWENTY-TWO

No, he didn't know anything. Waiting a few seconds more, he then went to Tammy's room. She was already sitting up.

She fixed her beautiful hazel eyes on him. 'Daddy,'

He passed a hand over her forehead - still a little warm - then took her out and sat with her in the rocking chair. 'If only you could talk and tell me about this crazy story.'

'Mmm... mama.'

'Yes, her. I'm confused and so very cross. And damn it, I can hear her crying.'

'Mama.'

'You love your mommy very much, don't you? But if she's telling the truth she's not even that to you either. So you are just a little girl with no one, but her to care for you.'

She started rubbing her eyes.

'You are supposed to be sleeping.' Holding her lovingly, he rocked her until she fell asleep again. Sister or not he could not think of her away from him.

He stood against the wall, not certain what he should do, but that sound... Unable to listen any longer, he went to roam aimlessly downstairs as he pondered over the startling revelation. He asked himself, now why should the knowledge change how he felt, and what was he mad about, that Tammy was not his sister, or that she was hers?

If things were as she said then that explained Charles' wish for them to be together, because any fool could see that he adored Gabrielle. The fact that he had left them nothing had been puzzling, Charles was not known for not caring about those he loved.

The idea of Charles touching her had driven him near insanity, so now that it was as he had wished, what was his excuse? There was none, he still loved her madly, but hell, he was furious, perhaps because she had wasted so much time. He cast his mind back, trying to see where and when she had lied; until that letter, she never had and he recalled the day well. She had been in total panic, with good reason if this was true. Realistically, how much better had he behaved? He too had been duplicitous.

He made hot chocolate, so with two mugs in hand, and half an attempt at a peace offering, he went to knock on her door. They needed to talk, to sort out this mess, to put it all behind, and start anew. Becoming aware of the silence, he knocked again. Receiving no answer, he tried the door. It opened. The room was empty.

He left the chocolate on some surface, as he made his way through the first floor, even going past Tammy again. Thankfully, her temperature had dropped, breathing was normal and she was sleeping peacefully. Getting to his room, he realised Gabrielle must have been there because the lights were off and the curtains drawn back. She too must be looking for him, also recognizing the need to straighten things out.

Down he went, trying to figure out where she might have hidden but as he turned, he noticed the dining room sliding doors open.

He walked past the pool, rows of rosebushes and continued towards the gazebo, knowing that she often went there. Rounding the short Ficus trees, he stopped to absorb the picture before him.

She lay on her back on the swing-chair almost naked. With an arm over her eyes, moonlight bounced off her skin, which meant that she had sleepwalked here, as she was not in the habit of trekking through the house and down the garden path without clothes. He might be upset, but the vision of her was the most potent turn-on he had ever experienced.

'Gaby,' he called. 'I'm sorry I've made you cry.'

Becoming aware of him, she sat up and patted the seat. 'Sit.'

He did and placed a hand on her shoulder. 'Are you okay?'

'Did you figure it out?'

'What?'

'The costume.'

'You want to know this?' They should be discussing everything else but considering she was in deep slumber, he had to follow her cues. 'It was a beautiful costume but I am not familiar with Nyx.'

'It's part of another Greek word, nyxta, pronounced neeggta. Do you know what it means?'

'No, but you wore black, had stars on the crown, forehead, and all the way down the sides of your mask, so she might be a night goddess.'

'See, it wasn't that hard. Her motto is; I bring the tumbling stars. Nyx is the daughter of Chaos, and sister to Erebus, darkness. She had a bunch of children and they include the Fates, and Keres – goddesses of violent deaths. The better known ones are: Hypnos sleep, Nemesis retribution, Thanatos death, and Moros doom. It pretty much describes me, don't you think? Look at the trouble I have brought you.'

'You are none of those.'

Her head dropped for a second then lifting it again, she threw her arms about her body and fixed her gaze on him. 'Why am I naked?'

There was Gabrielle. He touched her cheek. 'Evidently, you sleepwalked here.'

She leaned into the hand, took it to her lips and kissed it. 'Please forgive me for trying to trick you.'

She was as sweet as a kitten at that moment, in fact, far too good for him. He looked at his hand in hers and something churned in his stomach. 'Don't think about it anymore.'

Now that things were unravelling, he could see how the reason for their marriage had sent her into the world of secrets, but he understood something else too. She never did anything because she had to, so this little disaster proved one more thing. She meant to stick around, definitely wanted to make things work, even if choosing the zaniest way to go about it, and must trust and love him a whole lot if she was willing to let him become Tammy's father.

He felt like crap. He had been mean, insistent, unrelenting, constantly pushing towards the hunger he could not satisfy, so tonight's subterfuge, although twisted and unorthodox, made sense. Pulling her against his chest, he threw an arm over her shoulders. 'And I'm sorry that I made you sad, but don't ever doubt that I love you.'

A cloud arrived, hiding her for a few seconds in its shadow then drifting along moonbeams sparkled off her bare skin, as if she had smeared fairy-dust on. Holding her closer, he planted a kiss on her temple. 'You are cold.' Rising, he pulled her up and swept her into his arms. Feeling her skin against his, his heartbeat rushed up, his throat went dry, as if he had been starved of his own life force. Some people consumed peculiar things as aphrodisiacs; he didn't have to, she was enough, or perhaps more.

Striding through the garden, he went into the house, up the stairs, to his room, and put her down on her feet. 'This is our beginning, if you wish it to be. You know my heart is already yours, now I offer you my body to do with as you wish.' He told her in the moonlit room. 'And tomorrow, when I recall none of it, you decide what to tell me and how we proceed. I love you, I want you.' He closed his eyes then opened them again and smiled. 'After everything, I thought this moment would never come, but you are here, and so real.'

She smiled. 'Just love me.'

He ran his fingertips down her arms. It was as if he touched rose petals, soft and velvety, yet fire and strength existed within. Then leading her to the bed, he lay her down. 'I promise to make it memorable.'

He crawled to her and kissed her slowly, giving her time to respond. She not only let him in she pulled him in. He always felt crazy when touching her, especially when her breath was hot and quick on his skin and her mouth tasted like this. Stroking the line of her neck, he placed a finger at the base, where her pulse beat wildly.

She sighed. Now that he knew the truth, everything would be different. True, he would forget tonight but now they could build from her memories and she would tell him as if it were a fairytale. She reached out, traced a line from his forehead, down the side of the face and stopped on the bottom lip, looking into the blue eyes that looked deep grey, spellbound, bursting with desire in the moonlight.

His mouth explored every inch of skin; gliding, stroking, tasting. She was exquisite, precious, as soft as cream and as delicious, and again he thought of fruit as he made a line with his tongue from the collarbone, across the neck and all the way to her mouth. He drew invisible patterns on her stomach, feeling her skin react and tremble, and hearing her moan when he took her breasts into his mouth. He could never begin to explain what it felt like to touch her.

One hand descended to her legs and stroked them gently for a few seconds then found that secret place he had hungered after for so long and she was wondrously yielding. 'You intoxicate me.' He told her and began a deep kiss that matched the rhythm he was slowly teaching her.

How could she handle more pleasure, she was already beside herself. He was tender, loving, and so very careful, looking at her to see if she was okay. She had not known that passion could make one want to cry because she did.

He was hot and sweating, wanting wild, adoring her moans as her own need burst forth. He kissed her deeply, feeling her response. 'Gaby,'

Her hands went to his chest and her head swam, making it impossible to find words. Her body wanted to move but he would not let her as his hands and arms held her prisoner.

'I love you.' He held her closer and finally let the whole of him touch her. She whimpered and grabbed his shoulders so tightly he thought she had dug her nails through flesh. He adored everything about her, wishing to assimilate her into his being, to access this continuous rush. She thrashed a little and called out his name.

Entwining his fingers with hers, he too joined the wave that made him part of her, feeling his body dissolving into hers, experiencing an exhilarating emptying, an excruciating happiness forcing him to lose control, discovering that everything he was, was wrapped in this woman who had just given herself to him. That he no longer was one entity but half of something better. He felt limp, yet so very alive then held her close, and closer still.

She inhaled deeply, as one who had been weeping, and asked in a shaky voice. 'Are you going to sleep now?'

'Do you want me to?'

'No,' she started crying. 'I'm sorry I made you drink. I want you so much but didn't know how to tell you.'

'Doesn't matter anymore, you have me now.' He fought the sleep, lay holding her, and asked some questions. Then slipped off the bed and pulled her along. 'Come,'

The intention was to wash, so they would relax and wind down, but like all new lovers, they couldn't keep their hands off each other. They began an endless kiss, tongues sparring into a dance, feeling their desperation under the soft mist. Leaning against the wall, he pulled her to him and hooked one of her legs over his; her breath caught and so did his as they began moving in unison and neither knew that the other was crying as unspeakable bliss made it impossible to contain. They started drying each other then stopped abruptly. Tears running down their faces, they threw their arms around each other and sobbed.

'Please forgive me for all the stupid assumptions I made. I should have known that neither you nor dad would do what I imagined, that you truly are the angel I saw.' Picking her up into his arms, he carried her back to bed. 'Once in a blue moon, something extraordinary happens. I'm so glad it happened to me. Promise me that tomorrow you will find a way to tell me that you love me.' He begged.

'I will.' Her whisper floated tiredly.

Then he loved her slowly, tenderly, and wished he would never close his eyes, because when he did, all this would be gone, and he wanted to spend Saturday making love to her, then Sunday, and Monday, and every other day for the rest of his life. He had once watched a film where someone kept waking up on the same day; he wanted that experience of relieving this day for a thousand years to come.

For this was the sort of thing a man kept in his heart for all those times when they would get mad at each other because the closer people got, the more chances for fighting turned up. This had to stay in his mind so he could see it when she annoyed him, when she was being a pest, mean, or simply unreasonable.

He recalled how Amelia had always taken him to the edge but never been able to push him into the abyss of complete fulfilment. No one had ever done. He couldn't stop looking at her, touching her, tasting her, and he adored that she was as desperate for him as he was for her. Amelia was wrong; right here was everything he wanted. 'How are you feeling, my darling?' He asked softly.

She clung to him. If only she had not put all those foolish things in her mind and been so afraid. He was Charles' son, how could she believe he would be so fickle? It was inconceivable; she had loved Charles as a father and now loved his son as a husband.

Exhausted, he tucked her into his arms then resting her face on his shoulder, buried a hand into her hair and murmured some final words.

It was still dark when Gabrielle stirred again. Moving away from him, she gazed at his peaceful face. Amy was right; nothing equalled the feeling she had in her heart right now but sadly, soon, he too would awaken but recall none of it.

Never could anything or anyone make her this happy and it was not the mere fact that she had had the most astounding physical experience of her life. It was the knowing that he loved her with a wild intensity, that he meant everything he had ever said, and knowing that she too had given him something he had never had; fulfilment.

She had a choice; stay here and explain when he woke up, or leave and let things unfold, for ironically, she had achieved her goal anyway and could now *give in* any time she wished. No, she had not changed much, she was still the same fraud, and yesterday could never be relieved the same way again. Her eyes filled with tears of regret.

Getting out of bed, she ran a hand over his face and arm. He murmured her name but did not awaken. With a heart near bursting, she grabbed her things from the floor, gazed at him longingly and with a tender smile on her lips walked out, quickly checked on Tammy, and disappeared into her bedroom.

CHAPTER TWENTY-THREE

Sitting on the bed's edge naked, he ran his hands through his hair. He felt awful, as if he had run all the way home, and there was a bitter taste in his mouth, which meant, he had definitely had too much to drink. Gabrielle and her insane ideas, why the blazes had they imbibed champagne when he had had enough at the party already? He stared at his costume strewn on the bedroom floor. She must have helped him out of it because he barely remembered battling the buckles and leather.

A grin spread on his face. If he recalled correctly, after mystery woman turned out to be his adorable Gabrielle, she had just about confessed that she loved him. Why on earth had he not done something about that? Oh wait, there was that nasty bottle snuck in between and who knew now what he had done? He would have to ask her, since it had been her idea.

Getting to his feet, he picked the discarded leather pieces and threw them all together into a heap at the foot of the sofa.

The refreshing shower invigorated him and his mind wandered to the previous evening. She had teased him with her little disappearing act as a stranger and then played a game as she tried to tell him things with a song. One thing he got loud and clear, she was finally willing to give their relationship a chance. That fear he abhorred still hovered in the background but he was going to do everything he could to dispel her trepidation.

Yawning, he dried himself, feeling that he should crawl right back into bed because he was worn out. With a towel around his waist, he stuck his head out the bedroom door.

Not a sound, so Gabrielle must still be in bed. He tiptoed to Tammy's room and opened the door. Empty. Why would she be in there, she had set times for everything and Esther had guessed right that they were exhausted and already taken her downstairs.

He wanted to knock on Gabrielle's door, to ask her to tell him that she loved him, so they could start building on this thing, but if she felt half as drained as he did, then let her enjoy her rest. There would be plenty time later, as neither would be in the mood to go anywhere for the rest of the day, except perhaps to his mother, to give her a hand with cleaning up operations.

He dressed casually in jeans, linen shirt and espadrilles then went in search of breakfast. A smile spread on his face when he saw Esther playing with Tammy outside. Watching her try to run, he wondered if she was too young for a puppy. He hardly wanted her little hands to hurt the defenceless creature, although, puppy would probably sort her out with a strategically placed nip.

Gabrielle opened her eyes slowly, relishing the silent gloom. Never in her life had she had this feeling, the one of knowing that she was loved so completely. Even as a carefree girl in Switzerland, she had never reached this level of happiness. A frown crept onto her brow. Heaven knew how much or little Jonathan remembered this morning.

Throwing the bedcovers over, she became conscious of her nakedness. What a glorious freedom. Dropping her hands to her breasts, she felt their tenderness, evidently not used to as much handling as they had received last night. Jonathan loved them; but he didn't only love them, he loved all of her with a fanatical passion.

A faint smile crossed her lips. She recalled having made a vow when her mother died, that she would never love again. Funny how the world rose against you and made you change your mind. Because that very world she had disliked, despised and scorned as she complained about its unfair schemes, was now giving her this amazing opportunity at an incredible happiness.

Lifting an arm, she put it to her nose. Gooseflesh spread across her skin, she smelled like Jonathan. She closed her eyes, feeling a rush inside. Did this ever pass between two people? She hoped not; she wanted to feel like this forever, to want him always.

She preferred showers, but today, she pampered herself with a bubble bath. Last night, Jonathan kept telling her how good she smelled and tasted, so it was only right she used female guile to trigger his memory with another dose this morning.

"Interesting," she thought as she looked over her body. She had imagined that she had received a couple of bruises, but no, his hands stayed gentle even when demanding insane responses from a body that did not know much about the wonders of lovemaking. His final words had been a romantic declaration, as he held her close and whispered sleepily in the moonlight. 'I love you Nyx, my goddess of the night.'

He was outside, playing with Tammy when she arrived in the kitchen. Over weekends, they did not expect the servants to set out the dinner table for breakfast, or to go formal, so they usually found easy things to eat, such a cereals or toast. A smile spread on her face and heat filled her. To think that that gorgeous man wanted her, needed her, loved her.

Jonathan looked straight at her then, and she thought that she would go into convulsions as she tried to pour milk into a bowl. What did he recall? She would have to wait until he came inside and said something, which did not take too many minutes.

'Good morning my darling,' he greeted as he walked in with Tammy in his arms.

'Mama,' Tammy said and reached for her.

Jonathan dropped a kiss on the side of her face as he said. 'She is missing you, has been calling for you ever since she saw me.'

'Hey,' Gabrielle hugged her tightly. 'You love mommy?'

'I love mommy.' Jonathan grinned then fixed his piercing blue gaze on her. 'And apparently, mommy loves daddy too.'

She threw everything into perspective as quickly as her mind allowed. She had told him that at some point in the evening. She dropped her gaze, hiding the breathlessness he induced as he inched closer.

Tammy took her face in her little hands and plastered her nose against hers then did likewise with her lips.

'What are you doing my poppet?'

'That is adorable, she is kissing you.' As he said that, Tammy wanted him again. When he took her, she did the same to him. 'Okay, it's official; we have a very loving little girl. And she had better stay that way.' He said as he tickled her and she laughed with glee. 'So, do you?' He asked.

'Do I what?'

'Love me.'

She felt sad. Sad that she could not show him how they had said those words to each other endlessly. How they had cried with the intensity of that love. But there was nothing to do about that now. She could only start here, build further, and fulfil her promise that she would tell him so. 'Yes, Jonathan, I love you.'

'I knew you did,' he smiled tenderly. 'You just wanted to hide it all.' Pulling her with the free hand, he kissed her then complained in a lowered voice. 'What are we going to do about it? But first, tell me this; what did I do last night that I am so exhausted?'

It was as if he reached out and touched her. Her heart raced and images swam in, rendering her speechless.

'Sir,' Peter interrupted. 'Your mother would like to speak with you. She is in the study.'

'Ask her to join us here.' He said without taking his eyes off Gabrielle's face.

'I suggested it but she refused sir, making it quite plain that she wishes to see only you.'

'What's that about?' Jonathan put Tammy in Gabrielle's arms. 'I'll see you shortly.'

Jonathan took long steps to the study, wondering what this meant, but when he walked in, he instinctively knew that it meant a very bad thing because she looked agitated. 'Mom,' he tried to kiss her but she turned away. 'Okay, what is going on?'

Barbara inhaled deeply, turned to look at him, and her eyes glistened with a mixture of unhappiness and anger. 'Jonathan, please tell me that what that horrible woman told me yesterday is not true.'

'Huh... what horrible woman and what have you heard?'

'Your ex-girlfriend told me a most distressing story.'

'Amelia?' What had she done now?

'I don't like that woman, but she obviously knows things I don't.' She shivered involuntarily as she recalled the previous evening.

Barbara smiled as she gazed at Jonathan and Gabrielle on the dance floor, thankful that he had come to his senses. She would have never told him she did not approve of Amelia, as it was not her way to interfere in his life, but this turn of events... A shadow fell across her face, and glancing sideways, she realised who stood beside her. Think about the devil. 'Are you having a good time?'

Amelia gave her an incongruous smile. 'It is very grand.'

'How did you decide on your costume?' Something resembling a sea-creature was the choice for the bottom half of her body, just not quite fish, but so transparent that she could have been wearing nothing, which she clearly was not on her upper body, only the long blonde curls covering her breasts. She had at least used some type of bonding material because the hair seemed to be fixed securely.

'I have always been rather daring and this was the perfect opportunity to show off my skills, as I'm quite handy with few materials. My mind can cook-up just about anything and that includes in the kitchen, although, I don't like that too much. It makes me sweat, an activity best left for the gym or bedroom.' She laughed merrily. 'I'm quite the handy-work, and quite sought-after too.'

Barbara lifted a brow; both beautiful and vain. Sometimes, she did not understand men's ways of thinking. Jonathan had had an incredible array of girlfriends but never one who thought as highly of herself as this one did.

'Funny,' Amelia began. 'How I never got to know you before.'

'Charles and Jonathan were the outgoing types. I on the other hand, haven't always been sociable.' Barbara told her.

'Jonathan used to mention something, but never a lot. He was very stingy about discussing his family.'

'I'm glad the two of you have remained on friendly terms. As I hear from what happens out there, apparently people tear each other apart after their relationships end.'

'Well, don't be tricked into thinking wonderful flowery things where your daughter-in-law is concerned either.'

'Do you know Gabrielle?'

'Somewhat.' Amelia said.

'It's odd how men make choices.' Barbara turned to look at her. 'The extremes they vacillate between, especially Jonathan. He never dated anyone like Gabrielle, even when he was in school. So I was rather taken aback that he chose to settle down this early, and with such a sweet girl.'

'You know, no one is as good as you think they are, or as bad as they look.'

'This is true. As they say, don't judge a book by its cover.'

'As it happens, Gabrielle has some nasty little chapters in there.' Amelia told her sharply.

'None of us is perfect but Gabrielle is a breed apart. She is that rare jewel so many search for but never find.'

Amelia snorted. 'This is so typical of that kind. They come with their doe eyes, fluttering lashes, and enticing words. Butter wouldn't melt in their mouths, but what is it they do?'

A frown spread across Barbara's forehead. 'I understand that it must be difficult for you, especially if you had feeling for Jonathan.'

'Difficult? And they call me an actress. You have no idea what those three are up to.'

'Three... who are you talking about?'

'Paul. He's as prominent in this theatre production as they are and continuously covers up things. I wish I knew how she does it because she has them all twisted around her little finger.'

Barbara eyed the woman beside her. Sour grapes dripped like raindrops onto the ground. 'I understand it is upsetting letting go of a man to just see him take up with someone else, especially after a long relationship, and particularly one that leads to marriage. But if you are planning to have some type of friendship, you have to leave it all behind.'

'Friendship? I didn't come today to be friends with them, I came to see you. To tell you about what they are hiding from you.'

Barbara dragged herself out of her drifting, unwilling to recall the actual words the woman had imparted, and how much pleasure she seemed to feel while delivering them.

'Amelia always says more than she should.' Jonathan continued. 'She's an entertainer, always looking for attention.'

'That may be true, but I doubt she would concoct such a tale as the one she told me. Because she knows I would come here.'

'Which tale is this?'

'However painful, I want you to be honest. Who is Tammy's father?'

'I am.'

'Stop it!' She told him harshly. 'You are not. But—' she sucked in breath as a sob threatened to leave her. 'That Gabrielle was your father's mistress is one thing, but that you married her... How could you do such a thing? And— how could he go elsewhere for comfort and solace, while I sat in that house blaming myself for all the babies I could not have, and those I lost. Which now I see, was my fault because evidently he had no problem producing another healthy child.' She caught the sob.

'Mom, it's not like that.'

'Then how is it? Tell me that baby is not your sister.'

'She is that.' He dropped his voice. 'But what difference does it make now?'

'What difference?' She made an irritated gesture. 'How did I raise you? Where is it okay to take your father's mistress, marry her, and obviously have a life with, including sex? To go where your father has been; body and soul!'

That sounded so ugly that he blushed. 'Mom, I had to marry Gabrielle.'

'Why, did she lie to you first, telling you the child was yours? Was she playing both of you? And then what? Dear

God, and I thought Amelia was unsuitable. She looks like an angel in comparison. How did all of this happen?'

Never in his life was he more angry. That snake had to open her mouth and do this, when he had explicitly begged her not to. What in heaven's name did he do to take away that incredible hurt off his mother's face? 'So now you know; what do you suggest we do about it?'

She made an incongruous sound. 'Worst of all, that baby is nothing to me, merely your father's child. You made me love them even as you knew all of this; shame on you. It would have been more honourable to break my heart right at the beginning.'

'Mom, I can't change what is, so my question remains, what do you expect me to do about it?'

'Do you love Gabrielle?'

'You know I do.'

She covered her face with her hands. 'Amelia was right in that respect. All men love Gabrielle, including my husband.' Barbara broke into sobs.

He placed an arm around her shaking shoulders but she shrugged him off. She was not upset she was raging because she had never done that. 'Mom, you should go home to calm down and think things over.'

'Think? I have done nothing but since yesterday, so what else do you want me to do?'

'Okay, I understand, it's a nasty shock, you are hurting deeply but no matter what we wish, we cannot change it. Would you like to talk to Gabrielle?'

'I couldn't possibly right now.' She said quickly and harshly, 'I'm grieved and so very disappointed.' Then she grabbed her handbag and car keys. 'I must get out of your house because I cannot comprehend how you were able to do this.'

'Mom,' he intercepted her departure.

'I want to leave here now.' She glared at him with a mixture of anger and pain.

'This is what I need you to know.' He said, still barring her exit. 'I married Gabrielle because I wanted Tammy. You know very well that unwed mothers have all the power over their children and I could not bear to be out of her life completely. She's my little sister and I wanted a say and to help raise her. I could not simply abandon her when she cannot be blamed for her father's lack of judgement. Yes, it's unconventional, but when I did, it was just a marriage of convenience, which is why Amelia went along with it.

'But I have since fallen in love with Gabrielle and I can't change that. To tell the truth, I keep thinking that it must have been a one-time happening because she is not that kind of person, and if you look inside yourself, you know it too. And mom, what are you really upset about? Is it that dad had an affair, that he had another child, that I married Gabrielle, or that I love her? Perhaps you should think about these things and then come speak to Gabrielle.'

'Hold your tongue because I never want to see your wife or your sister again. You want them, have them, don't involve me, and as you seem to have already chosen, I won't come here again. I'll go see you at the office and you may come to the house, alone. I don't know, Jonathan, I just don't know if I can ever forgive any of this.'

'I am sorry that you hurt this much and sorry you heard about it as I never wanted you to. And mom, I understand completely because I used to feel the same way, until I got to know Gabrielle. She is not what Amelia is making her out to be.'

'Whatever she is, she managed to get a part of your father's love, a part that was only meant for me. And now, she has that part forever, and in my face.' Turning on her heels, Barbara rushed out.

Jonathan went out of the study and back into the kitchen. Empty. He went into the lounge. There sat Gabrielle, stiffly, deathly white. She had obviously heard part, or the entire conversation.

'I am so sorry.' She told him. How could she fix any of this?

He sat beside her. 'I'm the one who is sorry it happened like this because I never meant for her to find out but evidently, Amelia was chasing her revenge.'

'She will never be able to look at me again.'

'I was long past all this, so it doesn't affect me anymore but she will be aching for a while. I am as mad as hell, this should not be happening.' He grabbed his phone and dialled.

'Leave her.' Gabrielle suggested.

'Not on your life.' He waited a little longer.

'Hello Jonathan, fancy you calling me. You have not done so in a while.' Amelia's voice reached him.

'What did you do? What the bloody hell did you do? Are you insane? Did I not tell you that you were not to repeat this to anyone?'

'Wow, twenty questions. Listen lover-boy, if you thought that I would just let you waltz away by breaking our contract without compensation then you were mistaken and all that covering up was pretty annoying. Now, it's out in the open and your mom knows what a wonderful little girl you got yourself. Your father's trash, you must be proud. Be thankful I told only her, that I didn't rush off to the media. And don't provoke me because I might still do.'

'What the hell is the matter with you? I don't care if you hurt me. Fine, do it, all over the place if you wish but my mother... She was just starting to come out of her shell and you crush her like this. A woman you don't even know. You are cold, mean, and so very cruel.'

'Jonathan Knight, you have not yet seen the half of my fury. As for cutesy girl, no one messes with me.'

'I'm warning you, stay away from her because I swear I will hurt you if you hurt her. And how the hell did you think that this would take me back to you?'

'That was yesterday. Since then, I have realised that you did me in on purpose. You did not even have the decency to break up with me; instead, you used your father's shenanigans to toss me aside. What I am telling you is this, I have changed my mind and I will make you squirm.'

'Don't cross my path.' He threw the cell phone onto the nearest sofa.

'I don't know what to do.' Gabrielle said as she looked up at him.

'There is nothing to do.' He went to her and took one of her hands.

'Deny it all you want but I am so much trouble for you.' Her eyes filled with tears.

He pulled her closer. 'That is not true.'

'What if your mom makes you choose between us?'

'No, she simply needs time to process everything, to accept facts.'

Facts, funny word. She had a couple she would like to share but could not prove. And of all the ironies in the world! Yesterday, she had wanted to lose her virginity so they could be a couple, finally a family; today, she needed it back to restore that very family.

Of course Barbara was hurting, who would not faced with a bombshell such as this? Unintentionally or otherwise, she had broken Barbara's fragile heart, because how could she prove anything either way? She could take Tammy for the paternity test but that would take weeks and how did she make Barbara feel better in the meantime? She had messed everything up again. Giant tears dropped from her eyes. She did not know why but she was a bane to everyone named Knight.

Worse, she had to revert to secrets because how could she explain all this to Jonathan again, Barbara, anyone? And again she heard loud and clear how he had felt and why he married her, even if also admitting to loving her; it was a nasty wound to everything that had transpired the previous day. What had she done with a deceptive bottle of alcohol? There was no guarantee that he would react the same way as he had done last night. Her head hurt and she felt sick.

Jonathan watched the pale face become paler, as she obviously tried to figure out things. 'Everything will be all right.' He told her encouragingly.

'How?' She wiped her overflowing eyes. 'This is punishment for all the bad I have done and I am going to take it because I know I deserve it.' She sprang to her feet and ran upstairs to her room, locking herself inside.

He tried the door; locked. 'Don't do this to yourself. You made a mistake, you have the consequences and now we deal with them.'

She sunk against the closed door. 'I need to be alone for a while.'

'I still love you.' His voice dropped. 'Let me help you through this.'

'I am all right it's your mother who needs your help. Go to her, go tell her all the things she needs to hear, go hug and comfort her. And tell her that I am sorry for having hurt her so deeply.'

'You're sure you're okay?'

She swallowed a sob. 'Just go, she needs you.'

'But you promise that we will sit down and discuss all of this calmly when I get back?'

'Please go. I can't think of your mother alone, crying, feeling abandoned and deceived.'

'Okay my darling, I'll see you later.'

The house was quiet when he returned. Esther had already left because her car was no longer in the garage, and neither was Gabrielle's. That was odd, because she did not like taking Tammy out when she wasn't feeling her best. He walked into the house and wondered where Peter was.

He found him in the kitchen with a cup in his shaking hands. 'Are you all right Peter?'

'No sir, I'm not. And I apologise because I couldn't stop her.'

'What has Gabrielle done?'

'She left sir, just left. And it was terrible because her heart was breaking, and she broke mine because I—'

'Left...' Jonathan repeated, not understanding what Peter meant. 'Where did she go?'

Peter shrugged his shoulders. 'I don't know sir, she took two suitcases.'

'No...' he swivelled on his feet and ran to her room. Her cupboard door stood open, some clothes obviously missing, a few flung onto the bed. He rushed to Tammy's; some of hers also gone. He returned to Gabrielle's and sat on the bed's edge, dropping his head into his hands. He placed a hand on his chest; it felt as if he were about to have a heart attack, it hurt so damn much.

Getting to his feet, he went to her cupboard and grabbed the costume she had worn the previous day, burying his face into it. She couldn't be gone because— where would she go? She knew no one.

He grabbed his phone, dialled a number and waited. 'Hello Amy, have you seen Gabrielle?'

'Morning, Jonathan. No, why?'

He decided not to frighten her right away. Perhaps he had to give Gabrielle some time to return. 'She didn't tell me where she was going and I thought she might have gone to see you.'

'Sure it's me she would visit today? She has probably gone to your mother. I'm sure there are tons of things to do around the house.'

'You're right.' He disconnected. While he had been at the house, he had seen there was a mountain of work, but Gabrielle would not go there, for right there was the battlefield. He wanted to call Paul, decided against it and went into his room.

Sinking onto the sofa, he tried to figure out why she would do this and where she would go. He was getting to the why; she had put it into her head that she should not be in his life, as to the where. Then he saw it. There on his bedside table lay an envelope. Catapulting to his feet, he grabbed the thing and tore it open.

'Jonathan,

You are my knight, my rescuer, always will be, but I am petrified of destroying you.

I cry every day, not because you make me cry but because I know I am being unjust.

I don't know what you see in me, but I know what I am, so very bad for you, and not only you. I got your father into trouble and now I've hurt your mother deeper than anyone else ever could. Please forgive me.

Your loving wife, Gabrielle.'

Tiredly, he sank onto the bed and perused the note again. He was accepting nothing and needed to figure out this thing because she had to be somewhere, and he was going to find her. Grabbing the phone again, he dialled.

'Hello,' Paul said groggily.

'Are you still in bed?'

'Yes, I'm bloody exhausted. Your mother sure knows how to throw a party.'

'Whatever. Listen, do you have any idea where Gabrielle would go if she left me?'

There was a dead silence for a couple of seconds. 'What?'

'Gabrielle is running and I don't know where.'

'Whoa, reverse. What are you talking about now?'

'Amelia told my mother about Tammy.'

'You don't mean... crap, you do. Why the hell would she do such a thing?'

'Because she's mean, she hates me, and remember what you said? She wants to rip Gabrielle to pieces.'

'Shit! What happened?'

'My mom turned up here this morning wanting to know if the story Amelia told her last night was true. She is devastated.'

'Of course she is. Hell, that woman is mad. How did you not see this before? No, I know, she is so bloody good in bed.'

'If I could I would take it all back, but I can't, can I?'

'No, that's just the way it is. What happened with Gabrielle?'

'She has put it into her head that she is trouble for me, so she left after telling me to go look after my mother. After hearing my mother say some pretty awkward things.'

'Sometimes I think you do not deserve her, because hell, she's something I don't understand either. But no, I am wrong, you do because you love her and she loves you. It's quite crazy actually, because you would flay yourself for her and she— what she would not do for you.'

'You seem to know a great deal about my wife.'

'And none of it is important if we can't find her. You don't suppose she would leave the country?'

'You mean back to Switzerland? I don't know, I hope not, but I will have to check.'

'Do that so long. Have you tried Amy?'

'I called her first, but I didn't tell her why. Gabrielle is not there.'

CHAPTER TWENTY-FOUR

'Gabrielle,' Dimitri greeted surprised when he saw her on his doorstep. 'What are you doing here?'

'Did you mean it?' Her voice struggled. 'That I was welcome in your home day or night.'

'Yes, of course.' He noticed the suitcases. 'What have you done?'

'What I should have done before, but I— I can't ruin his life and deserves so much better than me, not someone full of problems. Not a liar like me.' Her shoulders shook.

He stood staring at her, not knowing what to do then came to his senses. 'Come,' he said, let her walk past him, then, picking up the cases, took them in, and closed the door. He turned around and saw her just standing there, crying softly. 'You are very lucky; I was getting ready to go to the club.'

'I'm sorry I'm here, but I didn't know what to do.'

'Did you fight with your husband?'

She shook her head. 'Not with him, but I had to go.'

'Do you want to tell me about this?'

She shook her head again.

He furrowed his brow. 'Okay, I'm guessing you mean to stay a while, or at least until this is resolved.'

'I don't know if it can be.' She told him. 'I'm grateful for your help but as soon as I can I will find my own place.'

'And I think you should be home.'

'Do you have a baby bed? But why would you?'

'As a matter of fact I do.' He smiled. 'It was both mine and my siblings', and it came all the way from Chelyabinsk. This used to be my parents' house before they returned to Russia, so a lot of their stuff is still around. Let me show you.'

Minutes, hours, days had passed but she felt no better. Her heart was empty, needing Jonathan to fill it again, as for hurt— the last time she had hurt this badly was when her mother died.

Dimitri was a kind host and she noticed that he was in fact quite smart. But she had already deducted that from his office at Red Bare. No one possessed so many books without having some kind of knowledge.

He stayed at the house until about twelve every day then asked if she needed something. After hearing her response, he left for the club. He came home very late, or early, depending on how one looked at it, and never intruded in her space or asked too many questions, just leaving her to deal with whatever she was going through.

Standing by the window, she knew that she had to start doing something for herself soon. She had the money Jonathan had given her, but it would not last forever if she started spending it. But she needed to stand on her own two feet and felt so very bad about needing it. She glanced at the time; Dimitri should still be home. She went to the lounge to wait for him.

He saw her sitting on the sofa. 'Have you been waiting for me?'

'Yes. I know that you are willing to help me indefinitely but that is not fair. So here goes; I need a job. I suppose I could find employment in some office but I am not sure how long that would take as the marketplace is inundated with office girls. I have no idea if you need anyone to do anything for you but I am willing. I need to carry my own weight until I move out.'

'Tell me something,' he lifted a brow curiously. 'Do you speak to your husband as you are doing to me?'

'I don't know what you mean.'

'You have this thing about you. As if you do not need anyone's help, even while you are asking for it. Sure you are not a Russian princess?' He smiled.

'Jonathan became very upset with me once.' She dropped her gaze. 'He told me that I could not go through life alone, that I am not to think I don't need anybody's help.'

'Yes, it's this aristocratic air about you. You are not stuck-up but there is this aura of I will do it myself. And Jonathan is right, you cannot be alone.'

'About the job—'

'You don't have to look, you can come dance for me.'

She went pale. 'Dimitri—'

'Oh, I apologise,' he said quickly as he saw her face. 'I meant it as a joke. I did not realise you would take it seriously.'

'What would you have me do then?'

'Can you waitress?'

'Despite how I come across I do not imagine myself above anyone else.'

'This is true; you are in fact a very humble person. You confuse me.'

'I will have to either get a nanny or take Tammy to a nursery school—'

'No, she must stay home. Besides, you are not going to stay long; your husband will come for you.'

'He shouldn't. And please promise that you will not tell anyone that I am here.'

He shook his head. 'You sort out everything and tell me when you are ready for work.'

'Thank you, Dimitri.' Who would have believed that this moment would come? How could she have guessed that one day she would need his help, which he offered so willingly and freely.

Jonathan could not work, so he either sat staring out the window, or dialled her number and prayed that she answered. Ten days had passed and had turned into pure misery. He needed to send her a message but how did he reach her? Perhaps he should contact the newspapers.

So far, he had been able to hide Gabrielle's disappearance from Amy and Barbara but he guessed that he would have two very different reactions when both discovered that bit of news.

Barbara would not be moved because she was angry, upset, everything else, and including hurting. Amy would take it badly because she believed in Gabrielle in ways even he did not understand. Curious, why had he never sat down with Amy to find out what she knew? She had been Charles' PA for ages so she might know how the affair had come about, and perhaps provide some information that would help his mother deal with this.

Someone knocked.

'Enter,' he called and looked up. 'Mom,' he went to her and wondered if she was at last receiving greetings. He leaned towards her and she did not pull away. Good, perhaps they would get over this obstacle.

'One question,' Barbara said straight away. 'Why has Gabrielle not tried to call me or see me? I know I would want to if I had done this. And I know she respects me, so I don't understand her silence. I do want to talk to her but she should approach me first. Or must I be the bigger person here?'

He swallowed hard. 'Huh, mom, I don't—'

She saw the distressed look. 'What is wrong?'

If only he could stop the ache. 'Gabrielle is not home. She left last Saturday while I was with you and I haven't seen them since.'

'Why? I thought you said you are standing by her and all that.' She made a gesture. 'Is she testing you, to see whom you love more?'

Jonathan shook his head. 'You don't know Gabrielle. She was very upset that she hurt you, me, everyone. And she has put it into her head that she is bad for us.'

Barbara shrugged. 'Perhaps she is not as mistaken as you think.'

'Stop it, mom, you know her a little, not as I do.'

'Knock knock.' Paul said from the door. 'Hello Aunt Barbara.' He went to kiss her cheek. 'Thank you that you are not as mad as I thought you were.'

'Oh, I am mad, I'm just not shutting you out, even though both of you should have known better.'

'Anything?' Jonathan asked.

'I don't know where else to look, but at least she has not left the country.'

All three turned their heads as they heard a knock. Amy stuck her head in. 'Since there seems to be a crowd in here, can I make you coffee, tea, get you something to eat?'

'Some strong coffee would be appreciated.' Jonathan told her then turned to Paul. 'Where else can we look?'

'Beats me. Who does she know, where did she live before? Does she have any university friends?'

'Not as far as I know. She was there only a couple of months anyway; the majority of her studies were done in Zurich.'

'Tell me to mind my own business but what are you talking about?' Amy asked as she set a tea tray.

'Gabrielle left home last Saturday. We don't know where she is.' Paul told her.

Tray and teacups landed on the floor; dozens of china pieces everywhere. 'Hell, Jonathan, and you tell me this now.' Amy said as her eyes filled with tears. 'Why?'

'Amelia told me about her affair with Charles.' Barbara informed her.

Amy went paper white and reached out for support. 'Dear lord,' one hand shook against her temple. 'I need to sit. And I knew that woman would not keep her mouth shut.'

Paul helped her to the closest chair.

'So, you also knew.' Barbara stated. 'And why did all of you think it was okay to conceal this from me?'

Amy put her hands to her head. 'Please tell me that none of you had a fight with her over this.'

'Fight, no, she has not faced me yet. It seems she takes care of everything by running.' Barbara announced.

Amy jumped to her feet. 'Are you all insane? What kind of rubbish do you believe? Oh Jonathan, you know she is better than this. All of you know it but how you came by this assumption only heaven knows. Who told you people that she had an affair with Charles?'

All three stared at her blankly.

'Well,' Amy continued angrily. 'Since this mess is upon us let me tell you the truth about Gabrielle. She is the most wonderful girl any of you will ever meet. And to put all your minds at rest, she was not Charles' mistress—'

'What do you mean?' Jonathan interjected.

'Jonathan, your father thought of her as his own daughter, even let her call him daddy. He promised Eleanor that he would not leave the poor baby alone in Switzerland; that he would look after her. Then she met that horrible man who was her biological father. And before long, there sat Gabrielle with a baby sister to care for—'

'Whoa,' Jonathan's hand went up. 'Baby sister?'

'Yes Jonathan, Tammy is Gabrielle's sister, not yours, and she is definitely not Charles' child. Why do you think she freaked when you asked for the paternity test? Tammy is not related to you. The poor darling became petrified when she discovered your silly reason for marrying her, and was expecting you to leave her.'

Paul sunk onto a chair. 'What the hell have we done?'

'Is this true,' Barbara's voice shook emotionally. 'Charles did not cheat on me?'

Amy took her hands. 'How could he, he loved you. But he also loved Gabrielle, just didn't know how you would react because of the past. Wait,' she stood up suddenly, went to a cupboard, rummaged through some CD's, grabbed one, slipped it into the DVD player, switched the TV on and pressed play. 'Gabrielle used to send these all the time, in pretty boxes with biscuits.'

'Gaby,' a woman's voice called. 'What are you doing?'

Seventeen-year old Gabrielle waltzed on-screen, dressed in a pretty ruffled dress. 'Mom, Luc doesn't want to dance with me.'

'I can't imagine why.' Eleanor laughed off-camera. 'He's a teenage boy, of course he doesn't want to do embarrassing things on tape.'

'Luc, come here.' Gabrielle dragged a blond boy into focus. 'You had better put your best foot forward.'

Luc made a face and said in decent English. 'Gaby, you kill me, and I will kill you if you tell my friends I make these.'

Gabrielle giggled then faced the camera. 'Daddy, this is my entry for the ballroom dancing exam. Since we are not allowed to film on the day, I wanted to show you. Oh yes, I wanted to ask you something and you can give me the answer whenever you are ready. When can I visit you in South Africa? I want to see the country where I should have been born but mom keeps saying maybe next year. But she's been telling me that for the last five years, so I don't believe her anymore. I will stay in a hotel if you can't take me to meet your wife, although I would really like to. She must be a nice lady if you love her so much. And Jonathan, well, he's a young man, who won't be interested in a teenager.' She smiled. 'It's okay, I like them anyway. Daddy—'

'Gabrielle, stop calling Charles that, he is not your father.'

'I know but he doesn't mind. And I like it when he tells me that he has two children he's very proud of.' She gave the camera a gorgeous grin. 'It's Jonathan and Gabrielle forever.'

'The things teenagers put in their heads. So, are you serious about doing this thing?' Eleanor asked.

'Mom, you know why daddy is always alone, why don't you tell me?'

'You are a young girl, please be happy and leave other people's sadness. Trust me, it will come your way faster than you will be prepared for it.'

'Was it very sad when my father died?'

There was a silence. 'Yes, very sad. Can I start the music?'

'Why don't you like to talk about my father?'

'Gabrielle, what kind of video are we making?'

'An interesting one. Mom, take a shot of your face.'

'Why, we are filming you. Luc, stand over there. Gabrielle, he is just about ready to run so do it now.'

Gabrielle laughed and grabbed Luc's hand. 'Okay, play the music.'

The two twirled about a couple of minutes then the music stopped.

'Mom, why didn't you ever remarry?'

'And why do you ask these questions?'

'Because I want to know,'

'Because men are not on racks in shops. Besides, I had you and some men are not keen on other men's children.'

'I understand if someone didn't want me but you are so beautiful, you cannot mean there wasn't a man who didn't look at you.'

'Maybe there were a few but I wasn't interested.' Eleanor said.

'Didn't daddy know anyone nice for you?'

'Gabrielle, Charles is a businessman, not in the dating business. And he already has done more than was necessary.'

'I have decided,' Gabrielle pointed a finger. 'Daddy, I am only marrying a man like you.'

'That reminds me, did Robert ask you out last week?'

'He did.' Gabrielle punched Luc's arm as he giggled. 'Stop it.'

'I can see from your demeanour that nothing came of it. What was wrong with him?'

'Nothing,'

'That is not what you said. She called him a mountain goat,' Luc said in hysterics. 'Because he was horny.'

'Mom, I don't care if he is your friend's son, I don't like him. And do I have to date anyone?'

'Gabrielle, I'm not forcing you to do anything, I just thought—' suddenly, the woman's hand turned the camera onto her own face. Serene but beautiful blue eyes looked straight ahead, 'Charles, when you do come, please talk to her because I cannot get her to do normal things. Now she has developed an aversion for boys, except Luc. But he's more her brother than anything else.'

'Daddy,' the camera turned again. 'Don't listen to her. Oh yes, I wanted to show you this,' she stuck a paper in front of the camera. 'My results; I did well. Sorry I call you daddy all the time when I know you are not, but in my heart you will always be. I miss you so much, and I wish I lived near you, but mom says it is quite impossible, and I don't know why.' Her eyes filled with tears, which she rubbed away quickly. 'Anyway, I don't know how long this thing is and mom is telling me to cut, so we are cutting. Give a nice kiss to Aunt Barbara and think of me. Not for Jonathan, he won't like a kiss from a girl. Or maybe he would, but not from me— Bye daddy, I love you.'

Amy stopped the CD. 'Now that you have seen that girl, and think of Charles, which one of you can see an affair here?'

'You said Tammy is her sister, her father's child, but I heard them say he was dead.' Paul pointed out.

'That's the lie Charles and Eleanor told Gabrielle, otherwise she would have dragged her mom here a long time ago. Her father was Malcolm Barker-Hayden.' She registered the shock on the three faces and nodded. 'Precisely why Eleanor hid in Switzerland with Gabrielle. Quite the notorious gambler, or whatever vice you want to look up, as for trouble— But when Eleanor got sick, her conscience wouldn't let her rest, so she told Gabrielle about him. After she died, Charles brought Gabrielle over and she finally met the weird man.

'Tammy was just another of his countless mistakes, with a drug-addict no less. So there was Gabrielle, trying to figure out what to do with a baby. The insane child went to Home Affairs and registered the baby as her own for fear of the welfare taking her away from the two useless parents, and then started bringing her to work because she did not trust them.

'Charles was so angry with Malcolm and not solely because of the baby, but because he took all of Gabrielle's money. It was a sort of trade; she kept the baby as her own and they took all her money. Next, she met the two of you and I cannot fathom who thought of this preposterous thing first. Then one Saturday, when she returned from shopping, both Malcolm and Charlotte were dead, murdered.

'I had no idea the two of you were deep in this intrigue. Then one day, you got married. But of course,' she pointed accusingly. 'You never let her know why. When Gabrielle told me about the paternity test— heavens, you scared her senseless with that thing. But then you were in love with her and she with you, but she couldn't—'

'Why not?' Jonathan asked eagerly.

She gave him a stern look. 'This is easy to figure out. How was she supposed to explain why she's still a virgin if she has a baby? One you believe to be your sister, the very reason for your marriage.'

'Dear God,' Barbara said. 'What have we done to that child. But she could have told me. No, perhaps not, I was too upset; I would not have listened to anything. Would have thought she was making it all up to run from taking responsibility. Jonathan,' she turned to him. 'Know this. You are an excellent judge of character, just as your father was. Yes, you had weird things in your head but you saw right into her heart and somehow knew that she could not have done this. I on the other hand,' her voice wavered. 'Did not trust my husband enough.'

'Jonathan,' Amy called. 'Are you all right?'

'No, I'm not. I'm missing her like crazy, both of them. I want my wife and my daughter back. Do you have a problem with this now, mom?'

Barbara's eyes filled with tears. 'No honey, none. And I'm so sorry for what I said. I was so mean and ugly to a sweet, sweet girl.'

CHAPTER TWENTY-FIVE

Dimitri watched Gabrielle as she cleaned the table at the end of the room. He did not like seeing her doing those things because she should not be doing them. She was supposed to be with the baby, in fact back home where she belonged because he had not been able to sleep for days. He knew he had feelings for her but also knew that if he did not find a way to get rid of her, from both club and house, it threatened to become something else and he was in no mood to pine for a woman who would never be his.

The little fool was pretending but he could see right through her. She loved her husband madly, missed him something awful, and cried more than she should. As for little Tammy, she cried for all sorts of things and Gabrielle often said that she was missing her daddy. Jonathan Knight was a lucky man.

'Just one kiss,' a man's voice said.

Dimitri found owner of voice and saw Gabrielle standing perfectly still.

'Please sir, do not touch me.' She told the man.

'Or you'll do what? It's a strip-joint; I'm going to believe you have some kind of morals?' Man and friend laughed.

Gabrielle took a deep breath. 'Sir, what you believe is none of my concern, what is, is that I am not to be fondled like your beer bottle.'

'This one speaks nicely.' Man's hand went to her knee.

'Sir, this is the last time I request you remove your hand from my person, after that you will have to deal with the consequences, and I assure you that it will not be the reward you are expecting.'

'Wow, she gets better as she gets angrier.' Man's hand moved further up.

Dimitri stepped in before she did what he knew she was about to. 'Okay, you two, it has been lovely to see you but it's time you left as we need your table for someone else.' He clicked his fingers in the air.

Gabrielle watched as Calvin walked over immediately. She always got a strange feeling around the man, as he often watched her surreptitiously. She could not explain it, she thought that she should feel uncomfortable, as he had been the one who made a pass at her the first time she met them outside her apartment but his bulk did in fact the opposite, making her feel safe. He had also never said another word on the matter, or made any other improper innuendos.

'Yes boss,'

'Calvin, please see these gentlemen to the door.'

Calvin grabbed the two by their arms and just about lifted them up as if they weighed next to nothing, took them to the door, and almost flicked them out.

'I could have handled it.' Gabrielle told Dimitri.

'I know, but I prefer not to let patrons see the girls smacking the losers senseless.' He grinned. 'And that is what he is here for.' He pointed to Calvin.

'They hadn't paid yet.'

'And I'm losing what? Besides, they will return so I'll get it then. Gabrielle, it's almost the end of your shift anyway, go rest in my office. Then go home, and I'll see you there.'

'Thank you.'

He watched her walk away; she did not belong here. When he went into his office thirty minutes later, she was asleep on the sofa. Leaning against the desk, he watched her. He knew why men did foolish things for women sometimes because he felt all of them lately. No, he could not do this to himself. Getting to his feet again, he left the office.

'So, did you believe me when I told you that I was coming to visit?' A voice asked as he sat in one of the velvet seats out front.

Dimitri looked up and grinned. Great, someone to take his mind off Gabrielle, or maybe not, this was one of her friends. What the hell! 'Paul, it's a pleasure to see you.' The men shook hands. 'I'm still recovering from that party. How are you?'

'Okay.' Paul glanced around. 'You changed a few things since I was here last. It looks good.'

'Just a bit of refurbishing. You are alone?'

'Quite. I just needed to get away from things.' Paul sighed deeply.

'Looks like you have a heavy mind.'

'You could say that, you remember Jonathan.'

'Yes, good guy. Something happened?'

'His wife has gone somewhere and we don't know what to do.'

'You know women are very emotional. Did they have a fight?'

'Not really. And boy,' Paul sighed again. 'Did we all mess up.'

'You mean the fight is not just between the two of them?'

'And it's a shambles. By the way, you never told me how you know Gabrielle.'

'I knew her father.'

'Which one?'

Dimitri furrowed his brow. 'This is a funny question. What do you mean which one? How many fathers can a person have?'

'If you are Gabrielle, you apparently have two. Biological and another one you simply pretend is your father.'

'Oh yes, Charles Knight, a very good man. He got her out of some trouble her real father got her into.'

Paul studied him with interest. 'Oh yes, it was to do with your boss. What happened?'

Dimitri nodded. 'Calvin and I were the ones who went to see Gabrielle on his behalf. As I told her later, if it was today, I would have tried to find a different way, but I didn't know her back then.'

'She didn't have any money, Charles had to pay.'

'I know, and I am sorry it transpired as it did. But she and I have moved past that, which is why I was at the party.'

'And since then a nasty piece of business turned up and all hell broke loose.'

'What kind of trouble is this now?'

'It was all about the baby.'

'What do you mean?'

'You say you know Gabrielle, so do you also know who the baby's father is?'

'Of course, it's Gabrielle's own father. He and Charlotte were quite the high pair. I know drug-addicts but that woman— how that baby survived no one knows.'

'So it is all true.' Paul nodded his head.

'What is?'

'That Gabrielle and Tammy are sisters.'

'Self-explanatory,'

'Did you always know that? Wasn't there a story that the baby could be someone else's?'

'I know that baby and she was born to Charlotte. What a greedy woman she was. Do you know that she practically sold the baby? But Gabrielle is a funny girl; she does not see money like other people.'

Paul nodded. 'Anyway, none of that matters now. What does is that we don't know where she is. Jonathan has tried to contact her, but she does not answer her phone.'

'Can you explain this misunderstanding?'

Paul did. '...that is what went down Saturday morning after the party.'

'I can see how it broke her heart she loves her husband very much.'

'*Very much* does not cover what those two have.'

Dimitri gazed at him then smiled. 'I see you and I belong to the same club, we can only watch them love each other.'

'You too, huh? It is the most horrible feeling. Don't you know some nice girls?'

Dimitri winked. 'Perhaps we will ask Gabrielle if there is a place we can go find ourselves some. But talking now, there is something I want to show you.' He rose to his feet and beckoned to Paul to follow him.

'Have you got some special drink from mother Russia again? That time you gave me... what the hell was it?'

'It was Everclear and it's not Russian. Though, I did give you some potent Vodka as well.'

'I remember it well. Jonathan had some too and got himself into the biggest muddle with a woman. He gets alcohol amnesia, so he had no clue who she was, where she came from, or what they did. Not exactly the best foundation to start a relationship.'

It was providential Paul was here because he wanted this thing ended. She must go home, and he could start trying to get over the feelings that were growing far too quickly. He would keep his word and not say anything, merely open the door and let Paul see her, case closed.

Dimitri opened the office door and walked in. Where was she? Evidently, she had left, as her handbag and jacket were also gone.

'What are we toasting today?'

Since he could not do anything about Gabrielle, he might as well drink something with Paul. 'Give me a moment.' Taking a small bunch of keys from his pocket, he opened a cabinet. 'Now, let's celebrate our first getting drunk together to get over Gabrielle.'

'Hear, hear. I second that and tell you to pour a bloody tall glass; we're going to need it.'

Jonathan turned in bed. He did not know why he bothered to climb into it because he could not sleep. It was his heart; it was having trouble dealing with her absence, with both of them gone. He wanted them home. He wanted to walk down the passage, go into Tammy's room and see her little face, hear her laughter, see those gorgeous hazel eyes.

Hazel eyes— Gabrielle's. He wanted to look into them and tell her that everything was all right. That she did not have to hide, pretend, or be scared because he knew all that was important and loved her so much more.

Knowing he was not about to close his eyes in the next two hours, he went downstairs. He made himself hot chocolate and smiled, recalling another she had made and that it had looked like mud. Suddenly, his next movement was arrested; he could smell her fruity scent.

Taking the cup, he went to the lounge and sunk onto the sofa, realising as he did, that the scent had followed him. His brain must be recalling it, as he missed her so much and was sitting where she always sat.

'Open it,' he heard her voice then heard himself ask what they were celebrating. He felt as if he were in a brain pipeline, because voices, sounds and words were swirling.

'I need to tell you with how many people I've been.'

'I don't care, or does it matter to you that I know?' He shook himself; it felt crazy real.

'None,'

With a clatter, he dropped the cup onto the table, leaned back on the sofa and closed his eyes. His skin became one giant mass of gooseflesh and the hair on his body stood up. Oh, he knew what this meant, the missing hours were returning.

For this was part B of the phenomenon he shared with alcohol. After drinking, he forgot everything when he went to sleep, but eventually when he least expected, it all suddenly fell into his head with mindboggling clarity. He recalled tastes, colours, scents, absolutely everything there was to evoke. Like a movie, their episode with the removal of his costume started pouring into his mind.

Catapulting to his feet, he ran to his room and threw himself across the bed. He could see her, hear her, feel her, smell and taste her. Like an avalanche and with equal speed, he found her in the moonlight at the bottom of the garden. He started panting and calling out her name then grabbed the sheets, feeling his body convulse as the sensations swamped him. Sweat pouring out, he writhed in ecstasy, as tears streamed down his face.

Completely spent, he discovered that he could not move merely stare at the ceiling, as he experienced her love. When he eventually moved, he rose slowly – also comprehending why he had felt exhausted the following day – and pulled the cover off the bed, rolled it into a ball, threw it aside and went to take a shower.

Returning, he sat in the armchair staring at the bed. Right there, she had given herself to him and he had in turn made himself hers forever. He gulped as he recalled how many times they had told each other how they loved. Never had he known such ecstasy.

She had been right; sex and lovemaking were different. Not only had his body been in it, so had his heart and soul. His eyes filled with tears.

He wanted her back regardless but now that he recalled this rapture, he felt his heart pound and his breath quicken. He needed to see her smile, to taste her mouth, to hear her whispers, to feel her soft touch, to smell her again.

Down the stairs he went and into the study. Opening his laptop bag, he took out the CD's he had brought from the office. No one had not known they existed until Amy had made them aware of them. He took one and slid it into the drive. Her bruised face appeared.

'Look daddy, I had to have my wisdom teeth pulled out. Too wise for words, apparently.' She made a face. *'Looks like I went boxing and still hurts when I laugh. I told my friends that I was in a fight with Luc, they wanted to beat him up.'* She giggled. *'I have been eating only ice cream, I'm tired of it now.'* She panned the camera over the table. *'Anna is baking for you.'* A clock struck four in the background. *'Sorry, I have to go to dancing class. Will record more later, bye.'*

Jonathan moved forward thirty minutes. It had to be a different day because her face was no longer bruised.

She smiled. 'Daddy, remember you asked me what I wanted for my birthday? I have an idea, but mom says no.'

'I would like to be part of this too.' Luc made a quick appearance in front of the camera and waved. *'Hello Mr Knight.'*

'Know what I saw the other day? A hot-air balloon floating through the African skies. That is what I would like, to go visit my rightful country and see the land from a balloon, maybe even some wild animals. Mom says I'm fanciful, but why is it wrong to dream?'

'I'm dreaming too.' Luc interjected.

Gabrielle glanced at her watch. 'Luc, je suis en retard pour mon course de danse.'

'Oui, we cut. Bye Mr Knight.'

Jonathan fast-forwarded but realised there was nothing else after that. He took that one out and chose another with a more recent date in.

'Gaby, why do we make these?' Luc queried, showed his face and waved at the camera. *'Hello Mr Knight.'*

'Memories,' she waved a pink hat and plonked it on her head. *'But these stink. Daddy, mommy is very sick.'* Her hazel eyes shone brightly and then the tears fell.

'Please don't cry.' Luc placed the camera down. *Grass and flowers came into view. 'I know it's hard but you will make it.'*

'It hurts so much.' She sobbed.

'This is always. Remember when my father died? I thought I could not live anymore but I am here, and I smile again.'

She grabbed the camcorder and focused it on him. 'I don't want daddy to see my blotchy face. Tell him something.'

'Like what?'

'Tell him about your motorbike.'

Excitement poured from Luc as he started talking about his off-road bike, even forgetting what language he was supposed to be using. He disappeared into French and when hearing Gabrielle giggle, changed back to English. 'I don't know all these words.'

Jonathan removed that one and grabbed the one he had watched at the office and fast-forwarded to where he wanted it.

'I know but he doesn't mind. I like it when he tells me that he has two children he is very proud of.' She gave a gorgeous grin to the camera. *'So, it's Jonathan and Gabrielle forever.'*

He forwarded it almost to the end.

'Give a nice kiss to Aunt Barbara and think of me. Not for Jonathan, he won't like a kiss from a girl, or maybe he would, but not from me—'

He stopped it there and ran his fingers over the screen, following the line of her brow, her nose, down to her smiling mouth. 'Yes Gaby, it is Jonathan and Gabrielle forever. But you are wrong, it is only your kisses that I want.'

CHAPTER TWENTY-SIX

Dimitri was surprised to find her still up when he got home. It was very late. He and Paul had finished that bottle of Vodka and neither felt better at the end of the mind-bending trip. There was solace in knowing that he had a partner in this misery. 'Why are you not in bed?'

'I can't sleep. Sorry I left but I was tired.'

'It was the end of your shift anyway.' He regarded her for a few seconds. 'I must tell you, Paul came to the club after you left.'

She looked keenly at him. 'He does know you and he has been there before. Did you tell him about me?'

'No, but I wanted to, especially after Paul told me something.'

She saw he meant to add on. 'What did he tell you?'

'They would like you back. And that includes Jonathan's mother.'

'What do you mean?'

Dimitri looked at the ceiling, as if the answer was about to drop from there. 'Your friend Amy explained everything that needed to be explained. Paul said everybody is upset that they have hurt you, especially Jonathan's mother. The lady cried and apologised many times, and told Jonathan that she does not care what it takes, but he has to find you.'

'Is this true?'

'Why would I lie? Besides,' he gazed at her gorgeous face. All he wanted to do was reach out and kiss her, but perhaps it was the alcohol. 'You know my feelings are growing, why would I try to get rid of you?'

'Is that what you are doing?'

'Yes, you must go. You love your husband, he loves you and both Paul and I are out of this picture.' He gave her a lopsided smile. 'He and I will recover and drink a lot of Vodka or Everclear while doing so. As tomorrow is Friday, come past the club for Tammy to visit with her grandpa and then go home.'

'Are you making this up?'

He shook his head. 'How would I know all this if Paul didn't tell me? Amy helped them to understand and now they know you never had an affair with Mr Knight and that Tammy is your sister. You never told me why you left.'

She nodded. 'Regardless, I should not be in Jonathan's life.'

'Why not?' He asked curiously.

'Because,' she made a helpless gesture. 'I'm full of nonsense and he should not have to deal with someone like me.'

'I will tell you why he's willing to put up with you.' He said seriously. 'Maybe it is true that you come with a little drama but you will never break his heart – except for now of course, you are ripping it out of him. You will not cheat, you do not ask for things, you will be devoted. Your beauty is not only on the outside but also inside, and a man appreciates that. You make a man happy because he instinctively knows that he can trust you. Apart from all of that, he loves you. And even as sweet as you are, I know that none of us is perfect for anybody; we have to make things work, you just happen to be better than most at it.'

'Where did you get all of this, women's magazines? It's just psychobabble.'

'Well, then they got it from my mother.'

'But Jonathan must be so angry with me—'

'He's not angry, just sad that you are gone and missing you very much. And by the way,' he furrowed his brow. 'He has apparently been calling you non-stop but I notice that you do not carry your phone around.'

'I didn't bring it.' She told him as she dropped her gaze. 'I knew I would not be able to deal with that.'

He shook his head. 'So you have been driving around at night without any means of communication.'

'Maybe you can get me one.'

'No, you must go home.'

It was her turn to shake her head. 'I can't go.'

'Why not?'

'Because,' she got to her feet. 'Jonathan will be in so much trouble if I do.'

'Explain yourself.'

She didn't want to tell anyone, but Dimitri had an oddly forceful way of asking questions. 'Amelia threatened me. She wants to tell the media what I've done.'

'And what have you done?'

'I told you, I registered Tammy as my child.'

'That story again. But didn't you also tell me that Charlotte signed her over?'

Gabrielle nodded. 'I didn't trust them with anything. They were dangerous, not only to themselves but also to her. She had no inoculations, wasn't even registered, so when I went to do it... I know it's wrong but I wanted to protect her, to be responsible for her.' She broke into sobs.

'I see Amelia thinks she has the perfect weapon to keep you away from Jonathan. A very beautiful but mean woman.'

Gabrielle looked at him tearfully. 'So you do understand what a scandal I can cause Jonathan.'

'And let me tell you,' he gave her a faint smile. 'Jonathan will go through it willingly. I also told you before that doing the wrong thing for the right reason is something I understand well, so this is what we are doing. Tomorrow I am visiting Amelia—'

'No, you must not hurt her.'

He put his hands up. 'Oh no, I'm not touching her. The same way she scared you I can scare her.

'No, Dimitri, this is not your fight.'

'Are you trying to do everything alone again?' He queried as he raised a brow. 'And I will repeat what Jonathan said before. You cannot go through life without the help of others. And do not worry, she will not turn up dead or whatever other images you have racing through your head.'

'Isn't that blackmail?'

'I'm glad you have a name for what she's doing. But after she hears what I'm going to say she will never bother you again. Now, there is something you have to do when you return home.'

'What is that?'

'You and Jonathan have to go to a good lawyer and explain this story. You have to adopt your sister so you never go through this again. Or have you forgotten Valk?'

'No, I have not forgotten about him.'

'Okay, but perhaps now, you will actually be able to sleep.'

'Thank you for everything you have done for Tammy and me.'

'Yes, yes, go rest,' he waved dismissively. 'Tomorrow is going to be a very emotional day.'

Gazing at him, she could tell that he wished to walk over, take her in his arms and kiss her, and probably do so much more than that. He was right she could not hang around here and tempt him relentlessly.

Two weeks since Jonathan's birthday but it felt as if it had taken place an eternity ago. Standing in the bedroom where she and Tammy had spent much of their days, she knew she would not miss it, but she would think of it as the refuge she had needed and been so kindly offered.

She arrived at Red Bare early and while parking felt calling Jonathan. She missed hearing his voice but today, she could not.

She was surprised when Snoop appeared alone to visit with Tammy. 'Where is Valk,' she queried but was glad he was absent.

Snoop waved a hand. 'Somewhere,'

He looked better, had new clothes, hair trimmed and clean. At least he was spending money on the right things.

She kept glancing at her watch, anxious to get home, but she could hardly rush the old man. Thankfully, two hours had to end and she was about to leave when Dimitri walked into the office.

'Please tell me you did not really go see Amelia.'

He nodded. 'Of course I did.'

'You didn't threaten her,' she sighed. 'What did you tell her?'

'Nothing that concerns you,' he smiled. 'But don't worry, no threats just a good talking to. Trust me, neither you nor Jonathan will hear from her again.'

'I don't think you understand how grateful I am.'

'It is the least I could do for a friend. And the invitation still stands, anything, anytime. But your husband is going to hang onto you and the two of you,' he grinned. 'No, the three of you will be very happy. Good luck.'

'Thank you Dimitri.' Unable to contain herself, she threw her arms around him and kissed his cheek.

'You must stop this, Jonathan will be jealous, and then he will stop you coming here.'

She laughed through some tears that decided to fall regardless of her intentions. 'You just pretend to be bad. See you next week.'

'Bye, Gabrielle.'

The breeze felt different when she drove up the driveway, freedom filled her heart and an incredible pounding pressed her ribs tightly. She wondered if she should have gone over to her mother-in-law first but although she wanted to tell Barbara that all was forgiven, her anxiety was foremost for Jonathan. First, she would get Tammy settled in, think of all the apologies she had to make then surprise Jonathan when he got home.

Peter came running with a wide grin on his face. 'Madam, I am so glad to see you. And may I suggest I take the young lady?' He offered.

Gabrielle smiled, touched by his concern and care. 'Thank you, Peter.' Then she understood why he wanted to take Tammy. Right there, across the yard, stood Jonathan, staring at her, as if she were an apparition. 'Jonathan,' she called out and started walking towards him.

He hesitated a second, as if uncertain then ran to her, catching her into his arms as she threw herself at him. 'Gaby,' he said as he squeezed her against him. Then his mouth was all over her face. 'Thank you that you have come home.'

'I'm so sorry.'

'Sshh,' he told her as he placed a finger on her lips. 'Everything is fine.'

'Daddy,' Tammy called.

Jonathan turned and without letting go of Gabrielle, took the little girl from Peter. 'How I missed you.' He kissed her little face, his eyes filling with tears. 'And I can't explain how glad I am that you are both back.' He dropped a kiss on top of Gabrielle's head. 'Come, let's go in the house.'

'Why are you home?' Gabrielle asked curiously.

'I have been sleeping badly all these days you were gone, so I am exhausted. And then last night—'

'Madam, would you require some nourishment?' Peter enquired.

'Thank you but we are both fine. I'm guessing Esther isn't around.'

'Oh but she is. Comes in every day in the hope that you would be home.' Peter informed her.

Gabrielle swallowed. How had she thought that she could simply walk away?

'She has been most upset but she will be very happy now. I'm taking little Tammy to her immediately,' Peter continued with a twinkle in his eye.

'Thank you.' She watched him walk out then turned to Jonathan. 'Did I make you worry very much?'

'I hardly made it through the days.'

'Is your mother all right now that she knows the truth?'

'She's fine but remorseful about all those harsh words... How do you know that?'

'Huh,' Gabrielle took a step away from him. 'I don't want to lie or hide things anymore. I went to Dimitri.'

'Dimitri,' he shook his head. 'I'm a little blank right now.'

'Maybe he's not a friend but you have been in his place before. He owns the Red Bare.'

'That Dimitri?' This was an interesting and unexpected development. 'How on earth do you know him?'

'He and my father had business and I was tricked into owing his boss a lot of money.'

He caressed her face. 'You were safe?'

She nodded. 'Truth be known, Dimitri is more crazy than dangerous, even if bordering on being part of the Russian mafia. Anyway, a while back he offered that if I ever needed help to ask, so I did. Then Paul turned up there last night and the two of them got as drunk as skunks and discussed all this. When Dimitri got home, he told me that everything was out in the open and my stay was ending in the morning. I am sorry for making you miss work and worrying you so much. But now I have to call your mother—'

'She has been blaming herself and feels awful for hurting you. But what she is especially mad about is that she believed her husband cheated on her. I don't know if talking to you will be enough. She was in therapy before, she may need to return.'

Gabrielle shook her head and placed a hand on his chest. 'Your mother will feel much better to hear that she didn't make me leave, someone else is responsible.'

'Who?'

Right now, she couldn't give two hoots about Amelia and her drivel, her family was important. 'Amelia.'

'What?'

'She sent me a message.' Gabrielle pointed to the ceiling. 'When I was in my bedroom— telling me that she was going to drag your name through the mud if I stayed.'

'What the hell are you telling me?'

'Can we forget her? I just want you to know that I was going to tell the truth and was planning to take Tammy for blood tests to prove she is not your sister. So everyone would find peace in your dad's memory.'

'I want to kill that woman.'

'I think the best form of punishment is to ignore her.'

'You are way too sweet my angel and Amelia is getting better than she deserves. But I will go call mom, while you deal with that.' He pointed to the door and smiled. 'Esther is first going to shout at you and then kiss you.'

The blubbering woman appeared with Tammy, who was resting her head on the comforting bosom. 'Oh madam,' she said completely overwhelmed and threw her arms around her. 'Please do not scare us like that again.'

'I promise I won't.'

'My baby lost weight, then, she was crying and telling me that she did not like to be away.'

'I'm sure she did. She was very unhappy and missed you very much.'

Esther nodded. 'I know. She must not be away from me again, but now I go with my baby.'

Gabrielle laughed emotionally as she watched Esther leave the room. 'Her baby,'

'Of course she is.' Jonathan said as he got off the phone. 'Did you notice her little hand holding onto the dress tightly, making sure no one is taking her out of Esther's arms again.'

'I never realised,' Gabrielle said. 'I no longer can do things merely for my convenience. I need to consider her first.'

'And I am happily going with my daughter's wish to be home, where she belongs.' Jonathan put a hand to her chin. 'So you see, it is already two votes,' he grinned now. 'What does mommy say?'

'She says yes. Is your mom on her way?'

He nodded. 'Prepare yourself; it is going to be one long crying session.'

Saturday afternoon turned into a celebration, as Jonathan also called Paul, Amy and her family. He found it taxing, not because they were there but because he could not tell Gabrielle that he remembered the most beautiful encounter. Every time he touched her hand or part of her body, the images drove him near madness.

As the day finally ended and evening arrived, his heart twisted peculiarly as he could see that she was so very uncertain about things again. Refusing to rush, he went through the evening routine of getting Tammy happily settled down and they returned to the lounge.

She liked the night silence in the house, as it always made her feel safe but as she sat down, she wondered how she was supposed to tell him about his birthday.

He turned to her. 'Gaby, I need to tell you something.'

'As do I,'

He smiled and reached for her hand. 'If I'm not mistaken, I think we are about to talk about the same thing. Or maybe, there will not be much talking involved.'

She knew what he wanted, had been obvious from the moment she had walked in the door. He was going to tell her yet again how much he loved her. Would also tell her how he could not live without her. If he felt anything close to what she did, she believed him. 'Go ahead, you can tell me first.'

He took a deep breath then lifting her hand to his lips turned it over and kissed the scar on the palm. 'I never finished telling you about part B of my alcohol problem. It happened last night, which is why I could not move myself this morning.'

'Something else happens apart from forgetting?'

'Yes, when I least expect it, it all comes back.'

She had a blank expression now. 'It all comes back.'

'I recall everything.' He leaned into her and brushed his lips against hers.

She blushed furiously under the intensity of his gaze. 'Then...'

'I remember how sweet and beautiful you were when I found you at the bottom of the garden. How much we told each, how wonderful it was to feel as if I were dying in your arms. I never want anyone else for as long as I shall live and I will willingly walk through hell for you and with you. Do you believe that?'

She nodded. 'But I still think I am unnecessary trouble.'

'Unnecessary trouble? You have it all upside down. I am in trouble without you.' He stood to his feet while holding onto her hand, pulling her up with him. 'What I care about is that you are mine and I am yours, so how about we take a shower together? I have sweated enough for one day, desiring you like a maniac.' Sweeping her into his arms, he began the walk upstairs.

She giggled as she held tightly onto him. 'You are so silly.'

'You have that right.' He said as he dropped her onto her feet. 'Utterly silly for you.' His hands went under her hair as he tilted her face and began a tender kiss.

Now that she knew this heaven, few things would please her as much because when his fingertips touched the bare skin, she thought she would collapse from an overload of pleasure. They fell across the bed, their hands feverishly exploring all the secret places, gazing into each other's eyes and crying out their love and passion. They emptied themselves, took the other in, and became different entities.

CHAPTER TWENTY-SEVEN

Jonathan looked up as Amy entered his office. He had never seen her grin as broadly as that. 'You look happy, what happened?'

'I was on the phone with Gabrielle. I am ecstatic that you two are finally on the right track.'

'And I am exceedingly grateful that you are such a loyal friend. But I think that I haven't thanked you properly for saving me from being a complete jerk.' He walked around his desk and hugged her. 'The chaos I could have caused further if I had continued believing all that junk.'

'You are very welcome.' She returned the hug. 'Just keep loving her because you do know that you got the most wonderful girl in the world.'

He grinned sheepishly. 'She's just fantastic.'

'I see she has been surprising you in quite a few ways.' She teased.

Jonathan turned bright red. 'Please don't make me think about it because I will burst right here, or run all the way home. Why do you think I am taking time off to go on a proper honeymoon? It's all we can think about.'

She laughed. 'I'm so glad. And please be patient, it's not as if she knows everything.'

He nodded. 'I know. As I said, thank you for being the best friend she could ever ask for.'

'Stop this nonsense now; you are not making me cry.'

'No?' He lifted a brow. 'I didn't tell you then.' He whispered something in her ear.

'What?' Amy's eyes filled with tears right there. 'You just had to mess my make-up.' She accused as she tried to wipe her face.

'And you'd better not tell her.'

The intercom buzzed.

'Yes,' Jonathan called.

The girl from reception announced. 'Sir, security just called up. They say there is a very angry man downstairs who is demanding to see you.'

'Does this man have a name?'

'I think they said Valk. He is apparently refusing to go away, talking about a baby, and some stolen something.'

Amy put a hand to her mouth. 'It's him!'

'You know something about this?' Jonathan looked at her.

'It's Charlotte's husband. He's not Tammy's father but he can cause so much trouble. He must be looking for money again.'

'Money?' Jonathan queried.

'Never mind now,' a worried look spread on Amy's face. 'But how did he find you?'

Jonathan was silent for a moment then recalled the bank manager's call weeks ago, informing him that his wife had drawn two-hundred-thousand Rand. He had been curious but never asked what she used it for. 'Has this man ever asked Gabrielle for a payout?'

Amy took a deep breath then nodded. 'This is exactly what she was concerned about and wanted to avoid at all costs.'

'Okay,' he told the receptionist. 'Tell them to let him up.'

'Are you serious?' Amy asked nervously. 'He's also very dangerous. Has been to jail a number of times, and killed people.'

'If he wants money he's hardly thinking of killing me. Just go back to work, I'll be fine.'

Amy did not like it one bit. Sitting at her desk, she grabbed the phone and waited a few seconds. 'Gabrielle,'

'Amy, did you forget something?'

'Please stay calm, but I think Valk is on his way to Jonathan's office.'

'What? How— Why? But... why would he go there?'

'This is exactly where he would go if he's looking for money.'

'But... they promised... is the old man there as well?'

'I don't think so. It sounds like a solo thing.'

'Jonathan is not really planning to see him...'

'Oh he's seeing him all right, already told them to let him come up.'

Gabrielle swallowed her breath. 'This is bad, very bad.'

'Maybe he'll be happy with a hundred-thousand.'

'Amy, just ask security to keep him under surveillance at all times, I need to think.'

Valk stepped out of the building with a wide grin on his face. The meeting with the rich young man had gone well, no, very well. In fact, better than he expected, and neither Gabrielle nor Dimitri could say that he had broken that stupid thing they considered a contract. Besides, he had not bothered her, and from the look of things, he would not have to again. But had she really believed that he would not figure out who she was? All it took was patience, and he had learnt enough of that in prison.

He had simply waited until she visited the club with the baby again, followed her home, and after that, used his smarts. He did not loiter around the area but he did ask pinpoint questions from the servants and security guards as he pretended to be delivering a parcel in the neighbourhood. Now if all went well, he would be set for life, perhaps start his own strip-joint, one just like Red Bare.

Dimitri... there was a smart guy with good business sense but who had always been careful not to get himself into too much trouble. A smart move, as his grandfather Alexei had been a notorious crime lord and run an underworld organisation that dealt in all sorts of unspeakable activities since the sixties. Dimitri's father on the other hand was an indecisive man. Yuri had never been certain if he wanted to be clean or break the law, vacillating between the two in an annoying fashion. He eventually returned to mother Russia with his family and perhaps it had been the best decision he had made regarding Dimitri's future, who then joined the organisation.

Dimitri did not have the reputation of all-out criminal but Valk had known the family long enough to believe that he could push the younger man to a certain degree. Valk grinned again. Dimitri was besotted with Malcolm's daughter and that bit of information could easily be used accordingly and yield him huge benefits. Mr Knight would not take kindly to some two-bit club owner having yearning eyes pegged on his wife. But that was a last resort.

Men lusted. After women, drink, drugs, money and all the carnal desires places such as Red Bare provided, and for him, it was the one thing he craved above all else; had done for a long time, seeing the immeasurable possibilities. Blackmail, extortion, manipulation, the sky was the limit. All he needed were the gorgeous girls with lithe bodies, sparkling eyes and wide smiles to bring in the saps. If he could make Dimitri an offer he could not refuse... because he had to admit, Dimitri had style, and had created something with more potential than even he was aware of.

It was in fact astronomical but Dimitri never showed interest in pushing it to the limit of debauchery, which was why so many upper class men frequented it. It was not raunchy or tawdry like just about every other one in the city, but that was the market. Getting to know those influential men, finding their weaknesses, setting them up, and milking them for every cent he could because all had much to lose when the threat of scandal loomed. Valk took a deep breath, maybe his ship was finally coming in.

Someone tapped him on the shoulder and he turned. 'Dimitri!'

'Hello, Valk.'

'What the hell are you doing here?'

'Funny you ask me that because I was about to ask you the same.' Dimitri gazed up at the building. 'Do explain what you are doing outside Knight Industries.'

'You know what is funny? You pretend to be a criminal but are not really one. There are things I do that you are not willing to do.' Valk turned and started walking down the street.

Dimitri caught up to him. 'If I'm not mistaken you are actually threatening me. I am glad you finally found the guts to do so because I have been waiting impatiently. Obviously, I intimidate you somewhat because you never have dared before. So Valk, what were you doing in there?'

'*Jy het vir my gelieg.* I'll bet pretty lady has more money than you claimed but that's beside the point because her husband definitely has more than anything I could have asked from her.'

'I see. So how much did you ask for to stay out of their lives?' Dimitri asked sarcastically.

'Three million,'

'Wow, and did he agree to give it to you?'

'You know this love thing is a great weapon, it makes people do all sorts of things, good and crazy. Of course he's going to pay and do so willingly. He wants her to be happy and for that she needs her sister, so there is your answer.'

'I have wondered for a while and I think that I have it right. Where were you when Malcolm and Charlotte were killed?'

'You are becoming personal, she was my wife.'

'Which makes you the ideal suspect,' Dimitri noticed they were heading towards an alley. 'You have been searching for that money since but in the meantime your greediness drove you to Gabrielle.'

'You think you know a lot but all this is conjecture, circumstantial, and you can't prove anything.'

'You are the one who is mistaken. Right now I have three choices on how to deal with you.' Dimitri came to a halt. 'But I will pass on the first one because soiling my hands with your blood—' he shook his head. 'Besides, Gabrielle would not like that, even if she wishes that you would disappear.'

Valk smirked. 'You definitely do not have your grandpa's guts. There was a fearless man and I'm proud I still did some jobs for him before he was dragged off to jail in 1980. I believe that is the year you were born? Your father,' he waved a hand. 'Not quite willing to carry the family name to greatness either and never knew on what side of the fence he sat. A very confused man, which in turn made your brother a confused boy, as for your sister— I guess she turned out normal enough.'

'I hardly need a family history lesson.'

Valk laughed. '*Yessum*, I liked your grandpa, but your mother did not like all these things. So this is how you also ended up this way, neither here nor there.'

'You underestimate me and no one knows better than you that that is a very dangerous thing to do. Let us get back to choice number two. I could tell people where you are but I'll pass because a few of my employees already did. Your old enemies know you are back and they have been asking about you. So you see I don't have to do much.'

'Who is looking for me?'

'Some of the people I know you don't want to run into, including Erasmus' brothers. You remember them, don't you? They swore revenge and we both know they are men of their word. Oh and of course, Max, who has not been able to deal with his best friend's death. As for the little accident of you killing his father on the same day— No, he is not a happy man. As you can hear my choices are getting progressively worse.'

'What is number three?'

'On second thought, I'm keeping that one to myself because you are definitely not worth the knowledge. You would just be a huge waste of money and for what?'

Valk stared at him with his strange eyes. 'And you are a big disappointment to your grandpa's memory. Completely spineless and this nonsense—'

'Nonsense you say? You are going to trip this time and the fall will be your last. From that one you will not get up again, that I guarantee.'

'You talk big but you can't do one third of what your grandfather did. Have you ever stolen money, and what about pulling the trigger? Or even held a gun? I think that club runs way too clean. Where are the drug-dealers, the prostitutes, the racketeering that is supposed to be going on?'

'That is true but I have never been much into that sort of thing and everyone knows it. I suppose that my grandfather being such a well-known kingpin sort of took the wind out of my own sails.'

'True, you are no Siberian Tiger, just one big pussy,' Valk rolled his eyes. 'They say the apple doesn't fall far from the tree?' He laughed merrily. 'Geez, they can be so wrong. You fell down, rolled off and landed in another field.'

'What do you know you actually said the first right thing today. So, are you going to tell me how you killed Malcolm and Charlotte?'

'Why do you want to know this stuff? And why would I tell you anything?'

'What if I told you that I think I know where the money is? We could make a trade. You tell me your part and I tell you mine.'

Valk looked at him curiously. 'You would make this stupid trade if you knew where the money was and you could have it?'

'I have a pretty good idea where it is but I can't really keep it, can I? It is Gabrielle's.'

'This love business is so crazy.' Valk laughed. 'I cannot believe the things men do for it.'

'It is better than living with no purpose. So, interested?'

Valk nodded as he pointed a finger. 'You just told me that you can't have it because it's Gabrielle's, why then would you offer it to me? It does not make sense.'

'This is how I see it. She doesn't know where it is and what is a million or two in Gabrielle's life right now? Her husband can look after them just fine. So let's forget about the other three you just went to ask from Jonathan.'

Valk stopped walking and faced Dimitri. 'Nuh, nuh, nuh, nuh, you are trying to trick me. This is what I think; you don't know where the money is but are also trying to discourage me from the other three million. Have you fallen for this woman so hard that you are willing to put your life in danger? Because that is what you do when you make me mad.'

'All this time and you haven't even spat at me, must be getting soft.'

'You are pushing your luck.'

'You have no idea what you're supposed to be doing. All you want is money. I have a suggestion. Why don't you actually do some work for a change?'

'Jy soek vir my.'

'You're full of crap. That's what I believe you're full of.' Dimitri turned and walked away.

Valk's hand gripped his arm.

'What now?'

'No one has ever insulted me and lived.'

'Is that what Charlotte did, turned her back on you and laughed?'

'She was always a floozy, cheating on me every time I was in. But this time she crossed the line. Living with another man and then had his kid? What am I? Maybe he had money and position once but he was a loser.'

'Then I am taking it that their death was your handiwork. But admit it Charlotte did not become an addict by herself. You learnt all those things a long time ago, I'd say that you taught her all she knew. You were just a little tougher and didn't fall as hard as she did.' Dimitri grabbed one of Valk's arms and pointed. 'The tattoos cover some of the tracks but not all.'

Valk yanked his arm away. 'There is something strange about you and I have never liked you.'

'I am shattered.' Dimitri told him sarcastically.

'Yes, yes,' Valk nodded and pointed a finger. 'You are too cocky, something is just not right.' Sticking a hand in his belt, he pulled out a knife. 'What are you all about, Dimitri?'

'Put the stupid thing away.'

'Or you do what?' Lunging for him, Valk plunged the blade into the arm.

Dimitri stumbled in shock and pain then tried to reach for his gun but Valk had the upper hand and stabbed him again on the shoulder.

A shot rang out and Valk staggered. Falling to his knees, he stared at Dimitri. 'I thought you didn't know how to use it.'

Dimitri sucked in a painful breath. 'Considering I'm holding my shoulder and not a gun, you should wonder how I shot you.'

Valk doubled over. 'Then... who...'

Dimitri glanced around and located the shooter. 'Apparently, you have just discovered choice number three, my partner.' He grimaced as the newcomer reached him. 'What the hell Calvin, playing Miami Vice in broad daylight?'

'I'm sorry, did you prefer to be convulsing at death's door instead of just having two stab wounds?' Calvin queried as he pointed to Valk. 'Good thing I followed you.'

Dimitri sunk to his knees and ripping Valk's shirt open, studied the ugly wound. He shook his head. 'You did a good job all right he is not going to make it.'

'So... you... Are...' Valk stuttered as he spurted blood.

'Amazing, you are the first living person to hear this. My partner and I are undercover. So you see you were right about how apples fall. Sadly for you, you will not be able to blackmail me as you have, what— five minutes to live?'

'But... your grandpa, he was... the bloody Russian mafia.'

'Imagine that. I guess I was simply influenced wrong.'

'Were you... telling the truth... about the... money?'

'It could be where I imagine.'

'And where is that?'

Dimitri shook his head. 'It does not work like that. Not unless you tell me who killed Charlotte and Malcolm.'

Valk nodded. 'I was there... But... they decided... not to tell.'

'How did you kill them?' For all he knew Valk was lying, just to get his wish to hear where the money was.

'Charlotte's... syringe. Malcolm was weak... easy. They... didn't feel much...' He spurted a mouthful of red. 'Where... is... it...' he stopped breathing.

'Right,' Calvin said as he got off his phone. 'Get into the ambulance as soon as it gets here and I will explain this to the captain.'

'Why were you following me today?'

'Because you switched your wire off and I knew you were about to do something foolish because of that girl.'

'Sorry I broke the rules but I had to. This nut case had just been practicing extortion.'

Calvin looked around the alley, noticing a few curious passersby gathered at the entrance. 'It didn't turn out so bad, we solved two murders.'

Dimitri nodded. 'Let's hope no one followed you.'

Calvin grinned and ripped Dimitri's shirt open on the shoulder. 'Ugh, this one is deep. And this,' He studied the first wound, tore the sleeve off and wrapped the arm. 'You won't be able to use that hand for a couple of weeks.'

'Yes doctor.' Dimitri grimaced.

'Get yourself fixed up and I will keep an eye on the club until you get back, there are other big fish to fry. That reminds me, how far is the *boss'* new deal?'

'A couple of months at least,' Dimitri looked to the entrance of the alley as they heard a siren approaching. 'I have to call Gabrielle...' he swooned.

Calvin shook his head. 'Why did you have to fall in love with her? You, the Russian mob's trusted number one.'

'I'll just have to fall out of it, won't I?' Dimitri said bitterly.

'Can you?' Calvin placed a hand on the bleeding shoulder and glanced at Valk. 'At least that one can be scratched off the list.'

'You have no idea how relieved I am it turned out this way. That mad man chasing after Gabrielle is not a thought I relished, especially as I can't keep an eye on her.'

'Yes, she will be safe now.'

CHAPTER TWENTY-EIGHT

They were back at the game reserve. Jonathan had made certain they got the same tree house and now they found it impossible to keep their hands off each other. She recalled him suffering a little hell when they were first married but pretending she was oblivious to it. He kept asking if it was possible to die from an overdose of pheromones, hormones, adrenalin, serotonin and everything else associated with good feelings.

She couldn't help it, there was a permanent smile on her face and she loved registering his satisfaction as his eyes zoomed in on her and never let go. As he slid up to her and simply stood there smelling her with a pleasure she didn't fully comprehend. How he drank her in when they kissed, or tasted her when they lay naked in each other's arms.

He had done one thing she found utterly romantic. When they got to *their* tree house, she found one of the beds had been moved out to the overhanging platform and adorned with a mosquito net, so they slept most nights there, except for one when it rained.

She turned in bed, where was he? He never let her wake up alone and never got out before they made love. She could hear him talking to someone.

It took him ten minutes to come up the stairs with a breakfast tray, which he placed on the table. He smiled as he saw she was awake. 'Good morning, my gorgeous.'

'Morning,' she stretched and sat up. 'Where have you been?'

He kicked his shoes off, dropped his pants and unbuttoned the shirt. 'Were you dreaming of me?'

'No, I was dreaming of Santa Claus. So I've decided what I want and he'd better bring it because I've been a really good girl.'

'I can vouch for that, if he needs signatures.' He grinned and climbed into bed. 'Breakfast, or me first?'

'You know,' she grinned. 'It's when you have a choice that things get difficult. But is it hot?'

He laughed. 'Do you mean me or breakfast?'

'I did mean breakfast.' She snuggled up to him. 'Where did you go?'

'Today is a special day,' he grabbed the tray and brought it over to their lap. 'I know, a little different but I had to get the man early so he understands our needs.'

'Who are you talking about?' She asked curiously and began on the fruit salad.

'I managed to arrange a fantastic surprise for you.'

'That's wonderful, thank you. Now have your breakfast, or did you eat already?'

'I had an apple.' He grabbed a slice of toast. 'We have some time, so don't rush.'

'Can I guess what the surprise is?'

'Be my guest,' his lips curled. 'But this time I get you.'

'When did I get you?'

'When I tried to guess your costume. Any ideas?'

'We've been on safari, seen the elephants, went down to the watering hole and canoed down the river. We've done just about everything there is to do here. Oh wait, you said you saw someone. Have some new animals been born?'

'No. Continue,'

'Please, nothing to do with spiders.' She begged.

'Heaven forbid and no, no arachnids.'

'Okay, I'll wait.'

'Almost done?'

'Thank you, it was very nice. So, what's next?'

'Need you ask?' He took the tray away and pulled her into his arms.

Excitement poured out as she walked down the path, feeding off his energy, wondering what he had in store for her. She couldn't hear or see anything so any guess was a complete waste, but when they rounded the thorn trees, she let out a scream of joy. Right there, in the middle of the clearing, awaited a rainbow-coloured hot-air balloon.

'Jonathan,' her eyes sparkled. 'Are we going up?'

'Yes. Mr Wilson has been very kind to take a day off his schedule to take us up.'

'But—it's incredible.' She said excitedly. 'This is one of my lifelong dreams.'

'I know.'

'How is that possible?'

'Well, I have a secret. I have all the CD's you sent dad and I heard you tell him you wanted to do this.'

Her mouth opened in astonishment. 'He kept them all?'

Jonathan nodded. 'I'm pretty sure it must be all of them.'

'Thank you Jonathan. I love you.'

'I know. So, let us go float through the African skies.'

Mr Wilson smiled at Gabrielle's undisguised excitement at being able to do something she had dreamt about for so long and winked at Jonathan. Then he had to restrain her and explain that she could not dash about the wicker basket as if she were standing on a veranda.

Jonathan roared with laughter, glad that he was the one granting her this wish.

They had been enjoying the amazing views and running animals beneath them for about half an hour when he pulled out a small basket from the corner. 'Okay,' he said as he grabbed a bottle.

'No,' Gabrielle said. 'I don't want you to forget.'

'Neither do I, it's sparkling grape juice.' He poured some into two champagne glasses, handed her one and returned the bottle to the basket. 'Now, for the second part of your surprise.' He fell down on one knee in front of her.

'What are you doing?'

'I'm proposing to you. We did things crazily before, so I'm correcting it.' He stuck his hand in his pocket and pulled out a ring. 'So, my darling, will you marry me?'

'Can we do it again?' She said as she stared at the ring and then at him.

'Well, we are married but I want a second ceremony. I want to see you in a proper white wedding gown, flowers, dancing, the lot.' Seeing the face of protest, he placed a finger on her lips. 'You are not going to say what's on your mind. You should have had all those things. So, your answer my lady,'

'Of course I'll marry you again.'

'And this time, we will have your friends from Switzerland come over—'

'Anna and Luc?' Her eyes danced happily. 'I love you so much.'

He slipped the ring onto her finger. 'Fantastic, that's what I wanted to hear.' Then rising, he twirled her around, pulled her into his arms and kissed her.

'You are never going to bore me.' She told him breathlessly.

'I should hope not. Right, now, I know you sent a request to little old Father Christmas, so what is it you've wish for yourself?' He asked as he still held her in his arms.

'You want to know it now? Christmas is still months away.'

'What if it's something difficult, something I have to travel to China to get, or I have to go diving with the sharks to find it?'

She laughed. 'I appreciate that you'd be willing to do all of those things for me but thankfully, you do not have to endanger your life to give me this.'

'Oh good, that's a relief.' He grinned. 'So, what is it you want?'

'I'd like to go back to university, to do my honours and masters. Is that okay with you?'

'Good grief,' he said with a twinkle in his eyes. 'And I thought travelling to China and sharks was bad. All those hormonal male students just staring at you, trying to date you, writing you little notes, texting you to tutor them in heaven knows what.'

'You are silly.' She laughed. 'That's mostly a first-year craze and I'll be nowhere near any of them. Besides, I have the most gorgeous man this side of the equator and I'm going to look at them, for what exactly? What can they give me that I don't already have?' Her hand went to his jaw lovingly.

'That's what you want for Christmas?'

She nodded. 'That's all I want.'

'No, it's not the students I have to worry about; I think it's the professors this time. They're the ones who are going to be dreaming about you.'

She giggled. 'Stop it, Jonathan, you're inventing nonsense.'

'Just so you know; I'm getting a really hot student. Do you have a problem with that?'

'None whatsoever,'

THE END

 Athina Paris lives in South Africa but spent her formative years in Mozambique, where she was born. Years in convents and boarding schools prompted a deep curiosity, which quickly developed into an avid interest in reading and storytelling and led to a lifelong obsession with the written word and books. By fifteen, she had discovered ancient civilizations and became fascinated with various mythologies; a love she has kept to this day.

She studied Interior Design then turned to Creative Writing and followed that with Scriptwriting.

She became a spectator of human nature, quiet and shy, she preferred recording conduct and so built a treasure-trove of observations from which she drew the plots and settings for her romantic novels.

Set in faraway and exotic places, Athina's romantic works take her characters on voyages of self-discovery while dealing with catastrophic love lives in an imperfect world.

A stint as a high school English teacher polished her skills, a position she has vacated to concentrate on her professional goals of writing, editing, and proofreading.

If you enjoyed reading this book, please leave a review and let Athina know.

Here are more titles by Athina:

 Love & Madness

 When Dani Smiled

 All I Ever Wanted: Jessie

RockHill Publishing LLC

There are some lessons that only time can teach, but you do not learn talent, you only perfect it over time.

www.rockhillpublishing.com

www.ingramcontent.com/pod-product-compliance
Lightning Source LLC
Chambersburg PA
CBHW071736190726
48292CB00003B/771